ACCEL·WORLD

02

THE RED STORM PRINCESS

REKI KAWAHARA
ILLUSTRATION BY **HIMA**
DESIGN BY **bee-pee**

"Aaaah!"

HARUYUKI

Boy in the lowest
school caste

"Big brother, you have some pretty cute qualities, don't you?"

TOMOKO SAITO

"Little sister" taken in by Haruyuki's family

"So, you're not running, huh? You sure got guts."

SCARLET RAIN

Red avatar who challenges Haruyuki to a duel

"Haruyuki, all things are experiences."

"Wh-what?!"

KUROYUKIHIME

The Black King
Umesato Junior High School
student council vice president,
operator of Black Lotus

"I don't think there's any harm in trying this Armor of Catastrophe subjugation mission."

"K-Kuroyukihime!!"

SILVER CROW
Haruyuki's duel avatar

HARUYUKI
is the...

"Silver Crow"
in the
Accelerated
World.

"Haruyuki Arita"
in the
Real World.

"Pink Pig"
in the
Umesato Junior
High School's
Local Area
Network.

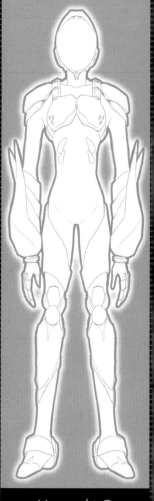

Haruyuki @
In-school local net
Pink Pig

Haruyuki @
Real World
Haruyuki Arita

Haruyuki @
Accelerated World
Silver Crow

▶▶▶ *ACCEL·WORLD* 02

THE RED STORM PRINCESS

Reki Kawahara
Illustrations: HIMA
Design: bee-pee

YEN
ON

NEW YORK

■ Kuroyukihime = Umesato Junior High School student council vice president. Trim and clever girl who has it all. Her background is shrouded in mystery. Her in-school avatar is a spangle butterfly she programmed herself. Her duel avatar is Black Lotus, the Black King.

■ Haruyuki = Haruyuki Arita. Seventh grader at Umesato Junior High School. Bullied, on the pudgy side. He's good at games, but shy. His in-school avatar is a pink pig. His duel avatar is Silver Crow.

■ Chiyuri = Chiyuri Kurashima. Haruyuki's childhood friend. Meddling, energetic girl. Her in-school avatar is a silver cat.

■ Takumu = Takumu Mayuzumi. A young man Haruyuki and Chiyuri have known since childhood. Good at kendo. His duel avatar is Cyan Pile.

■ Tomoko = Tomoko Saito. A girl taken in by Haruyuki's family. She calls Haruyuki "brother" and clings to him. Her hobby is baking cookies.

■ Neurolinker = A portable Internet terminal that connects with the brain via a wireless quantum connection and enhances all five senses with images, sounds, and other stimuli.

■ In-school local net = Local area network established within Umesato Junior High School. Used during classes and to check attendance; while on campus, Umesato students are required to be connected to it at all times.

■ Global connection = Connection with the worldwide net. Global connections are forbidden on Umesato Junior High School grounds, where the in-school local net is provided instead.

■ Brain Burst = Neurolinker application sent to Haruyuki by Kuroyukihime.

■ Duel avatar = Player's virtual self operated when fighting in Brain Burst.

■ Legion = Groups composed of many duel avatars with the objective of expanding occupied areas and securing rights. The Seven Kings of Pure Color act as the Legion Masters.

■ Territory Battle Time = Time for fighting with special rules, set up for each Saturday evening. Rather than the usual one-on-one fights, groups battle other groups of the same size, regardless of level.

■ Area Control = Privilege given by the system for having a better than 50 percent win average during Territory Battle Time. Within Controlled territory, Neurolinkers are given the right to refuse a duel even if connected globally.

■ Normal Duel Field = The field where normal Brain Burst battles (one-on-one) are carried out. Although the specs do possess elements of reality, the system is essentially on the level of an old-school fighting game.

■ Unlimited Neutral Field = Field for high-level players where only duel avatars at level four and up are allowed. The game system is of a wholly different order from that of the Normal Duel Field, and the level of freedom in this Field beats out even the next-generation VRMMO.

■ Enhanced Armament = Items such as weapons or personal armor owned by duel avatars. Can be obtained in ways such as: being credited as initial equipment at the start, acquired as a level-up bonus, or purchased in the shop at the Unlimited Neutral Field.

▶▶▶*ACCEL·WORLD*

Haruyuki stared through the eyes of his pig avatar at the gray, counterclockwise streaks making helixes within six steel holes. Nothing existed in the space around him. There were only white floors and white walls and a white ceiling encompassing him—a vast, empty room.

The bluish hunk of steel alone in the center of the room was a large automatic handgun. The hairline-finished slide, the checkering carved into the grip, the overwhelming weight and density of the weapon, and the very coolness of the thing could all be seen and felt, but of course, it was not the real thing. This device of unknown make and model was a virtual substitute Haruyuki had selected at random, from gun polygon elements placed here.

But it did shoot bullets. For that purpose, he had it pointed at the brow of his avatar, which stood a mere twenty meters away.

He had cobbled together this VR training app, referring constantly to the manual as he did, and the dreariness of the perfectly white room had actually depressed him when he first dived into it. What he had really wanted to make was the roof of a skyscraper, with a dark-suited hit man holding the gun, but the burden of creating all that was too much for a simple gamer still in junior high.

Had he asked her—his teacher, more experienced at these

things than he was—she likely would've slapped it together for him in seconds, no matter how elaborate the specs. But Haruyuki hadn't asked. He'd been afraid she would wonder why he was practicing such remedial stuff this late in the game. In the end, he'd managed to create a substitute that was the epitome of dreary: a single, clumsy handgun floating in a room that was so totally and completely white it literally made his eyeballs hurt.

But when he actually used the program, he wasn't entirely displeased with the way it had turned out. Either way, the gun was the only thing in the room other than himself. Whether he wanted to or not, he had no choice but to focus on its muzzle.

Crouching in the body of his pink pig avatar, Haruyuki slowly spread his arms wide, all the while staring intently at a single black hole.

He'd long since lost any sense of time and had no idea how many minutes he'd exhausted carrying on this way. The app's programming was exceedingly simple: Once he positioned himself and called out, "Start," the handgun automatically targeted Haruyuki and fired a single shot within a thirty-minute time frame following a five-second countdown.

Naturally had this been the real world, he'd just die, unable to do anything. But this was a virtual space created by his Neurolinker. The bullet's speed and distance were calibrated to allow him to avoid the projectile if he reacted the instant he saw the muzzle fire.

The issue, however, was that he had absolutely no idea when in those thirty minutes the gun would discharge. Nothing existed here to allow him to read the ball's trajectory or timing, unlike in the virtual squash game at which he was so adept. All he could do was keep his eyes open and maintain his concentration.

But this was exceptionally difficult. Right from the jump, his ability to focus for long periods had been nothing to write home about. When he started this training a month earlier, the nervous tension of the situation had broken in a mere two or three minutes, after which he would unconsciously start going through the

Kuroyukihime album in his mind, and just when he was smiling faintly to himself, he would take a merciless slug from an invisible assassin.

But Haruyuki had made this app himself, which was exactly why he stubbornly persisted with the training.

At any rate, his opponent was a single, stationary gun. Given that Field duels were fought for a full thirty minutes by battle-seasoned stalwarts whipping out a variety of awe-inspiring and overstimulating techniques, this training was almost easy.

Haruyuki's plan had been to increase the number of guns to five within a month. But here he was, still struggling with a single bullet fired from a lone pistol.

He had no talent. He'd known that right from the start. But if he didn't even try to train and stretch what little talent might lie buried within him, she would forever be higher than him—he would never stand shoulder-to-shoulder with her.

Damn. Dammit! I have to get faster, I have to be stronger. For her. So I can keep being her partner.

The impatience growing in Haruyuki's heart turned to noise, stiffening his avatar's limbs.

Almost as if the gun had been waiting for this, the trigger moved with a faint, metallic rasp. The hammer hit the firing pin. The slide recoiled, and the muzzle spit out an orange flash.

"Ngh.....!!" Haruyuki threw himself into a leap to the right, but his initial reaction was the tiniest bit off, and the spinning bullet gouged his left cheek up to his ear.

The impact, on par with getting slammed by a massive hammer, sent him flying helplessly. He yelped at the searing pain ripping through his body all over again as he bounced across the white floor.

"Ah! Aaaah!!" He held his head in his short hand and continued screaming as he rolled across the floor.

He had slapped an illegal patch on this app, one pulled from the net to neuter the default pain absorber built into his Neurolinker. He'd also cranked up the gain on the pain generator, so this shooter app he'd built could deliver a shock to the diver essentially equivalent to actually getting shot.

"Ah...ah!!"

Haruyuki writhed on the floor, tears in his eyes, his entire body convulsing. This made three times today that he'd endured this pain. Since embarking on this training a month ago, he couldn't count the number of times it'd happened. But he felt like he would never get the least bit used to it, no matter how many times it seared him. On the other hand, he was currently operating at what was basically the upper limit of his pain threshold as he'd quickly acclimated himself to the previous levels he'd set.

However, an adverse effect of this was that occasionally Haruyuki's Neurolinker would detect these abnormal brain waves, activate the safety, and automatically disengage the full dive. This function was hardwired, which meant it couldn't simply be hacked. The Neurolinker hit that hard limit now, and the white room before him disappeared without warning.

Gravity's axes suddenly changed. The real world rushed back from the depths of darkness, dragged out like a starburst. Tears were spilling out of Haruyuki's real eyes, and what met his blurred, distorted vision was the utterly familiar blue-gray door of the boys' washroom stall.

Although he could dive during school now because she had exorcised his bullies, leaving no one around to play tricks on his body while he was in a full dive, Haruyuki would be in serious trouble if a teacher found out about such a dangerous program. But he had an even more important reason for diving in the washroom, if only when using this app. The lingering remnants of intense pain and the shock of being abruptly yanked out of a full dive threw Haruyuki's nervous system into such confusion that everything around him spun slightly—the mere thought of which was enough to send his stomach careening upward.

"...Hrngh!" Haruyuki clamped a hand over his mouth, dropped to the floor from his perch on the closed lid of the toilet, turned around, and flipped the lid up.

He just barely made it, and the backward flow from his digestive organs was entirely confined within the region meant to contain it. After those organs had repeatedly emptied themselves, he stretched out a limp hand and pushed the button on the wall.

Haruyuki felt the whirling water close to his face but couldn't muster the energy to get up, and he stayed slumped over the toilet. The tears running down his face slid off to be swallowed up immediately by the toilet's flow.

These tears weren't just the byproduct of the extreme pain and the vomiting. His own weakness frustrated him, and Haruyuki clenched his teeth tightly, shoulders shaking.

This training was only supposed to improve his basic reaction speed—in duels, depending on who your opponent was, you could be showered by rapid gunfire in the space of a few seconds. And yet despite the goal of his training, Haruyuki was a month in and his evasion rate had only barely increased, from 20 to 30 percent.

She said he should take his time, get stronger at his own pace. But Haruyuki couldn't help but fear that the depths of those eyes actually harbored a deep disappointment.

It had already been three months since Haruyuki first used a function hidden in his Neurolinker to accelerate his thoughts, obtained from the fighting game Brain Burst—where one fought on a battlefield that was half reality—and become a Burst Linker, a player in that game.

Initially, Silver Crow, the duel avatar he controlled, had been able to leverage the enormous advantage of being the only avatar with the ability to fly to make easy progress. He'd reached level two after a mere week; within a month, he'd moved up to level three. He'd even started believing he might actually be a real hero in that world.

But it was all just fleeting glory, gone the moment someone figured out his weakness: Flying also meant your whole body was constantly exposed to enemy eyes. Faced with sharpshooting abilities wielded by a sniper so fast and accurate it would be nearly impossible to see the bullet, he was nothing more than a sitting duck.

When Haruyuki finally made it to level four, he became mired in a series of eternal stalemates. There was a total lack of progress on their current objective—the expansion of the domain held by his Legion, Nega Nebulus—and just maintaining their sovereignty over the area around his school required their undivided attention.

Territories—areas controlled by Legions—were recognized by the system when a Legion maintained a better than 50 percent win average in the Territory Battle Time set aside each Saturday evening. During that period, groups challenged rivals of equal number, regardless of level. Members of a Legion were given the right to refuse a duel in territories under their Legion's control, even when their Neurolinkers were connected globally.

But as a result of other Burst Linkers studying Silver Crow's unique abilities, the enemy teams that came after them during the group fighting time invariably included a duel avatar with impressive antiaircraft abilities, leading Haruyuki to hang up basic flight. Which meant that Silver Crow was nothing more than a close-range fighter who couldn't take a hit to save his life. His win rate dropped before his eyes, and his teammates, Cyan Pile and Black Lotus, were constantly forced to cover him.

Which was the reason for the special training.

If he could dodge at least half of the antiaircraft attacks, he could identify the shooter's position and then crush them with his superpowerful sudden-drop attack. That's what he'd been thinking when he put the app together, but he didn't feel like he was getting any results at all. If he couldn't dodge a bullet even when he knew exactly where it was coming from, how was he supposed to avoid an anti-aerial assault coming from the shadow of some obstacle on the duel field?

She didn't show any impatience or annoyance on the surface. On the contrary, she gently encouraged him every time he racked up another ugly defeat in the Territory fights. But the disappointment that was surely building inside her scared Haruyuki half out of his mind.

And if I end up dropping even further...

Lately, he'd catch thoughts like this popping up, shocking even himself. If he was just going to let her down, it would have been better if none of this had ever happened. His old habit of running away reared its ugly head, and little by little, the desire swelled in the very bottom of Haruyuki's heart.

He'd thought he could change. For a time, he'd believed that the moment he'd accepted that copy of Brain Burst and become a Burst Linker, he'd turned into someone different. But in the end, it was just same old, same old. School or virtual battlefield, wherever he went, he seemed destined to be nothing more than the very lowest of the losers.

Jiggling, round body still crouched in the toilet stall, Haruyuki squeezed his eyes shut and tried to banish his negative thoughts. He forced his voice from his throat, which still burned with the pain of his gastric acids.

"...Still...I..." But he couldn't get out the words that came next. This Haruyuki lacked even the strength to talk himself down.

As the dismissal bell signaling the end of school rang directly in his head via the local net, Haruyuki muttered silently.

...I want to be strong.

I want to be stronger.

1

"Big brother! Welcome home!"

Arriving home, Haruyuki had taken his shoes off and trudged about halfway down the hallway to his room when he heard a voice from the living room to his left.

"Thanks," he muttered automatically, almost unintelligible. He took another step, then another, and on the third, he yanked up the emergency brake hard.

Huh?

What was that?

As far as Haruyuki knew, the thirteen years and ten months since the birth of the human being known as Haruyuki Arita had been an unbroken chain of only-child-dom. And he thought he was grateful and happy for this fact, rather than have it be a source of dissatisfaction, but perhaps the truth was that he nurtured an unconscious loneliness, which had finally resulted in auditory hallucinations.

I'm no one's big brother, am I? Especially not a girl with a cute voice like that? Little sisters only show up in horror movies, right?

Haruyuki was still standing there awkwardly quizzing himself when he heard the sound of the impossible once again.

A singsong humming. Small slippers slapping against the floor. He even smelled something sweet. Hallucinated...scent? Was that possible?

The bag on his shoulder fell with a thud, and he whirled around a hundred and eighty degrees to stumble clumsily into the living room.

And then his hallucination even became visual.

There, in the kitchenette immediately to the left when you entered the room—a space almost never used for its designated function under normal circumstances—was where it hovered.

Probably about ten years old. Skinny enough as to be surprising and wrapped in a white blouse and navy skirt, obviously the uniform of some elementary school. The look was completed by suspenders and a pink apron over the top. Pigtailed red hair hung finely on both sides of its head, and the face below the round, smooth forehead was a shape that was nothing other than cherubic. Possibly biracial? Little freckles scattered across the milk-colored skin, the large eyes also a red-tinged green. His overall impression in sum was...

An angel? A vision from the heavens?

He stared, slackjawed, robbed of his ability to think. The girl flashed him an adorable smile before saying, "I'm baking cookies right now. You just wait a minute, okay, big brother?"

"Aaaah!" Haruyuki decided it was time to scream and tucked his round body behind the living room door. Unable to make heads or tails of the situation, he warily poked out just the top half of his head.

The girl tilted her own head to one side, looking perplexed, but soon smiled once again before turning around to peek into the oven. The two gatherings of red hair shook gently as she did, shining in the winter light coming through the window.

Having gotten to this point, Haruyuki finally decided that she was no hallucination. However unbelievable the situation seemed, the girl was too real. Which meant...she had to be malware uploaded to his Neurolinker. An ultradetailed 3-D model had been added to his vision, with extra false data for the sounds and smells. Although he couldn't see why anyone would do something like this.

I mean, there's no way I actually have a sister.

If it was a polygon fake, there was no reason to be afraid. Chuckling to himself, Haruyuki stepped into the kitchen and reached his right hand out toward his "little sister" as she looked up at him with a smile. He then grabbed a freckle-spattered cheek and yanked.

The Neurolinker, communicating on the quantum level with the wearer's consciousness, was capable of generating a virtual world that was, for all intents and purposes, indistinguishable from reality if limited to the senses of sight and hearing.

But when it came to reproducing the other senses, touch in particular, research still lagged due to the difficulty in assigning numerical values to these senses. Even with unlimited memory and CPU capacity, the creation of a single person took all of the Neurolinker's processing power. It was impossible to perfectly re-create in a virtual world the complex sensations of the texture of skin, the resistance of muscles, and the reflexive contraction in a human cheek. So when Haruyuki pulled on her cheek, the only thing his fingertips would feel would be lifeless rubber—

"Fwah ah you doon?"

"Holy crap?!" Haruyuki yelped, let go, and fell backward, hitting his butt on the refrigerator.

The illusion was perfect. Soft, velvety, young. In other words, a sensation of pulling on the cheek of a ten-year-old girl that was nothing shy of perfect—although he had never before had such an experience—was generated in his fingertips.

Staring into the saucer-sized eyes of the girl puffing up her cheeks in sudden outrage, Haruyuki reached a shaking hand up to the Neurolinker on his neck, released the lock, and ripped it off in one go.

The augmented reality information, like the clock, calendar, and app icons, were wiped from his vision.

The girl did not disappear.

"Haruyuki, I'm sorry, but..."

So began the message from his mother that Haruyuki belatedly noticed on their home server. Neurolinker reequipped, he stood stock-still and listened to it.

"I'm sorry, but the daughter of a relative is going to be staying with us for a few days. You know them, don't you? The Saitos in Nakano? My cousin? He said it was a sudden business trip overseas. And I already told you, I'm in Shanghai from today. I'll be back in a couple days, so you keep an eye on her, all right? Mail me if you need anything. Bye."

His mother, Saya Arita, worked in the trading department of a bank that had its home office in the United States. She was never home before the clock struck midnight, and she was always flying overseas, leaving Haruyuki alone for days at a time. Although it was unclear how much of this travel was work and how much was getaways with the man she was dating. Haruyuki sometimes thought that if the divorce seven years earlier hadn't been because his dad was cheating, it would've been exceedingly strange for the family court to let her have custody.

Thus, ever since elementary school, Haruyuki was often taken in by the Kurashimas—Chiyuri's family—two floors down in the same condo. If Chiyuri's mom and dad, who always welcomed him warmly, had ever shown him even the slightest hint that they were inconvenienced by this, he would have been crushed. He would have had nowhere to go and probably would've ended up bullied ten times more than he was.

Thoughts like this filling his brain, Haruyuki watched Saito's kid whirling around busily in the kitchen.

The oven timer sounded lightly, and the girl opened the door to pull out a metal tray. The sweet scent hanging in the air became even stronger. Apparently, the source of the fragrance was the cookies.

After carefully transferring the dozen or so cookies via tongs to a large plate covered with a paper towel, the girl exhaled sharply, as if relieved. She took the plate in both hands and turned around, looking up at him. "Um... I'm sorry for using the kitchen without asking. I thought my big brother Haruyuki would be hungry when he got home... so I..."

Her voice is even smaller than before, Haruyuki thought. *Oh, duh, she's probably worried that the "big brother" in the place she was abandoned looks put out by her. She's insecure. I'm the older one, I shouldn't be so freaked out, just meeting a girl.*

A formless pain deep in his chest, Haruyuki did his best to put a smile on his face. "Oh, thanks. I'm starving."

And just like that, the girl also grinned, ice melting. "Um, I'm Tomoko Saito. I'm in fifth grade. I figured you maybe forgot me since we haven't seen each other in years, but... I think we're second cousins. Um... I'm sorry to just barge in on you like this, but I hope we can get along." Still holding the plate reverently with both hands, she dipped her head neatly, causing Haruyuki's pulse to skyrocket and his sweat glands to open to their fullest.

But he quickly remembered the conclusion he'd just reached and somehow managed to respond with something along the lines of a coherent greeting. "Right! Um, I-I'm Haruyuki Arita. M-me, too, I—I hope we'll get along, Miss Saito."

Immediately, the girl declared, "You can call me Tomoko!" with a grin, and Haruyuki frantically reined in his distant thoughts, which were moving out into nowhere land at a dizzying pace.

If he was honest, the only memory he had of the Saitos in Nakano was a vague sense that such relatives existed. Which was, he supposed, par for the course when it came to your parents' cousins.

"So. Are you an only child, too?" he asked, and Tomoko nodded pertly.

"My dad is the only family I have. He had to go away on business suddenly, and I said I could stay home by myself, but he said he would worry. So he brought me here from school a little while ago and then went straight to the airport," Tomoko replied as she placed the plate of cookies on the table.

Haruyuki checked without thinking. "Oh, so you didn't see my mom, then."

"No. I just got a spare key to your house."

That was extremely good luck. That mother of his wouldn't have hesitated to shoot Tomoko a look of pure, venomous, and complete annoyance had they met.

However.

Right. So, then, that means...for the next three days, I'm supposed to live alone with this girl, right? No, no, no, no need to panic, you big dummy. She's in fifth grade. There's a full two years separating us... Two years...so? So then...?

Tomoko seemed unaware of the sudden uneasiness swallowing Haruyuki, and she smiled again with a "Please restrain yourself until they cool" smile before stepping back. She quickly washed up the bowl and other dishes in the sink while she waited for a pot of water to boil, returning in a few short minutes with a tray of tea. She was clearly already more at home in this kitchen than Haruyuki.

Marveling at how incredible girls are, Haruyuki shook his head abruptly. *She's a kid, a kid. She's just a kid.*

But the cookies were so delicious, they could've been sold in a specialty shop. Making short work of a rather large portion of them—nine, to be exact—he sipped the tea Tomoko had made for him, wondering exactly how many years it had been since anyone had baked him any treats.

On the other side of the table, redheaded Tomoko blew little puffs of air over her cup with a serious look on her face, a mannerism both unsophisticated and touchingly lovely. Just watching her, Haruyuki felt a kind of warm glow.

"Thanks for this…Um…Th-they were delicious," he managed to say in a somewhat normal tone, and Tomoko flashed him a broad smile, as if relieved.

"Really? I'm so glad! You weren't saying anything, so I was a little worried."

"S-sorry, I just spaced out while I was eating."

Chuckling softly, she rose halfway, reached out, and plucked off a cookie crumb stuck to Haruyuki's cheek. Which she then popped into her mouth, smiling again.

Haruyuki heard a weird heart-popping sound effect in his head and frantically rubbed at his mouth. "U-uh, um, okay. R-right. What should we do now? P-p-play video games? I have a ton of them, some from, like, forty years ago—" he said, before remembering that the majority of them were bloody hellscape–type things.

Fortunately, however, Tomoko shook her head lightly, still beaming. "Um, I don't really play video games. I'm not very good at full dives."

"H-huh." Shifting his gaze as she spoke, Haruyuki finally noticed that there was no Neurolinker, that essential tool of modern life, around her thin neck, which was covered by a blouse buttoned tightly all the way to the top.

He knew there were more than a few families who avoided daily Neurolinker wear while the kids were in elementary school, because the infinite global net was also a hotbed for all kinds of criminal activity. Even with the parental control function, it was hard to completely block harmful information.

He could also understand being scared of a full dive, with the way it blocked all input from your actual senses if you usually only used the audiovisual mode in classes at school. That being the case, he was beginning to seriously wonder if there was anything they could do when his eyes finally landed on the large-panel monitor attached to the living room wall.

Haruyuki pointed at it. "O-okay, we could watch a movie or something? And I've got some pretty good 2-D programs from way back, too."

But Tomoko shook her head slightly again and said, as if embarrassed, "Um...instead of that, would it be okay if we talked? Like, about your middle school? I'd like to know about that." She stood up and navigated around the table to sit down next to him.

A sweet scent like milk tickled Haruyuki's nostrils, activating now of all times the antigirl force field he had cultivated over many years, and he reflexively threw himself backward. His chair tilted precariously, and he waved his arms out at his sides to pull out of what was nearly a side-fall onto the floor.

Tomoko stared intently at him as he thumped back down into his original position before giggling, "Big brother, you have some pretty cute qualities, don't you?"

—*Aaah.*

Listening to the sound of bubbles burbling up from his mouth, Haruyuki sank deeper into the bathtub.

Bathing being a particular love of his mother's meant that the Arita bathroom was ridiculously large. So, too, was the bathtub, and even Haruyuki, with his ample frame, had room to spread his arms and legs out without feeling boxed in. He took a deep breath of moist air, smelling the scented bathwater through his nose, held it in his lungs, and exhaled slowly.

Although he'd been fairly tongue-tied at all the wrong times, his throat hurt from having spoken at such length after so long. Interrupted only by the curry and rice Tomoko had made for dinner, he'd somehow spent a total of four hours basically talking nonstop. He was mildly impressed that he could find that much in his regular life to talk about.

In the end, he'd spilled nearly every detail about his life, starting with the various systems at Umesato Junior High all the way up to random episodes with his two childhood friends, plus this and that about a certain older student dressed in black, who happened to be the most important person in the world to him. The only thing he didn't talk about was the bullying that had plagued him until just a few months ago. That and anything related to the other world.

And Tomoko had listened intently to every bit of it, conversation that couldn't have actually been all that interesting, occasionally laughing out loud.

Haruyuki reflected seriously that this might be what it was like to have a real little sister. At the same time, he hated himself for not being able to get rid of that last nagging doubt that something was off.

It was just—it was too perfect. One day, he comes home from school and he suddenly has a little sister who makes him cookies, curry and rice, and—the clincher—she's all "I want you to talk to me." Not to mention that it would be just the two of them for three days?

His mother hadn't raised him to simply accept surprises out of nowhere without question. But if there was some ulterior something behind this, who on earth could have put it together and what was the purpose? And how was he supposed to find out?

After thinking on this a little, Haruyuki pulled himself out of the water and picked up the aluminum Neurolinker hanging on the rack beside him. It was water-resistant, but just in case, he wiped the water from his neck before attaching it from behind. The arms of the U-shaped device swung out lightly from inside and locked around his throat.

He turned it on, and the start-up symbol sparkled before his eyes, the brain connection check continuing for about twenty seconds before his virtual desktop opened. Swiftly moving a finger on his right hand, he opened a window for the Arita home server.

Haruyuki hesitated slightly before he opened the family album in data storage. They hadn't taken any photos or anything as a family these last few years, but there had to be hundreds of images buried in there from before he puffed up into his current physique, back when his mother and father were still in love. He'd rather have died than look at those. He went back a level and instead opened the external nets connected to his home server.

Several three-dimensional access gates opened to fanfare, all home nets of Arita relatives. Naturally, you couldn't just go poking through the server data willy-nilly, but you could leave messages and view schedules and things made public for the family.

However, there was no "Saito in Nakano" house among the access gates. Most families used the top screen to collect family photos and recent news, so he thought he could double-check there, but of course, only his mother's parents and siblings were connected, with a few aunts and uncles; apparently, cousins weren't covered.

Haruyuki momentarily shifted his gaze away from his desktop and listened for noise on the other side of the bathroom door. He could faintly pick up the sound of the panel TV in the living room. Apparently, Tomoko was still watching a family-friendly variety show. He felt bad for not getting out of the bath sooner after she had so firmly insisted he get in first. And he felt even guiltier that the reason for his long soak was his doubt that she was really his second cousin.

He focused on his desktop once again and opened the access gate in the middle of it—his mother's parents' home net. Ignoring the peaceful family photos taken against the backdrop of a farming village in Yamagata, he clicked on the gate to connect to the net interior. And naturally, a confirmation window popped up to block Haruyuki's progress.

Here he entered the ID and password his mother had given him. Because this login would be recorded on the other end, his mother would find out he used her ID if her parents asked her why she'd logged in, and he'd be in serious trouble. But he didn't imagine that his grandpa and grandma, who ran a cherry orchard, would actually check their home net's access log. Still, it was obviously best to get the job done as quickly as possible. Haruyuki hurried to dive into their home net and open the album folder.

There was an enormous catalog of photos collected over several decades. Annoyed, he applied a filter for date and number of people, narrowing down the total number of images. He dimly recalled that the entire Arita family had gotten together at his grandpa's seventy-seventh birthday party five or so years earlier and felt like he'd said hello to the Saitos from Nakano then. In which case, Tomoko, who would've been about five at the time, should have been there, too.

His search filtered soon enough, throwing up several thumbnails. He flicked one after another with the tip of his finger.

Not this one, not that one, either... Oh, around here? Like the next one maybe.

"Big brooooother!"

A singsong voice came out of the blue from his right, and Haruyuki reflexively twisted his neck around. His right index finger froze in midair.

At some point, the door to the bathroom had been opened slightly, and now Tomoko was standing on the other side, face and right shoulder peeking through.

His eyes fell from her head—reddish-brown hair wrapped in a towel—to her face, with its somewhat bashful smile, then down to her slim neck and the smooth skin of her shoulder. "Wha—wh-wha—"

She turned a faintly cherry-colored smile on him as his jaw flapped furiously. "Big brother, can I get in with you?"

"Get... in... That's—"

"It's just, you're taking so long. I'm tired of waiting!" Without waiting for his reply, Tomoko stepped into the bathroom, giggling.

Haruyuki frantically pushed his body under the water with a splash, shut his eyes tightly, and cried out, "S-sorry! I'll get out right now! I-I-I'll get out right now, so just wait a second more!!"

"It's fiiine. I mean, we're cousins and all."

It's totally not fine at all!! he screamed in his mind, but his bio-optical visual processing units—that is to say, his eyes—betrayed their master's intention, and his eyelids lifted slightly of their own volition. Tiny bare feet stepping across the ivory tiles leapt into his field of view, and he stopped breathing.

His focus shifted upward automatically. Calves drawing out a surprisingly thin, smooth line. Round knees, supple legs. The base of those legs was just barely obstructed by a pink bath towel, and he wondered momentarily just what was going on before his gaze continued traveling upward, and he cursed his own idiocy. The towel covered the small torso perfectly, with minimal bumpiness, and a delicate collarbone jutted out, smooth skin above the seam in the fabric—which threatened to unravel at any second.

"That's exactly why I'd be grateful if you didn't look so intently at me right now!" From the freckled face, finally, eyes turned downward, as if embarrassed.

It was this view that Haruyuki compared to the Arita family photos from five years ago still displayed on the right side of his field of vision.

The children, including himself, were clustered together in the front row. After all this time, he had absolutely no clue who was who, but fortunately, photos from that period were already using technology to embed data in the pictures. If he unfocused slightly, the names popping up in front of each child would disappear.

The name he was looking for showed up on the sixth kid in line. Tomoko Saito.

When he fixed his gaze on the name, the photo automatically zoomed in on the child who bore it, enlarging the image to the same size as the Tomoko in front of him.

Five years old at the time. And girls change, so I mean, her face, in five years could have…

There's no way.

Haruyuki took a deep breath and held it, before exhaling at length. Then he turned toward the puzzled girl calling herself his second cousin and spoke to her with a sad smile. "Tomoko…"

"What is it, big brother?"

"…You're a new Burst Linker, aren't you?"

Her reaction was immediate and graphic.

For a brief instant, the look on Tomoko's sweet face was the very definition of surprise. Her cheeks were probably dyed red for reasons other than bashfulness, and her right eye twitched convulsively.

But impressively, the girl, who age-wise was definitely at least around ten, cocked her head and said in an even sweeter voice, "What, big brother? What are you talking about? Berr…st? What's that?"

"Tan," Haruyuki murmured in response.

"What?"

"You've got clean tan lines on your neck. About the same as me. That's the kind of tan you can't really get unless you've been wearing one constantly from the time you were born…A Neuro-linker, I mean."

Tomoko—or rather, the girl who was likely not Tomoko—covered her neck quickly with both hands.

"And," Haruyuki continued, "there are still pictures from five years ago on my grandpa's home server. Tomoko Saito's in them, too, you know? I'll just say this, you're about ten times cuter."

The girl's face spasmed again before devolving into a look that was actually complicated. Finally, her flickering expression settled down into a sulky grimace, light-years from the naive mask she'd been showing him up to then.

"Tsk!" She placed both hands on her toweled hips and clucked her tongue fiercely. "And after I went and checked the albums here. Never expected you to go and dig them up at your grandpa's. You're pretty suspicious."

Flustered at the sudden change in her tone, Haruyuki somehow managed to reply, "Y-you went too far. I'm assuming the mail to my mom from Saito was a fake, but what if she'd decided to double-check with him?"

"All mails and calls generated from your mom's Neurolinker are set to be intercepted and sent to me. It took me three days to get everything ready."

"Well…good, job, I guess…" An incredulous voice slid out from between Haruyuki's lips as he clung to the edge of the bathtub.

The only way to get a virus into someone else's Neurolinker was to connect directly with a cable. Most likely, this girl had been tracking Haruyuki's mother's movements and had connected to her Neurolinker in the locker room of the gym she always went to.

Naturally, he wasn't exactly pleased that something like this had been done to a close relative, but honestly, he was impressed. A lot of Linkers called themselves hackers or wizards, but most of these soldiers weren't too keen on leaving the safety of their own homes to tackle some social engineering in the real world—becoming another person, the ultimate hacking to break security off-line.

Perhaps hearing the praise contained in Haruyuki's voice, the girl smiled confidently, almost smugly.

Looking up at that smile, Haruyuki continued spelling out his hypothesis. "I guess you went to all this trouble because you want to use me as a stepping-stone to hack her, but you're too optimistic. She'd have realized you're a fake the second she saw you. Unlike me taking five hours…And you know, I totally get how you'd be feeling like you'd lose if you just went and challenged her to a fight as a Burst Linker. I mean, you'd be going up against *the* Black Lotus."

When Haruyuki finished his grumbling speech, wishing the whole time she would hurry up and get out, the girl's attitude changed abruptly once again. Her eyes glinted fiercely, shining the same shade of red as her hair. Glossy lips twisted into an unbecoming sneer, revealing the tiniest hint of white teeth in the gap.

She looked down at Haruyuki with an expression that could only be described as arrogant and said in a low voice, "Hey, hold up. *What'd* you just say?"

"Huh? I—I said…if you were to challenge her—"

"I'd lose? Me? And that's why I'm here on this superannoying, secret, real-life hack?"

Is it not? As Haruyuki asked the question with his eyes, the girl reached up with her right hand and ripped the towel off of her head. She threw it on the floor and shot her index finger out at him.

Her red hair, nearly crimson in the steam, was practically standing on end. Short, it rippled like fire as the girl threatened, "God! Enough! Let me lay it down for you: Lady Scarlet Rain here's gonna take that insult outta *your* tanned hide, so you stay right there like a good little lamb while I go get my Neurolinker!!"

Tucking her index finger back into her hand, she stuck her thumb out, turned it downward, and then yanked it off to the side before whirling around forcefully. Her right foot, poised to take a step forward, encountered the towel she'd just tossed aside and slipped.

"Hyaa?!" High-pitched shrieking.

Looking up at the girl falling, essentially somersaulting backward, Haruyuki cried out, too. "Whoa?!"

His arms shooting out automatically, he caught her just as she was about to crash into the edge of the bathtub. But his foot slipped in the bath, and Haruyuki also went tumbling backward.

Splooosh!

A magnificent clamor went with a tall pillar of water and a large bath towel fluttering alongside it.

Haruyuki bumped his head on the wall behind him and closed his eyes tightly, riding out the pain before raising his eyelids slightly to assess the damage.

Himself in the large tub flat on his back. The redheaded girl using his plump belly as a cushion. His arms wrapped tightly around that slim torso.

And both of them butt naked.

"Aaaaah?!" Haruyuki cried, which was drowned out by the girl's "Eeeeeeeeee!!"

Writhing frantically, she escaped the tub in a single leap, employing the propulsion from a foot stomping down on Haruyuki's stomach. She grabbed the bath towel from the floor and flew into the changing room before showing her face again.

"I'm going to beat you to death."

Listening to the sound of her footsteps as she dashed toward the living room, Haruyuki was stunned.

I saw her. I touched her...

No, wait. She's probably an assassin from one of the Legions of the Six Kings. And what she just said now, that probably means she's coming to challenge me to a duel.

In which case, maybe he ought to take off his Neurolinker and avoid her? But if he was going to have to face her as an enemy at some point, it would be better to find out what was going on sooner rather than later. Now that he was just barely level four, he wouldn't lose too many points if he failed to win one duel. And he didn't have to worry about his defeat being too embarrassing if his opponent was a child.

Although 80 percent or so of his brain was in a state of total confusion, the remaining 20 percent had managed to reach this point, and Haruyuki recalled the name she'd given him.

"Scarlet Rain." He was pretty sure he'd never heard it before.

She was probably a distance-attack red on the color circle, but he would be rash to jump to the conclusion that she was a Red Legion Burst Linker based on that alone. He'd be able to confirm that soon enough if he got into a duel with her now, but he wanted more information.

He probably still had a minute or two before the girl equipped her Neurolinker, turned the OS on, and finished the quantum connection check. He muttered voice commands, still seated in the bathtub. "Command. Voice call. Number zero one."

Instantly before his eyes, the holo dialogue A VOICE CALL WILL BE PLACED TO THE REGISTERED ADDRESS 01. OKAY? popped up. He promptly pressed YES.

His interlocutor picked up on the second ring. *"It's me. What's wrong, Haruyuki, calling so late?"* In the background behind the smooth, graceful voice with its musical intonation, he could hear the sound of water splashing.

Oh, so she's in the bath, too... This thought flashing through his mind, Haruyuki began speaking to the person on the other end of the call, Kuroyukihime. She was one of the strongest Burst Linkers, Black Lotus, the Black King.

"Sorry to call so late. I was just hoping you could tell me something."

"Oh? And what's that?"

"Do you know a Burst Linker called Scarlet Rain?"

The answer to his question was a slightly long silence.

"Uh, um, are you okay?"

"Oh, sorry. So you're seriously asking me that?"

"Serious? Of course. I wouldn't prank call you at this time of night."

"I see. Hmm. I suppose this is an oversight on my part. We only use nicknames; I haven't told you any real names, have I? But, Silver Crow, this is a bit of laziness on your part as well."

"Huh? I... What do you—?" Cocking his head, Haruyuki could hear tiny feet trotting down the hall over Kuroyukihime's cool voice.

"Scarlet Rain. Immobile Fortress, Bloody Storm…The second Red King herself?"

Huh? Both eyes popped open, his jaw dropped, and his brain stopped.

As if on cue, the redheaded girl reappeared, nearly slamming into the bathroom door. She looked pretty furious, in nothing more than a cute underpants set. But she seemed uninterested in hiding anything anymore, and she proudly revealed her white body, crossing her arms in front of her.

Reflexively averting his eyes, Haruyuki noticed the one item other than underwear on the girl's body—wrapped around the slim neck, sleek, with a transparent red sheen—and stared incredulously.

The girl flashed him a ferocious grin and cried out in a voice full of both sweetness and menace, "Burst Link!!"

Skreeeeee!!

Although the screeching filling the world around him was familiar to him now, it never failed to send a shiver up Haruyuki's spine. Instantly, his real-world senses were disconnected, and the words HERE COMES A NEW CHALLENGER! blazed up in the darkness before his vision returned to him.

But what he saw was no longer his own bathroom, ivory cosmetic panels attached to the wall, but an expansive flat space, such that he could only assume that several floors had been knocked out of his condo building.

Haruyuki was deep in a full dive into the virtual world created by Brain Burst, the thought-accelerating, fighting game application in his Neurolinker. The world around him was a virtual duel field recreated from images from the social camera net laid out all over Japan.

But because, as a general rule, there were no social cameras in people's homes, including Haruyuki's, the game came up with this kind of supplementary extrapolation—in other words, a fabrication by the software. This time, the condo appeared to have been sent back to a time when it was still being built. Sprawling floors of bare concrete were pierced only by intermittent steel-frame girders.

In this stark space, Haruyuki and the girl faced each other in the flesh, albeit for a mere half second. Soon, however, the color and form of their bodies began to change. Into their alternate selves, their fighting duel avatars.

A silver glow reached up from the tips of Haruyuki's rounded limbs, enveloping and narrowing them at the same time, stretching them thinner and thinner while giving rise to mechanical arms wrapped in silver armor. The transformation immediately spread to his torso, cutting the girth of his stomach in half in an instant. As his superfine metal body neared completion, an orb of white light swallowed his head, encircling it in a smooth, round, mirrored helmet.

Aware of his own body's transformation into his duel avatar, Silver Crow, Haruyuki stared intently at the girl standing several meters in front of him.

Her arms and legs, slender like a doll's, were suddenly enveloped in a scarlet radiance. As the circle of light climbed upward, it was replaced by clear, ruby-colored armor. Her perfectly flat stomach and chest were also subsumed by the semitransparent armor, with dark gray and ruby as the two highlights. Finally, in a flash of brilliance, an android-like head appeared.

A mask with nothing more than two rounded eyes. Antennas shaped like bundles of bound hair protruded from both sides of the armor. The pigtails bounced pertly; the eyes shone sharply, a vivid red.

This is the Red King?

Still standing bolt upright, Haruyuki looked intently at the duel avatar several meters ahead of him. She was small. She couldn't have been more than a mere hundred and thirty centimeters. The only thing weapon-like about her was a handgun that looked like a toy dangling from her right hip.

"Uh, um." His mouth moved spontaneously, and a voice with a metallic effect leaked out from beneath the mirrored helmet. "You're really…"

Are you really one of the Six Kings of Pure Color, a level-nine Burst Linker, one of only seven in the Accelerated World, a powerful ruler leading an enormous Legion?

It was when he tried to ask this question that the space behind the cute girl-shaped avatar abruptly warped and distorted.

Four rough blocks glittering a deep crimson appeared, as if called up from the ether. They quickly covered the girl's arms and legs. Armor plates followed, rolling up from the sides, completely concealing the slim body.

"Wha…" Haruyuki gaped at the crimson avatar, which had, in an instant, gained several times his own mass.

However, the arrival of the extra armor didn't stop there. With a low, heavy banging, enormous hexagonal pillars, cylinders, plates, and more appeared in rapid succession and converged on each other. The avatar grew to nearly ceiling height instantaneously, quickly bridging the two meters to close the gap with Silver Crow, who hurriedly stepped back. Then it exceeded three meters.

A few seconds later, when silence finally returned, the thing towering before Haruyuki's eyes could only be called a tank, or maybe a fort. Two enormous gun barrels slowly rose, extensions of the original arms, and white smoke puffed out from cooling vents here and there. In the center of this weapons cache, two red eyes, barely visible, glowered brightly.

"No way…," Haruyuki muttered, as the word FIGHT!! glittered before his eyes in a flaming font before exploding and dissipating into nothingness.

Whatever! For now, just run!! Haruyuki thought immediately, turning to speed off in a fierce dash—before just barely stopping himself.

The enemy's affiliation was long-range red. This enormous fortress-shaped duel avatar was, without a doubt, a demon when

it came to distance attacks. In addition to the gun batteries on the left and right, the housings on both shoulders were most likely missile pods, and the short gun barrel protruding from the front was probably some kind of machine gun. Getting distance from an opponent like this was sheer stupidity.

Having made this judgment and mustering what little courage he had, Haruyuki turned again to face his opponent. He stood stock-still, exposed to the crimson gaze of the fortress avatar Scarlet Rain.

"So, you're not running, huh? You sure got guts," the Red King uttered in a voice that was both metallic and adorable.

"I-I-I'm too freaked out to move," he replied pathetically, earnestly running his gaze over every centimeter of the king.

In games, the usual attack strategy for this kind of enormous and heavily armed boss was to stake your life on close approaches from blind spots to take out weak points. Charging her from the front was clearly off the table, and her sides were most likely within range of the adjustable main arsenal. In which case, he'd have to go in directly behind her. If he could put everything he had into a dash around her and attach himself to her back...

Perhaps realizing what Haruyuki was thinking, perhaps not, Scarlet Rain giggled. "You say the cutest things! But you haven't forgotten, have you?"

"Huh? F-forgotten what?"

"The fact that..." The main weapon on her right suddenly squealed into motion to target Haruyuki. "...I told you I was going to kill you, you friggin' perv!!"

"That was an act of God, okaaaaaaay!!" Haruyuki screamed back, kicking the ground savagely. He charged like a bolt of lightning toward the enemy's left flank, turned sharply, and headed for her back.

Scarlet Rain's swiftness turning as she followed Haruyuki was surprising given her enormous size, but even so, it wasn't enough to keep pace with the rushing velocity of Silver Crow, a duel avatar singularly specialized for speed.

"And you were the one who just came waltzing into the baaaaaath!!" Raising his voice in a cry once more as he dashed in close, Haruyuki plunged unhesitatingly forward, his enemy's back finally coming into view.

As expected, her rear harbored nothing more than very long radiation fins and thrusters; he didn't see any weapons. He set his sights on the place where the armor looked thinnest, the area where a missile pod connected with a fin, raised his right fist, and—

Thrusters?

The second this thought flashed through his mind, the four black jet nozzles began emitting intense flames.

"Gaaaahot!!" Haruyuki shouted, instantly engulfed in the blaze, which produced an overwhelming sensation of heat and whittled away at his hit point gauge in the top left of his field of vision.

But he couldn't stop his charge now. The damage wasn't on a level he needed to worry about. Silver Crow, affiliated with the metallic colors, was resistant to heat attacks.

"Fire doesn't work on Silver Crow!!"

Got you! Haruyuki channeled all his energy into a Punch, pummeling the joint in the rear armor. But…

"Wishful thinking, kid!!" Scarlet Rain roared so gleefully he could almost see her laughter written in the air while the lids on the casings on her shoulders popped open.

Seeing a barrage of countless little missiles let fly, Haruyuki's eyes widened in shock.

How…This…We're in a…building…

In a flash, the concrete ceiling and floor, the steel pillars—everything was engulfed in the bright red blossom of an explosion. Above his head as Haruyuki desperately dodged a missile headed straight for him, cracks lanced through the concrete like a net, and the whole structure began to crumble.

"No way!" He just barely avoided an enormous chunk of debris falling toward him, the floor below his feet collapsing at an unbelievable pace.

"No way?!" Screaming, Haruyuki dashed for all he was worth. He couldn't just stand there worrying about getting too much distance from his enemy. They were on the twenty-third floor, far above the ground. If he got swallowed up in the collapse, his HP would probably vanish in a blink.

Because the only parts of what was formerly Haruyuki's condo remaining were the floor and the pillars, he could see the light that led to the exterior several dozen meters ahead. Zigzagging over the collapsing floor and pulverizing the falling lumps of concrete with his fists and his head, he glanced up to check the special-attack gauge below his health bar.

Neither the damage he was inflicting nor sustaining were very serious, but perhaps because stage destruction points were also being counted, his gauge was shining about 20 percent green. Which meant—

He could fly!!

Haruyuki took a deep breath and concentrated his power in both shoulders. The metal fins folded up on his back deployed with a crisp click. He vibrated the fins at a high frequency and accelerated his dash.

"Geronimooooooooo!!" Crying out, he turned to the gray sky approaching before him and threw himself headlong into a dive.

Haruyuki's place was very near the top of the skyscraper complex. Therefore, the moment he leapt from the building, the city suddenly lay spread out before his eyes, from Koenji to Shinjuku. It was a picturesque panorama, but like his own condo, the buildings had all been transformed into drab affairs, steel frames jutting out of cement. So this was probably a Weathered stage. He was pretty sure its attributes were: breaks easily, dusty, and sudden gusts.

Mulling this over, Haruyuki eased up on the acceleration of his metal wings and hovered in the sky. He glanced over at his special-attack gauge; there was only a little left. At this rate, he should have had enough for three minutes of continuous flight.

When he looked back, the condo's enormous tower was in the process of splitting in half at the middle, another stage in its progressive, merciless collapse.

"Aaah...My house...," he muttered unconsciously. Of course, that "house" was just made of polygons generated by the system, but this was the first time his own home had been destroyed in a duel.

"Honestly, this is ridiculous." Shaking his helmeted head, Haruyuki watched the condominium reduced to a mountain of rubble below him. The Red King had apparently gotten caught up in the massive destruction she herself had initiated and was nowhere to be seen. So even a fortress avatar was helpless before this kind of devastation.

He cocked his head to the side, wondering exactly what she had been trying to accomplish, and started his descent when he noticed something and shuddered.

Scarlet Rain's health gauge had not dropped. Although it was somewhat less full, on the order of 30 percent less, it wasn't an amount that could properly be called damage. And her special-attack gauge was shining brightly, fully charged.

Of course. Destroying such an enormous geographical landmark would have given her a huge bonus. Which meant that the Red King's reckless and random missile fire hadn't been intended to disrupt Haruyuki's attack on her back or to entangle him in the collapse.

All of a sudden, several rays of red light surged out from the rubble under his nose. At the same time, a shrill voice shouted, "Heat Blast Saturation!!"

A strange sort of resonance pulsated the air, a thunderous

sound that nearly burst Haruyuki's eardrums as he watched a line of red fire pierce the ruins of the condo, stretching straight up into the sky.

"Eeeeaaaah!!" he cried, vibrating his left wing as hard as he could in an attempt to avoid the beam with a tailspin dive. But...

The field of fire was just too huge. Unable to completely avoid the beam, which was basically as wide as he was tall, Silver Crow hit the flickering thermosphere with his left arm. There was a sizzling sound just below his elbow, and his lower arm steamed out of existence.

His HP bar plummeted 15 percent, and he was racked by an unrelenting, scorching heat. But Haruyuki was largely unaware of either of these things.

Because he was focused on the heat beam passing right by him, he didn't see it extend toward the east of the stage and blow away the top half of the Shinjuku government office towering over the area three hundred meters above the ground.

"No way..." The same stunned words he had uttered too many times in this battle slid once more from Haruyuki's mouth. Jaw agape beneath the silver surface of his helmet, he shifted his gaze and stared at the remains of his condo.

The Red King emerged majestically from an enormous gash cut through the rubble. The beautiful ruby armor covering her body was perfectly untouched. The thrusters on her back and undercarriage glittered lightly with the emission of flames, and white smoke trailed from the slits in the gun of her left arm.

"Ooh, you're flying! High in the sky!" the Red King half sang, looking up at Silver Crow with round eyes from the gap in her front armor. "I always wanted to try this stuff, antiaircraft fire. Looks like so much fun in sci-fi movies and whatnot. Just sends everything flying all over the place."

Ka-chak.

With a spectacular metallic clack, the missile casings on both her shoulders flung wide, her right main weapon came up, and the angle of the four machine guns on her front changed.

Trembling violently, Haruyuki recalled scenes like this from movies and anime. The tiny mecha soldier tries to slip past the enemy fortress's overwhelming curtain of antiaircraft fire and get closer. They were almost always shot down like little bugs and exploded, calling out a lover's name or something.

I'll go with "Kuroyukihime," then. Although that's just a nickname. But still, her real name would be embarrassing.

While he was busy losing himself in this kind of escapist thinking, the enemy's main armament began to charge, rumbling deeply. What looked to be a hundred small missiles rose up from the launchers, seeker heads glittering.

In contrast with his enemy's special-attack gauge, which was full again—likely from the bonus earned by destroying the government office—Haruyuki's had less than 5 percent left. He would probably be able to fly at full power for a couple minutes at best. It wasn't his style, but he was in a position where his only choice was to bet everything on a simple, straightforward suicide assault.

"Well, let me just tell you that everybody knows it's always the lone mecha that brings down the enormous battleship!" Psyching himself up, Haruyuki took a dash position in the sky.

"As if a mecha with a perv in it could do anything like that, stupid!" The Red King spat her comeback at him and added in a shriek, "Hailstorm Domination!!"

Zzgrrm! Tat tat tat tat tat! Krr krr krr krr!

Three kinds of gun reports thundered simultaneously as her main weapons, the missiles, and the machine gun unloaded as one. It was basically a "greatest hits" look at the sorts of long-range anti-aerial assaults that had been causing Haruyuki such grief. Last week and the week before, too, he had been forced out and shot down by firepower not even a tenth of this.

And yet, for some reason, it was only now that he wasn't scared or disheartened. Maybe it was complete apathy in the face of an enemy so much more powerful than himself, but for the first time in an incredibly long time, Haruyuki was overtaken by heat, as if all the blood in his body were boiling. And that heat was excitement for the duel.

"Nnngyaaah!!" With a war cry, he first dashed in midair to the right, somehow dodging the superheated beam of the main weapons. If he got hit dead-on with that, he'd sizzle up instantly. The beam narrowly missed him, passing immediately by his side to open up a huge hole in either Park Tower or the NS Building.

But his enemy seemed to have anticipated this maneuver. Countless small missiles closed in ahead of him, seekers twinkling.

Taking a deep breath, Haruyuki put everything he had into super-high-speed maneuvers. To draw the batch of missiles flying in a straight line, he turned back sharply, more than ninety degrees. Rocked by the explosion of the missiles that had lost their homing target, he lured off the next group, avoiding that detonation as well. Silver Crow flew on, carving out a zigzag in the sky like a UFO, countless explosions blooming behind him.

Strangely, he felt he could clearly make out the trajectory of the missiles and the barrage of the machine guns. He wasn't sure if this was the fruit of his training in that white room or not...

At the apex of the limit of his high-speed flight, Haruyuki felt suddenly deeply annoyed with himself. Why couldn't he have been moving like this in the Territory Battles at the end of every week? Why, when just a lone rifle was pointed at him, did his legs—no, his wings—cramp up and leave him grounded? If he was going to chalk it up to pressure, he should have been under much greater pressure now, engaged in a one-on-one battle with the notorious Red King.

I'm this fast. I can fly like this. So why do I end up eating bullets like a total klutz when it really counts? I need to get stronger. I have to be stronger, up my levels, and then she'll—

".....Ngh!" He gritted his teeth beneath his helmet, and his flight speed decelerated slightly, such that he failed to trace a single escape route. The remaining thirty or so missiles were converging from all directions ahead of him. At his back was the barrage of machine-gun fire. And on the ground, Scarlet Rain's left main weapon had finished charging and was beginning to track him.

"D-dammit!"

Haruyuki kicked down a missile closing in before him, blowing off the tips of his toes in the explosion. Using the reactive force, he altered the angle of his body and dropped into a sink-or-swim dive straight down. But the enormous maw of the main weapon was waiting there for him.

At that moment, a stormy wind blew across the battlefield, a geographical effect of the Weathered stage. A large cloud of dust rolled up from the naked concrete and the surface of the ground, and his vision was instantly obscured to a single shade of gray. The missiles around him lost their target and were forced to detonate one after another.

This is it!!

Haruyuki opened his eyes, focused his entire being on the ruby color glittering in the depths of the sand storm, and plummeted in a spiral.

The beam of the main weapon fired, piercing the center of this trajectory, but burning nothing other than empty space.

"Aaaaah!!" Battle cry torn from his lips, Haruyuki changed his posture and became a streak of light, plunging forward feet first. He was betting everything on a Kick to the gap between the two missile launchers he could vaguely make out on Scarlet Rain. If he managed a critical hit, he could come back from this.

But.

"Wha—?!"

As the tips of his remaining toes pointed swordlike converged on her, the enormous fortress-shaped avatar suddenly fell to pieces. The casings and main weaponry separated and disengaged along with the armor plates. The slender girl's avatar appeared at the center and regarded him before sidestepping like quicksilver and avoiding Silver Crow's Kick.

Haruyuki drilled a large hole into the ground with a grinding crash, falling awkwardly, and something struck his helmet with a clunk. Turning his face, he saw the muzzle of a small gun. Scarlet Rain's real body, the tiny girl avatar, leveled a crimson pistol at Haruyuki with her delicate right hand.

The second she avoided that Kick so easily, I lost. Although he admitted this in his heart, Haruyuki had a hard time surrendering and barked: "You think a toy like that's gonna pierce my armor?"

Conveyed only through the lenses of two round eyes, a smile blossomed clearly across the Red King's mask. "If I said that this gun is my most powerful weapon, would you believe me, big brother?"

Haruyuki took a deep breath, exhaled all at once, and held up both hands—even though his right hand had already been completely severed.

"I believe you. You win, Scarlet Rain."

The Red King laughed once again and asked, "Then will you do me a favor?"

"Huh? A favor...?"

She couldn't be asking him to betray the Black Legion. That was definitely off the table. Haruyuki panicked in his mind, but her response was completely out of the realm of the expected.

Suddenly threatening, the girl demanded haughtily, "Let me meet your guardian. In the real world...Both of us, flesh and blood."

2

A bright January 22. Thursday, 12:05 PM.

Rubbing eyes that hadn't gotten enough sleep, Haruyuki walked down the hallway on the first floor of Umesato Junior High School toward the student cafeteria.

The night before, he had, in the end, slept in his own room while his second cousin Tomoko—or rather, the Red King in that guise—slept on the sofa bed in the living room. But he clearly lacked the intestinal fortitude to sleep soundly in such a situation.

What exactly was the Red King's objective? Why put on the sweet younger sister act at first and bake cookies? And what was she planning to discuss when she met Kuroyukihime, otherwise known as the Black King?

Although he tried to seriously contemplate these and other questions, no matter what he did, the scene in the bath kept repeating in Haruyuki's mind. *Aaaah, that makes me a real perv, but I can't help it. I'm a thirteen-year-old boy, after all. But I have Kuroyukihime...*

Dawn broke with him still agonizing, so Haruyuki tossed back a breakfast of cereal, trying not to wake the deeply sleeping Red King, and left the house early. He managed to make it through his morning classes somehow with the help of the alarm on his Neurolinker, but as lunch break drew near, he roused himself a bit through self-interest, excited at the prospect of seeing Kuroyuki-hime again that day, enough that he flew out of the classroom the second the bell rang.

Stepping into the still nearly deserted cafeteria, he weaved around several long tables that were lined up and practically ran into the adjacent lounge.

She was seated at the farthest of the elegant, white, round tables arranged in a circle. Haruyuki forgot to breathe as he stared at the black-clad silhouette perched there. She almost looked as though she was glowing faintly, radiating softly from the mid-winter sunlight falling on her as it poured in through the window at her back.

He had seen this same scene countless times over these last three months, but the painful throbbing that filled his heart every time showed not the slightest sign of abating. He even felt as if the fact that this tableau, a perfect painting, existed again today was akin to a miracle.

Resting her chin in her hands gently, looking down at an enormous book that rested upon the table, the girl called Kuroyuki-hime finally lifted her head soundlessly. The soft sun sparkled as it slid along the long black hair flowing over her shoulders. Her beautiful face broke into a light smile, a ring of flowers blooming in an unsullied snowy plain.

"Hey. Morning, Haruyuki."

Even in the midst of his bliss at hearing his name spoken in her low, silky voice once more, Haruyuki felt ashamed recalling his recent and copious clumsy defeats, so as he walked over to the table, he bowed his head.

"Good morning! You, uh—"

You look beautiful again today.

Was what he desperately wanted to say, but he was completely incapable of uttering anything like that using his actual voice. He was forced to let something else emerge from his mouth. "You're early again today, huh? I've never been able to get here before you."

"It's only natural. The seventh-grade classrooms are on the

third floor, and the eighth-grade classrooms are on the second floor, after all." Her face clear, she shrugged lightly.

After pulling out the chair next to her and sitting down, Haruyuki replied, "I—I guess that makes sense. So then every day, you—"

"And rather than make you wait, I prefer to wait myself. That way, I can remember every instant of this precious time, right from the moment you appear at the entrance." She smiled again, her lips the petals of a black lily opening.

Joyful and daunted in equal measure that those words and that smile were directed at his fat, ugly self, Haruyuki slowly exhaled through pudgy lips the breath he'd momentarily held.

I seriously can't believe it. That this dreamlike, amazing upper-classman and the demonic Spartan instructor in the Accelerated World are actually the same person.

He personally would rather have spent as much time as possible with the former, but he expected that wasn't likely to happen today. Once he explained the situation spilling over from last night, there was no doubt that the gentle Kuroyukihime would immediately transform into the terrifying water lily of black death.

He was just thinking how he wanted to stare at her for even a second longer, like a love-struck little girl, when she opened her mouth.

"That reminds me. When you called last night. What was that? You suddenly stop talking in the middle of the conversation, and then you abruptly say good night and hang up. I believe... I believe you were saying something about the Red King?"

"Oh... um... right..."

During that one second when I was silent, I was fighting the Red King herself.

She wouldn't believe him if he just blurted out something like that. Because the level-nine Kings no longer had any need to earn Burst Points in normal duels to level up, they almost never appeared on the battlefield.

With no other options, Haruyuki resigned himself to telling her everything. The whole kit and caboodle, from start to finish, beginning with the "Big brother! You're home!" part—although he'd have to omit the problematic scene in the bath.

Several minutes later.

Kuroyukihime, her expression now a mixture of 30 percent amazement and 70 percent anger, raised a tightly clenched fist into the air while slowly inhaling.

That fool! Goddamn her!

She very nearly shouted in anger and pounded the table but checked herself at the last minute because there were several other students carrying lunch trays into the lounge now. They shot glances at Haruyuki and Kuroyukihime, the usual expressions of disbelief despite the fact that it was a familiar sight by now, and occupied tables a slight distance away.

Unlike Haruyuki, Kuroyukihime paid no attention to the other students as she took several deep breaths, fist still poised five centimeters or so above the table. Finally, she brought the hand down with a thud.

"I really want to... I want to say, you should have seen through her right from the start, but... a social engineering attack like this is certainly beyond all expectation. And carried out by the Red King herself no less."

"Right? Right." Relieved to have avoided a serious eruption, Haruyuki bobbed his head up and down.

Her expression finally settling into a wide, bitter smile, Kuroyukihime shook her head several times and said in a low voice, "Well... it's not as if there isn't an aspect of this that isn't quite lucky. A direct duel with a King is precious. You could never buy such an experience, no matter how many Burst Points you accumulated. How was she then, the second Red King?"

"Ridiculous. With one move, she sent half the government building flying... and she smashed my place in one go basically." Haruyuki recalled again that transcendental heat power and shuddered all over.

Watching him, Kuroyukihime laughed softly. "That type of thing is precisely the might of a singular specialized ability. I've heard that Scarlet Rain put all of her level-up bonuses into enhancing her long-range heat attack. Which reminds me, did the Red King move during your duel?"

"Huh?" For a moment, Haruyuki failed to grasp the meaning of the question and blinked furiously before quickly realizing what Kuroyukihime had left unsaid.

Right. Now that he thought about it, the Red King Scarlet Rain had transformed into her duel avatar before his eyes, clad herself in that fortresslike heavy armament, and then hadn't moved an inch until she finally cut loose with her antiaircraft free-for-all after leveling Haruyuki's condo.

Abruptly, he stopped shaking his head.

That wasn't right. At the very end of the end of the duel, when she dodged Haruyuki's full-speed plummet attack, the Red King definitely moved, although only by a single step—

"Oh, she did move. But it was only, like, five centimeters or so."

Hearing this, Kuroyukihime finally grinned again and clapped her hands together. "Well! That's really something! Scarlet Rain's other name, Immobile Fortress, was given to her not because she never moves, but because she never *has* to move. According to the rumors, in a large-scale battle—large enough to rouse the interest of the second Red King—she slaughtered nearly thirty enemies without moving one step from the coordinates where she appeared."

"Whoa…" Haruyuki gasped reflexively. And there he was, charging an opponent like that head-on. Ignorance was a terrifying thing. "I-if I'd known all that, I would've surrendered as soon as the duel started. I mean, you know you're up against a King, you flat-out say no before you even get to the duel. But from the whole 'Six Kings of Pure Color' bit, I just sort of assumed that the Red King was for sure a red something or other," he said.

Still with a smile on her face, Kuroyukihime replied, "Which is why I said on the phone that you need to study more. In the

Accelerated World, crowning the red symbol, none other than Red Rider—" Having gotten this far, she stopped abruptly.

Haruyuki stared, dumbfounded, as the vestiges of the smile on her lips melted away and disappeared. The blood drained from her white skin, turning it pale like ice.

"K-Kuroyukihime…?"

"No, it's nothing." The voice and wide eyes offering this reply to Haruyuki's question, however, were completely lifeless.

Ruled by an empty expression, Kuroyukihime slowly turned her face downward. He saw her right hand, still on the table, tremble, and he finally—and quite belatedly—realized the reason for her reaction.

The previous Red King. Red Rider.

This was the first time he had heard the name from her mouth. But he already knew why the Burst Linker with that name had left the Accelerated World. Two years earlier, Kuroyukihime— the Black King known as Black Lotus—had chopped his head off with her own hands. But she'd done so while they were at a meeting of the Seven Kings, rather than in the usual duel field, taking her speechifying opponent by surprise.

The cruel reality of battle between level-nine Burst Linkers was that if you were defeated just once, you lost all your Burst Points. Naturally, it went without saying that total point loss meant the permanent loss of Brain Burst itself.

Staring at Kuroyukihime's pale hands clasped tightly on the table, Haruyuki asked, half involuntarily, "Kuroyukihime…was the former Red King…to you, was…"

Was he not just a friend, but someone more special?

At the last second, he was self-aware enough to see that this question came from his own jealousy rather than concern for the person in front of him, and Haruyuki clamped his mouth shut in the middle of asking. He then bowed his head low. "I'm sorry. I'm being thoughtless. Last night on the phone, too…and this question now. I'm sorry, I really am."

"…No. It's fine. Don't worry about it." Her voice was husky, having lost all smoothness. "This is the path I chose. It's immature of me to react like this. Heh...I thought I had come to terms with all of this inside myself quite some time ago. After all, I made up my mind that every other Burst Linker is an opponent, that is, an enemy. But catch me by surprise, and look what happens. It's the height of ridiculousness." She laughed gravely and repositioned her right hand to rest on her knee.

Haruyuki spontaneously reached forward to envelop that hand. Kuroyukihime gasped and pulled hers back firmly, but Haruyuki resisted the tug with an uncharacteristic obstinance.

Although she was bathed in sunlight from the window, she was cold like a stone statue. So much so that he could practically hear the creaking as her tendons stiffened to their limits.

Summoning every bit of body heat he had to try and warm her hand, Haruyuki opened his mouth. "I—I..."

Despite the fact that he had a clear idea in his head of what he wanted to say, the ability to put it into words did not follow. As if unaware of the glances turned toward them from the lounge—which was quickly filling with students—Haruyuki moved his mouth desperately. "I absolutely will not fight you. I absolutely will not be an enemy. You're my 'guardian,' and I'm your 'child.' Before we're fighters, we're family, right?"

The silence continued momentarily before Kuroyukihime finally lifted her face, staring slightly upward at Haruyuki and nodding slowly. She smiled faintly, as if somehow sad.

"Shall we go someplace else?" She nearly sighed the words, but she did manage to return her right hand to its resting spot, unhindered this time.

She stood up smoothly and started to walk, carrying the hardcover book with her. Following her back, Haruyuki asked, "Wh-where?"

Somewhere we can be alone.

Instead, Kuroyukihime's response was exceedingly businesslike. "We can't exactly decide how to handle Scarlet Rain with just the two of us, can we? This type of thing has to be discussed by the entire Legion. We'll buy some sandwiches or something for lunch."

"Oh...r-right." Haruyuki bobbed his head up and down as he felt simultaneously disappointed and relieved by Kuroyukihime's return to normal.

The Black Legion, Nega Nebulus.

In contrast to the majestic scale of the name—Dark Nebula— the Legion was extremely small, made up at present of just three people, the last of whom responded to Haruyuki's mail with "I'm on the roof."

Pulling his neck in at the blast of cold air when he opened the steel door, Haruyuki was just able to make out a single person sitting on a bench way off to the side. Even as he hurried over, the figure sat so still that Haruyuki could almost imagine him as an actual painting, although of a different nature than Kuroyukihime's.

Tall frame, thin, but solid with muscle. The profile beneath the longish bangs, gently ruffled by a soft wind, held a calm sharpness reminiscent of a Japanese sword. Facing slightly downward, the fingers of his right hand were racing along in the air, likely operating a holo keyboard; but even this movement conjured thoughts of a samurai seated in Zen meditation somehow.

Hearing their footsteps, the young man raised his head, and Haruyuki lifted a quick hand. "Hey! Sorry for bugging you when you're studying. But do you have to do every single thing in this stupid-cold place, Taku?"

Takumu Mayuzumi—Taku, Haruyuki's childhood friend and battle companion—grinned from behind frameless glasses. "Doesn't the sun feel good today, though? You should get some sun sometimes, too, Haru." He then stood up briskly and bowed deeply to Kuroyukihime, who stood behind Haruyuki.

"Good morning, Master!"

"Mmm, morning, Takumu." Dipping her head, Kuroyukihime brought a wide, wry grin to her face. "As I've told you countless times, although it is true that I am the Legion Master, there is absolutely no need to always refer to me by that title."

"Apologies. But it really works best for me." Takumu took a slight step and gestured with his left hand toward the bench where he had been seated up to then.

Still wearing that same grin, Kuroyukihime sat, crossing her thin, black-encased legs before she arched a single questioning eyebrow, looked at Takumu, and said, "Excuse Haruyuki and me as we eat lunch here. And you? What about your lunch?"

"Yes, I've already eaten."

Haruyuki looked and saw a lunch box neatly wrapped up in a corner of the bench. He felt like he had seen the cloth covering it before and remarked lightly, "Chiyu made that, right? In which case, the two of you should have eaten together!"

Takumu turned a bitter smile toward him. "We're not like you and Master. We don't have the kind of relationship where we can be all openly lovey-dovey at school."

"W-we're not lovey-dovey!"

"We are *not* lovey-dovey."

When Haruyuki denied the charge in concert with Kuroyukihime, Takumu grinned and pushed his glasses up with a fingertip. "Talk about how you guys just sit and stare at each other in the lounge every day, this fluffy pink halo hovering over you, has made it all the way to my class even. Well, anyway, whatever. I've stopped rushing. I'll redeem myself bit by bit for all the things I need to redeem myself for."

Haruyuki put on a serious face and nodded. "…Right."

A mere two weeks earlier, Takumu had transferred from the school in Shinjuku he had been attending for seven years to Umesato JH the day the third term started. His old school was integrated from elementary all the way through to university, so Haruyuki had said it was a waste to transfer and tried to stop him. He remembered how hard little Takumu had worked for the entrance exam. But Taku's resolve was firm.

It wasn't for some pessimistic reason, like the fact that Shinjuku

was a battlefield under Blue Legion control. Takumu had decided
to put all of his time toward atoning for his crimes—hacking
the Neurolinker of his childhood friend and girlfriend, Chiyuri
Kurashima, breaking the rules of the Accelerated World, hunting Kuroyukihime.

An atonement that consisted primarily of always being by Chiyuri's side and continuing to fight desperately to protect Suginami, the territory of Nega Nebulus. Haruyuki wondered if even
the glasses he had started wearing this winter were a show of this
resolve.

As of the present, the year 2047, glasses had lost their original
function as a tool to correct vision and had become a fashion item
because the Neurolinkers on everyone's necks were equipped
with powerful visual compensation. But Takumu's blue glasses
were not an accessory. The lenses were the real prescription deal.
In other words, Takumu had stopped using his Neurolinker to
correct the nearsightedness that was a consequence of studying
too much with paper media and panel terminals.

As powerful as the Neurolinker was, it didn't have the power to
adjust the focus of the crystalline lens of a flesh-and-blood eye-
ball. Instead, it synthesized the blurry visual field captured by
nearsighted eyes with the images from the Neurolinker's internal
camera and corrected the perceived scene digitally in real time.
Which meant that over half of the world seen by people using
the Neurolinker instead of glasses was made up of virtual images
generated by the CPU.

Takumu had rejected that function and apparently decided to
see the real world with his own eyes. The real Chiyuri, the real
Haruyuki, his own real self.

*At some point, even Chiyuri, as awkward and weird as she still
is right now, is going to see how you feel, Takumu. You've already
shown her plenty what those feelings are.*

Haruyuki wanted to say this to his friend, but it was pretty
difficult. Despite what he said, Takumu sometimes got a look
in his eyes like he was still tormenting himself. The same look

Kuroyukihime got in her eyes when the topic of the previous Red King came up.

Shaking off these random thoughts, Haruyuki sat down next to Kuroyukihime and opened up his lunch bag. As he stuffed his face with a pork cutlet sandwich, he explained the situation once again, this time to Takumu, who was leaning up against the fence facing them.

Once he had finished listening to the whole story with wide eyes, Takumu nodded briefly. "Hmm."

"What do you think, Taku?"

"Well, even if we tried to guess what the Red King intends to say to Master, we don't have enough data to make those guesses meaningful. But I feel like I understand what she was planning to do if she had been able to keep up the charade for three days without exposing her true identity to you."

"Wow!"

"Oh ho!"

Haruyuki and Kuroyukihime let out exclamations at the same time, and Takumu turned toward them to continue speaking, the lenses of his glasses sparkling.

"Given your personality, Haru, if you had lived with her for three days, you'd have ended up fairly attached to your 'little sister.' And if she had said something along the lines of 'The truth is, I'm a Burst Linker. But because I'm a kid, all the big kids in the Legion steal the points I worked so hard to collect. Please, big brother, join my Legion and protect me!'…"

"Now really! That's ridiculous!" Kuroyukihime shouted, astonished. "Would anyone get tripped up by such an obvious trap? Quite the opposite, I would think; it would be plain as day that she would strip away all your points. However inclined Haruyuki might be, he would never…"

Here, she glanced over at Haruyuki.

"He…would never…"

She was speechless. Probably because she noticed Haruyuki was involuntarily tearing up.

"What is wrong with you?!"

"I-it's just…I mean, bullying, poor thing…"

As soon as he spoke, Kuroyukihime reached out with her left hand to pinch Haruyuki's cheek and yank it. "Whah haa ee oin oo do?"

"I'll tell you right now," Kuroyukihime whispered, glaring at him with eyes lit by an ember deep within. "You try anything noble like temporarily moving to another Legion to help your little sister, and you won't be coming back."

"Huh? Hai's aat?"

Releasing his cheek with a snap, the master of the Nega Nebulus Legion answered in a tone dialed up to evoke maximum terror. "You can't have forgotten. What was the fate of Takumu's 'guardian,' the senior Blue Legion member who disseminated that back door?"

"Uh, um…I'm pretty sure there was talk of a total point loss… so, uh, a revocation of Brain Burst…"

In front of Haruyuki, Takumu cocked his head and added by way of explanation, "About that 'total loss.' It's not as if he was thrown into duels and forced to fight until all his Burst Points were gone. In practice, that's just not possible. If you simply disconnected from the global net and removed your Neurolinker the moment the first duel was over and the acceleration released, you could escape the duels and the loss of points for the time being. Although the fate awaiting you after that would be being chased for the bounty, like Master here."

"Uh…uh-huh. Right."

"But you don't need to go to all that trouble. The Legion Master has a simpler method of 'executing' subordinates."

"Wh-what?! I haven't heard anything about that!!" This was complete news to Haruyuki, and he whirled his head around to look at Kuroyukihime next to him.

The older student, expression serene, opened up her right hand in a shrug. "It's written right there in the document shown when you apply to join a Legion. It's your fault for not reading it. And

I don't have any particular reason to execute you, do I? Other than, of course, if you cheat on me with some other girl."

Grin.

That smile, so full of affection, made him sit up perfectly straight. "I—I would never do that. B-but I kinda want to know this as a thing to know. Execution…what specifically does that…?"

"Mmm. Yes…well, we could call it a type of special attack. The moment you apply to the system to create a Legion and are registered as its master, it appears in your command list; the name of the technique is fixed. Very decisively, Judgment Blow."

"Judgment…," Haruyuki muttered, and Kuroyukihime turned her eyes softly from him, continuing her explanation with an increasingly serious expression.

"By joining a Legion, that is, a team, a Burst Linker obtains a large measure of security. Group battles reduce your risk and also stabilize your returns. As compensation for that advantage, there is the Judgment Blow. To participate in a Legion is to submit your life to its master. Legion members who receive this blow have their points zeroed out immediately and lose Brain Burst forever. The term of validity of this attack is during the period of Legion membership and one month after leaving the Legion."

"E-even a month later?"

"Mmm. That is to say, if you were disappointingly deceived by the Red King's social engineering, if you were to leave Nega Nebulus and join the Red Legion for even a short time, in that instant, you…It would be the same as giving her the power of life and death over Silver Crow."

"Whaaaat…" was all he could say.

In all honesty, he couldn't deny the possibility that he would have totally bought into the Red-King-as-his-second-cousin-Tomoko thing if he hadn't found that picture on his grandparents' home server. And after sleeping and waking up together for two nights like that, if she had come at him with the "Actually, I" attack Takumu guessed at earlier, he might have even given into his emotions and casually joined the Red Legion. It definitely could have happened.

However.

"But why?" Haruyuki spat out, looking at Kuroyukihime and Takumu in turn. "Why would the Red King go to all that hassle...?"

"And so we arrive inevitably at that question," Kuroyukihime growled. "Hmm... There's no reason to go so far as to put on this little suicide show, get Haruyuki to join the Red Legion, and obtain his loyalty by holding the Judgment Blow over his head. Not to mention that a Legion member with no sense of belonging to the Legion does no good and quite a bit of harm. Which means..."

Takumu picked up the thread as he pushed up the bridge of his glasses with his middle finger. "Which means there's something she wants to make Haru do just once. Just one time, and she could threaten him to make him do it. That must be what she was thinking. So then, this 'something' should be what the Red King plans to bring up with Master later. Since her little-sister cover was blown, maybe she's changed her strategy from the backdoor tactic she was working before?"

"Hmm." After growling in a low voice once again, Kuroyukihime looked up at Takumu. "How can I put this?... You're starting to look good for this."

"S-sorry? For what, Master?"

"The glasses character. How about we call you 'Professor' from now on, Takumu?"

Sliding his back down the fence propping him up, Takumu moved his head sharply from side to side. "N-no... I do appreciate it, but I'll pass."

Haruyuki worked hard to suppress the urge to laugh and said, "I-I think Taku's right. In the duel yesterday, the Red King could've mopped the floor with me, but she didn't. Instead, she told me to set up a meeting with Kuroyukihime. Which means she's choosing to negotiate as her Plan B, so isn't that basically a declaration that her intent is nonhostile?"

"You've finally said something sensible!" Kuroyukihime hummed and recrossed her legs. She crushed the paper that had been the wrapper for the sandwich she'd just finished and sank it in the garbage can a ways off, in an incredible overhand throw. "But, well, fine. If she wants to talk, I'll listen. At the very least, the sheer nerve of the King herself coming along, knowing full well that it outs her in the real world, is impressive, and in a child, no less. Haruyuki, call the Red King. The meeting will be today at four PM, the place—"

Here, Kuroyukihime cut herself off and stood up. She whirled around and grinned.

"Your living room."

Th-th-th-th-that's too soon I'm not ready we're honorable and just junior high students.

The confused, rambling refusal Haruyuki was preparing was dodged by Kuroyukihime with a simple: "It's all right for the Red King, but not me?"

Takumu invited Chiyuri to walk home with him, saying that he would come to Haruyuki's place after that, so inevitably, Haruyuki went home alone with Kuroyukihime.

Glancing over at Kuroyukihime as she walked along revealed her to be exchanging cheerful greetings with many other students while she kept one hand on her holo keyboard. She was most likely bringing student council work home as usual, but Haruyuki's thoughts were new and frantic.

Let's see, the living room, kitchen, and toilet should all be nice and clean. And we have tea and snacks. The problem is my room. Especially that blood-decorated, M-rated collection of games from the beginning of the century. If she saw those, I'd never be able to come back from that.

He had to defend his room to the last. No matter what happened.

He could not unlock that electronic key. Having made this resolution, Haruyuki glared at his condo building, just barely peeking out on the other side of the elevated Chuo Line track.

He got the unusually silent Kuroyukihime on the elevator, pushed a button, and got off on the twenty-third floor. All that was left was to walk a dozen meters along the shared outdoor corridor, and then they would be at his door.

"Um...my house is basically nothing special, it's just a regular house. We don't have any pets, either."

"I—I see. Not a problem. I hate shedding animals." Kuroyukihime coughed and stopped in Haruyuki's footsteps.

Please don't let anything happen! Prayer uttered, Haruyuki touched the unlock dialogue that floated up into his field of view. The click of the lock being released followed.

As soon as he yanked on the pull-type doorknob, Haruyuki's ears picked up the *rat-a-tat-tat* of the consecutive fire of a machine gun, a cry of, "Aah! Help me!" in English, and a girl screaming, "Yaah! Die! You're dead!"

"Aaaugh!!" Haruyuki cried in turn as he ran straight into the living room, removing his shoes being too much to deal with at that moment.

There he saw a previous-generation game console connected to the panel monitor on the wall, cases from his M-rated game collection scattered all over the floor, and the figure of the Red King sitting cross-legged on the sofa gripping a wireless controller.

"Wh-wha—My room...locked..." Haruyuki took a step into the living room, mouth flapping, and the Red King glanced back at him.

"Oh, you're home! Big brother, this is quite the hobby you've got. I love this kind of thing!"

Next to Haruyuki, standing stock-still with all thought processes stopped, he heard a slightly stunned voice. "Well, I can't say I hate it myself. The Western games from this era did have a certain philosophy. Mmm."

At exactly that moment, an older mafia don character was blasted away in a splash of blood on the large monitor.

"Yes! That's five cleared!"

Looking down at the elementary school girl posing triumphantly, Haruyuki muttered hollowly once again, "How...? It was locked..."

The Red King paused the game and finally turned her entire body around. She stared first at Haruyuki, then at Kuroyukihime next to him, before smiling like an angel, red pigtails bouncing. "I told you, didn't I? That your mom gave me a spare key for your place. It's easy enough to fiddle with that a bit and make it a master key. But don't worry, big brother. I didn't touch the other kind of M-rated games behind your reference books!"

His life was over...

His bag fell with a *thud* from his right hand, which had lost the ability to hold things. The Red King turned her gaze from the gobsmacked Haruyuki to stare at Kuroyukihime again, innocent expression wiped from her face.

Putting the controller aside, the girl lifted both legs and leaped down from the sofa. Her clothing was no longer the simple, pure white blouse and navy skirt of the day before. She was draped in a bright red T-shirt, black vest with a zipper overtop, and cutoff jeans that showed her slim legs right up to the base, accented with red and black-striped thigh-high socks. And around her neck glittered a Neurolinker with a semitransparent, ruby-like exterior.

The girl, clad in colors like the bright blaze of a fire, took a few steps forward, dangerous smile still playing around the edges of her mouth, and next to Haruyuki directly confronted Kuroyukihime.

In stark contrast in black, not a single color on her body as if she were an aggregate of cold darkness, the junior high school girl returned an aloof gaze and a cool smile.

He could almost see the blue-white sparks crackling between

the two of them and steadily retreated, momentarily forgetting the disastrous scene in the living room.

They're not actually going to just dive into a duel right here, are they?

He observed them with serious misgivings as the Red King placed both hands on her hips, lifted her sharp chin, and spoke without even a trace of the demure-sister act from earlier.

"Hmph, so you're the Black King. I get it. You sure are black. I wouldn't be able to see you at night, even if you were standing right in front of me."

Her usual sharp self, Kuroyukihime returned, arms folded, "And you are actually scarlet, Red King. It'd be interesting to hang you in an intersection and make cars stop."

The sparks increased a level in voltage, and Haruyuki took another step back, silently screaming.

These two were both level-nine Kings. Special rules applied if they got into a duel, and the loser would be unceremoniously stripped of Brain Burst. They certainly wouldn't enter into that fight lightly, but the low threshold of Kuroyukihime's flash point went without saying, and the Red King was doubtless a no less short-tempered personality.

I—I have to throw myself between them!

Haruyuki resolved to nobly sacrifice himself. "U-uh, I sure am happy I get to have a cute little sister and a beautiful older one all at once!" he said, scratching the back of his head with one hand. He turned a sheepish grin on them before he heard:

"I will kill you again."

"What is wrong with you?"

Two extracold voices lashed out at him simultaneously, piercing his brow and his heart.

No longer bothering to even glance at Haruyuki, staggering and crumbling, the two Kings continued to face off for another few seconds before finally averting their gazes together with disdainful sniffs.

After going a step further and clicking her tongue as if to nail an extra bonus, the Red King looked down on Haruyuki. "Hey, hurry up and make some tea. Don't you have any manners?"

"Oh, Haruyuki. I'll have coffee, black."

I like second cousin Tomoko from yesterday better, all baking me cookies and making me curry and stuff.

Honestly dejected, Haruyuki retreated to the kitchen on all fours, positioned himself where the two of them couldn't see him, and gently wiped the corners of his eyes.

Haruyuki and Kuroyukihime sat down next to each other at the large dining table while the Red King perched cross-legged on a chair on the other side. Just as they were sipping their coffees—Kuroyukihime's black, Haruyuki's with milk and sugar, and the Red King's essentially a café au lait made of milk alone—the door chime finally rang.

"Wow, this takes me back!" Takumu's cheerful voice called out as he came inside, the door unlocked remotely by Haruyuki. "How many years has it been since I came over here, Ha—"

And then he saw the devastation on the living room floor, immediately grasped that something of some import had happened, and clapped Haruyuki on the shoulder lightly, sympathy rising up behind his glasses.

Next, he looked at the Red King, and after narrowing his eyes for a moment, he set himself down next to her without a word. A cup of coffee with only a little milk was already waiting there for him, and he mumbled his thanks as he stretched out a hand. Affably, he offered, "First, how about we start by introducing ourselves? It would make sense for you to tell us your name, I think, Red King."

The girl sniffed quickly, but at the hard look Takumu shot her, she opened her mouth. "Well, whatever. I can do that much for you at least. I'm...Yuniko. Yuniko Kozuki."

She followed that with a snap of her fingers, and a crimson name tag popped up in Haruyuki's field of vision, inscribed with "Yuniko Kozuki" in a rather cute font. Although it was a business card sort of thing to give people you were just meeting, it was also a simple ID card. In the bottom right corner of the tag, a resident net certification mark glittered, and given the fact that even a wizard-level hacker would have a tough time forging this, the name on the tag had to be real.

The only other thing on the tag was her date of birth. Born December 2035, which meant she had just turned eleven.

There was often a discrepancy between the mental and physical ages of Burst Linkers, but in the case of the Red King—Yuniko— there was something that was hard to pin down. Sometimes, she seemed much more mature than Haruyuki, and other times, she was more like the girl her tag said she was.

"Hmm, Yuniko, huh?"

Tomoko-now-Yuniko gave the grinning Takumu a suspicious look. "Now what's your name, Cyan Pile?" Which meant the Red King had already done a fair bit of checking into Nega Nebulus.

Takumu had also likely made that assumption, and while his smile warped to include a hint of cynicism, he obediently voiced his real name. "I'm Takumu Mayuzumi. A pleasure." He slid a gentle finger, probably sending the Red King his name tag.

Yuniko momentarily stared into space, then turned her gaze on Haruyuki before her, jerking her chin.

"Y-you already know my real name, don't you? Haruyuki Arita."

"Gimme your tag," he was ordered, and he reluctantly turned to his desktop.

Finally, the eyes of all three fell on Kuroyukihime, who had stayed silent for this exchange. She lifted her face from her cup and blinked her long eyelashes slowly. "Hmm? Oh, is it my turn? I'm Kuroyukihime. Pleased to make your acquaintance, Yuniko Kozuki."

"Come on! That's not your real name!!" Yuniko shouted immediately, and Kuroyukihime flicked a finger coolly.

Instantly, a jet-black name tag appeared not only in front of the Red King, but also in Haruyuki's field of vision.

To the lower right of this, in a large Mincho font, the seal of resident net certification shone, and Haruyuki shook his head with a sigh. He really could not understand this girl.

The Red King released her breath slowly through her nose with an expression that was difficult to describe and finally clicked her tongue loudly. "Aah seriously, fine, whatever! I'll just remember you're totally shameless and actually have the nerve to call yourself 'hime' like a princess!"

Even if she was to force Kuroyukihime to give up her real name, Yuniko would have no positive proof that the next tag would be the real thing, either, since Kuroyukihime had clearly hacked the quantum cypher key of her tag.

Kuroyukihime finally smiled. "Much cuter than referring to oneself as 'King,' don't you think?" she asked, complacent and cool. "In any case, now that the introductions have been concluded without incident, perhaps you will allow me to get straight to the point." Her smile vanished, and her jet-black eyes were alight with a sharp gleam. "First of all, Red King—or rather, Yuniko. I must hear exactly how you cracked Haruyuki in the real."

First staring blankly at this unexpected opening, Haruyuki belatedly held his breath.

Right. This is the thing we should be concerned about more than anything else. How the Red King disguised herself as my second cousin Tomoko, not just the reason she did. Cracking the real is the ultimate taboo for Burst Linkers. Because it was directly connected to the safety of one's real-world self.

Glancing over at the now pale and easily read Haruyuki, Yuniko shrugged lightly. "You don't need to make that face. Even in the Red Legion, the only one who knows you're Silver Crow is me. I give you my word as King. As for how I pinned you down..." One corner of her mouth yanked its way up. "Same tech I used to sneak into this house. Social engineering. And in a way only an elementary school kid like me can do."

"Huh? What do you mean...?"

"Everyone knows you guys' territory is Suginami. And I guessed from the times you showed up that you were a junior high student. You following me so far?"

Because of the requirement that Burst Linkers must have been wearing a Neurolinker from birth, even the oldest ones were currently only sixteen. Strictly speaking, it was possible for some to be in tenth grade, but if they were students, the majority were in junior high, giving Yuniko's guess legs.

Nodding sharply, the Red King tucked her chin in slightly and continued. "So, then I used the fact that I'm in elementary school and systematically applied for school visits to every single junior high in Suginami Ward. Cuz if you get a visitor's pass, you can connect to the in-school local net. And then I just accelerate a bit while the teacher's showing me around and take a look at the matching list—"

"Which means you could discover Silver Crow at any point. Hmm, extremely troublesome, but your method makes sense," Kuroyukihime said, slightly vexed. "However, you couldn't have known anything more than that he was one of the three hundred students attending Umesato. How on earth did you determine it was Haruyuki here?"

At this, the Red King pursed her lips and fell silent for a moment. Face downturned, she gave Haruyuki a sidelong scowl before producing a voice that sounded very much like like she was excusing herself.

"Listen, it's not like I have any particular feelings for you one way or the other, okay? At best, it's your duel avatar I got business with, or more like just the wings on your back. I found Silver Crow at Umesato Junior High, I set up camp at a restaurant where you could see the road between the school gates, and I accelerated whenever students came out on their way home. I can tell you, I was pretty surprised when this guy was the person at the gate when Silver Crow appeared on the matching list."

Normally, this jab would've cut deeply, but right now, Haruyuki's resources were stretched too thin for that. His eyes grew round, and he flapped his mouth a few times before timidly asking, "Exactly how many Burst Points did you use...?"

"'Round two hundred maybe."

"T-two hundred!!" Haruyuki shouted, Takumu nearly dropped his cup, and Kuroyukihime offered a large, wry smile.

"I see. In other words, this is a method that only you, an elementary schooler who's also a King with points to spare, could employ. However, well...your tenacity's quite commendable. Have you really fallen so hard for Haruyuki?"

"That's not it!!" Irrationally, she kicked Haruyuki's shin with a bang under the table, and Haruyuki yelped.

"I told you!! My business is with the avatar, not the person inside!! I mean, if things had gone well, right about now I would've stolen him away and made him my subordinate!!"

"So, then," Takumu said quietly, still smiling, almond eyes filled with a cool light, "this 'business' is the ultimate reason you expended two hundred points, cracked Haru in the real, threw yourself into a social engineering project, *and* asked for this meeting."

As soon as he spoke, any hint of childishness was absent from Yuniko's face. "That's right," the Red King agreed in a low voice, shaking her neatly bound red hair, entrusting her slim body to her seat back.

Her dark green eyes shot straight at Haruyuki from beneath half-closed lids. The pressure of that gaze was more than sufficient to remind him that even if she was a small girl, she was still a King like Kuroyukihime.

"The wings on your back...I want to borrow your flight ability, just once. To destroy the Armor of Catastrophe."

3

Haruyuki couldn't understand the meaning of Red King Yuniko's words. Most likely, Takumu was in a similar state, eyebrows slightly furrowed behind his glasses. Only Kuroyukihime reacted with any intensity.

She abruptly clenched her right hand, which had been reaching for her cup. The Black King slammed her fist down on the table and shouted. "Fool! That armor...It's already been destroyed!!"

She fell silent, eyes staring off into space, and Haruyuki hesitantly posed a question to her pale profile. "U-um...What is that? The, uh, Armor of Catastrophe? It's a thing, not a person?"

For a few seconds, Kuroyukihime stayed silent, but finally, she leaned back gently in her chair and let out a long, narrow breath. Crossing her stocking-clad legs, she turned her upper body toward him.

"Yes...How to put it...It is a person, specifically, a Burst Linker; but it is also a thing, in other words, an object. I suppose you could describe it that way. Haruyuki, do you remember the first opponent you fought?"

"Oh, uh, yeah. The guy on the bike...Ash Roller, right?" Haruyuki nodded, an image of the splashy chopper motorcycle and the skull helmet floating up in the back of his mind. He still occasionally fought duels with him, a member of the Green Legion, which had its stronghold from the neighborhoods of Shibuya to Roppongi, sometimes winning, sometimes losing.

"His motorcycle. It's an object distinct from the rider himself but comprises the whole of the duel avatar. Which means that it ends up being a thing and a person, yes?"

"Umm...I guess so. Yeah." He bobbed his head again.

"In the Brain Burst system, this type of external item is called Enhanced Armament."

"Enhanced...Armament."

That...has a kinda cool name. Haruyuki felt a momentary thrill, which quickly changed into dejection. Because no matter how he looked at it, the empty-handed Silver Crow didn't have any.

As if seeing into Haruyuki's heart, Kuroyukihime smiled very briefly and somewhat bitterly before saying, "I don't have any, either. Don't be so down about it."

"I have some, though," Yuniko said, twisting her mouth into a sneer.

"Although in your case, it's rather that it has you at this point." Kuroyukihime's sharp voice rained down without missing a beat.

"Ooh! Those grapes are nice and sour!"

"O-okay," Haruyuki hurriedly interjected himself between the two girls' glares. "So those incredible heat-power lasers Scarlet Rain has...are those Enhanced Armaments?"

"They are. However, they are not such a rare item as this little girl boasts. There are actually four ways to get Armaments." Kuroyukihime stuck out the thumb on her raised right fist and continued. "The first is, you have some from the start as your initial equipment. Ash Roller's motorcycle is probably one of these."

"The Pile Driver in my right hand is one, too, right?" Takumu cut in, and Haruyuki cried out in surprise.

"What? You have some, too, Taku?"

"Yeah, well. Let's just listen."

"...I'll continue." The nail of Kuroyukihime's index finger stretched out, hitting empty space. "The second is, you obtain Armament as a level-up bonus. Although this is not possible if there are no choices for your bonus."

"...I didn't have any...," Haruyuki muttered, remembering the three times he'd leveled up so far. But even if there had been, he'd have followed Kuroyukihime's advice and poured all his bonuses into speed and flying time.

Her middle finger extended next, and Kuroyukihime continued with her explanation. "And then the third. You spend points and buy some in the shop. This one would be possible for you, Haruyuki, but, mmm, I don't recommend it."

"Huh? Shop... a store? Where is it?"

"Not telling. I can see only too well that you'll go crazy with all of your points."

"I—I..."

Takumu laughed out loud and nodded. "No doubt about it. When Haru goes into a store like that, his whole personality changes."

"Wh-what are you two even..."

The relaxed mood wafting out to the living room was cut short by a demand from Yuniko. "Hurry up and say the fourth!"

Although Kuroyukihime nodded as she met head-on the dangerous gaze of the Red King, she didn't immediately move to speak.

Consequently, Yuniko reached across the table and forced the ring finger on Kuroyukihime's right hand up while spitting out abruptly: "Four. Kill someone and take it."

"K-kill..."

"That's not an entirely clarified phenomenon, but...," Kuroyukihime added, a sigh-infused explanation for the benefit of Haruyuki gazing in wonderment. "If a Burst Linker with Enhanced

Armament loses in a duel and thus her burst points drop to zero and she is forever removed from the Accelerated World, in some cases, the ownership of the loser's Armament is transferred to the winner."

"One of the current established theories is that it's a randomly generated event with a low probability," Yuniko interjected, clasping both hands behind her head. "But 'maybe' isn't how it works for the Armor of Catastrophe. One-hundred-percent transferral rate—it's totes cursed."

"However," Kuroyukihime murmured, her teeth squeaking sharply as she ground them together. "That is impossible. It was destroyed. Two years ago, I saw the Armor... I witnessed the end of Chrome Disaster; I confirmed its annihilation!"

Chrome Disaster is the name of a legendary Burst Linker who had existed in the dawning of the Accelerated World, which is to say, seven years ago.

The story Kuroyukihime told began with those words.

Wrapped in the metallic gray, knight-like Enhanced Armor, Chrome Disaster possessed fierce combat abilities and made many Linkers crawl before him. His fighting method was, in a word, severe... or perhaps brutal; he was said to decapitate surrendering opponents, tear off their limbs, and perpetrate every outrage on them.

However, the end finally came for even him, he who had pushed countless duelers to the permanent loss of Brain Burst. The highest-level Burst Linkers—other than himself—joined together, targeted Chrome Disaster, and deliberately and repeatedly challenged him to duels.

In the end, his points dropped to zero, and in the moment he faced his "death" in the Accelerated World, he laughed loudly and cried out, "I curse this world. I dishonor it. I will be resurrected again and again."

Those words were truth. The Burst Linker called Chrome Disas-

ter himself left, but the Armor...his Enhanced Armament did not disappear. Ownership of it transferred to one of those who had subjugated him, and the mind of the Linker who equipped it, whether out of curiosity or giving into temptation...was hijacked. Despite the fact that until then this Linker had been beloved as a noble leader, in the space of one night—a single night—she changed into a ruthless slaughterer. Apparently, this wild figure was absolutely indistinguishable from the first Chrome Disaster.

There her words stopped, and after wetting her throat with coffee, Kuroyukihime continued gravely.

"The same events have, in fact, been repeated three times. Once the owner of the Armor has sown terror, they are subjugated, but the Armor, rather than disappearing, is transferred to the one who dealt its owner the final blow, and this transfer changes their personality. This Burst Linker is then referred to as Chrome Disaster, instead of their original name. Two and a half years ago, already occupying one of the seats of the Seven Kings of Pure Color, I participated in the subjugation of the fourth Chrome Disaster with the other Kings. The dreadful nature of that battle...Even now, my hair stands on end. I couldn't possibly communicate it in words."

She set her cup back down and stroked her arms gently over her uniform. "And that's it, Haruyuki." Her tone changed abruptly. "Sorry, but can you get two direct cables?"

"Huh, c-cables?! Two of them...?"

"I have one myself. As for length, I suppose a meter should do."

"O-okay."

Still not getting what she was up to, Haruyuki stood and trotted to his room, grabbed two of the XSB cables bundled up on a wire rack on the wall, and returned to the living room.

"I had exactly two. Um, the length is, this one's a meter, and this one's...ooh, ouch. Fifty centimeters." He dangled a cable from each hand, shrugging, and Yuniko stood up with an agreeable look.

"Ohhh, is that it? Okay, okay, I'll make do with the fifty-centimeter one." Smiling smugly, she grabbed the shorter of the cables from Haruyuki's left hand and plugged it into the connector on her own red Neurolinker. As soon as she had:

"H-hey! Enough! I'll use that one!"

"Noooope." Yuniko slipped smoothly past Kuroyukihime's outstretched hand and landed on Haruyuki's left arm. A body still hard like a boy's attached itself to him, its sweet and sour scent wafting upward as she aimed at the slightly stunned Haruyuki's neck. She thrust the plug at him.

He had no time to dodge, and the plug was inserted in his Neurolinker, causing a WIRED CONNECTED warning to flash before his eyes.

"Wh-whoa?! Wh-what—"

Yuniko looked up at the flustered Haruyuki and smiled boldly. "Come on, put that looooong one in and hand it to the girl there. Oh, and if you try and peek into my memory, you'll pay for it, so you better be careful."

At this, Haruyuki finally grasped the meaning behind the three cables. Kuroyukihime was trying to create a daisy chain among the four Neurolinkers present.

Takumu's and Yuniko's Neurolinkers were the lite type, with one external connection terminal, so the only way to connect all four of them was to have Haruyuki and Kuroyukihime—equipped with high-performance types with two terminals—come into the middle. Quickly grasping this, Yuniko had likely secured the shortest cable right off the bat to annoy Kuroyukihime. The effect was immediate, and Kuroyukihime's right cheek twitched as both fists trembled, and she cried threateningly, "Do not cling to him like that, you!"

"Don't have much of a choice, do I? Cable's too short."

"You were the one who chose it!" After raising her voice, Kuroyukihime finally sniffed with disdain and looked down on the Red King with her Kuroyuki smile and its temperature of absolute zero. "Honestly. This is why I despise children. Intimacy

being this or that depending on the length of the cable, it's really just nonsense!"

"Oh my, no one said anything about that, you know? I just figured there would be less signal decay with the shorter one."

"Th-th-this…"

Watching her aura suddenly rise from absolute zero all the way up to the temperature of the sun's surface, Haruyuki thrust out a cable with the other end connected and made desperate eyes at her, as if to say *Please forgive me somehow, your Highness!* Kuroyukihime took the cable, almost snatching it from him, and as she connected it to her own Neurolinker, she offered Takumu her usual two-meter cable, which she produced from her pocket.

Takumu, watching the proceedings half-dumbfounded, half smiling faintly, inserted the terminal, and Haruyuki heaved a sigh of relief when a second direct warning popped up, indicating that all four Neurolinkers were finally connected in a line.

"Um…so now….what are we doing?"

"First of all, sit down," Kuroyukihime commanded in an even more brusque tone. She promptly sat, tucking her legs under her and stretching her back up straight. Haruyuki hurried to follow suit, but the cable started pulling. Yuniko, still glued to him on the left, followed him down with a flop.

Finally, Takumu knelt, back straight, a reminder of his kendo team membership, and glanced over at Kuroyukihime. "Master, should we accelerate?"

"No, there's no need for that. After switching to full sensory mode, jump through the access gate displayed. Now, here we go. Direct link."

Watching Kuroyukihime's eyelids snap shut and her shoulders relax, Haruyuki hurried to shout the same command. "Direct link."

Immediately, the sensations from his entire body and the surrounding scene receded. His Neurolinker canceled out the actual information coming from his five senses, leaving only his consciousness to be called into the virtual space. In the darkness, he simply had a strong impression of falling. If he waited like this, he would go into a full dive on the Arita home net, but before that could happen, a round, shining access gate rose up before his eyes.

The instant he stretched out an invisible hand to touch it, Haruyuki's consciousness was sucked through the gate.

Light spread out, as if yanked from the center of his vision, and enveloped him. The scene that appeared was an infinite wasteland with nothing but rows and rows of strangely purple rocks.

Wondering where exactly this was as he turned his gaze downward, Haruyuki noticed that his body was not there and panicked a little. However, he soon realized that this was not the Accelerated World, but rather a VR movie; in other words, a recorded video that played directly inside his brain. As evidence of this, numbers counting out the play time and a slide bar floated small in the lower right-hand corner of his visual field.

"Um...Kuroyukihime?" he asked, and there was a response immediately to his right.

"I'm here. Takumu, little girl, are you also here?"

Although he couldn't see her, that was definitely Kuroyukihime's voice. Which was followed by the sound of two other voices: *"Yes"* and *"Don't call me that."*

When Haruyuki looked around again and confirmed that, yes, there really was nothing other than the weird rocks, he asked timidly, *"Umm... What is this movie file that's playing? If we're just going to watch a movie, why go to all the trouble of us directing?"*

"I don't want anything leaking to the outside, just in case. If I transmitted to all of you via your home net, it would remain in the cache of the condo servers."

"O-ohhh." He got the reason for the direct connection, but the

content of the movie was still a mystery. He cocked the head of his invisible body with the thought that it probably wasn't material that required any particular concern when he heard a sharp wind blowing suddenly in the sky above him. As soon as he raised his eyes, he saw a figure landing with a crunch about ten meters in front of him.

Jet-black, sparkling, semitransparent armor. Long, sharp, sword-shaped limbs. V-shaped head. There was no mistake, it was Kuroyukihime's duel avatar, Black Lotus.

"What? Kuroyukihime...?!" Haruyuki cried out unconsciously.

"Mmm," Kuroyukihime replied. *"It's me. From two and a half years ago, however."*

"Two...and a half years. No, wait...If you're in that form, then is this the Accelerated World? I mean, is this a recording of a duel...?" he asked, wondering if this was a feature in Brain Burst. This time, to his left it was Yuniko's voice that he heard.

"Thing called 'Replay.' You can record with a crazy-expensive item. Anyway, two and a half years ago—that means this is a replay of that battle you mentioned before, the Seven Kings of Pure Color versus Chrome Disaster? But there's just you alone?"

"No, someone else will come soon."

Before she had even finished speaking, a new duel avatar appeared from the left side of the field. Haruyuki strained his eyes as he wondered at the fact that it was a battle of many against one.

About a head taller than Black Lotus, its body was slim, but its arms and legs had serious volume to them. It carried a thick, rectangular shield in its left hand, and its right hand was empty. The color of the armor covering its body was emerald-like, deep and transparent green.

"What a beautiful green...Master, is that...?"

"Yes. The Green King," Kuroyukihime responded to Takumu's whisper. *"Affiliation is near and midrange...but the nickname more accurately expresses this avatar's particular nature. That is, invulnerable."*

"*Looks pretty hard. Rumor has it, all his losses were time-ups, and even then, his HP's never once been cut in half... Obviously a lie, though.*"

"*Watch and see,*" Kuroyukihime replied curtly to Yuniko's slight jeering, and the movie Black Lotus approached the green avatar, indicating with a gesture the shadow of a large rock beside them.

The Green King assented silently and slid into the shadow of the rock, pressing his back up against it. The Black King hid herself behind a rock a slight distance off. They were clearly planning an ambush.

Haruyuki watched over them, holding his breath even though he knew it was a video of the past, when he heard a sudden low crunch to his left. He snapped his gaze there with a gasp. *Crunch, crunch.* The dry sound of earth being trodden slowly drew closer.

A few seconds later, an enormous duel avatar appeared from between the strange rocks. It likely had another fifty centimeters on the Green King, and its chest, covered in bellows-shaped armor, was unusually thin and long, inclined forward, like a snake raising its head. Both arms were also almost impossibly long. Its hands, dangling down, held clumsy axes, thick blades nearly scraping along the ground. Its head was smoothly cylindrical, reminiscent of a massive earthworm, two black holes on the end. Dark inside, the eyes shone red and blinked vigorously over and over.

The armor on its body was a dusky silver. As the surface of it reflected the weak sunlight, the avatar, looking around at its surroundings, abruptly came to stare directly at Haruyuki. Standing stock-still, he instantly forgot this was a recording and cringed with fear.

What's going on? This... is this a Burst Linker? An avatar operated by a flesh-and-blood human being?

No way. It's like a robot... No, like a wild beast.

"*Is that... the fourth Chrome Disaster? It's completely different in form and size from the fifth one running wild right now,"* Yuniko murmured in a voice that was relaxed as always but tinged with faint tension.

"I suppose it would be. The black armor is Enhanced Armament, so the shape would change depending on the avatar equipping it. However, its characteristics do not change, no matter who inherits it. Essentially, an aggressiveness very close to madness," Kuroyukihime replied quietly, and as if guided by her words, the enormous black avatar wordlessly brandished its axes.

The blade's target was obviously the strange stone where the Green King was hidden. Whether by some unspecified means or by instinct, Chrome Disaster had seen through the ambush.

With a roar like a carnivorous animal, the avatar brought its ax down with ferocious velocity. The thick rock split like butter, but just before it did, the green avatar leapt sideways, slipping out from behind the stone.

The massive ax followed and was brandished once again. The Green King, turning and standing his ground, unable to flee this time, held aloft the square shield on his left arm.

With a metallic screech, the four corners of the shield expanded, and its rectangular shape became a large cross, large enough to basically cover the entirety of the Green King. The crude ax collided with the shield from on high with all the power its wielder's arm could muster.

A waterfall of sparks flew out, accompanied by the earsplitting *clang* of impact. Although the ax bounced back, the Green King dropped to his knees.

A cry indistinguishable between anger or joy leaping from his mouth, Chrome Disaster brought his ax down over and over with wild abandon. With his cross-shaped shield, the Green King efficiently and accurately continued his defense against the assault, which looked as though it could cut right through a body if it landed a single blow.

Here, Haruyuki finally noticed several deep cuts in Chrome

Disaster's dark silver armor. Each time the ax was swung, a black mist flew out of them and dispersed into the air.

"*He's injured . . . ?*" Haruyuki muttered unconsciously.

"He is," Kuroyukihime replied in a whisper. "*Right before this, he fought the other kings and was cornered in this place. In terms of his health gauge, he's on the verge of death. And yet he's still this wild. At the time, I feared him from the bottom of my heart.*"

I can totally believe that. Just watching the replay like this makes me want to run so bad. Muttering to himself, Haruyuki felt the hair on his real-life body, the sensations of which should have been cut off, stand up. In truth, it was unthinkable. A single-handed rampage against the kings, supposedly the strongest beings in the Accelerated World. And doing it while near death. Did this mean Chrome Disaster's true strength exceeded level nine?

Chrome Disaster growled, perhaps irritated at the Green King, whose defenses did not crumble no matter how many times the monster struck them with his ax. Even as he continued to attack, he stretched out his long head and wetly, abruptly opened his mouth.

Haruyuki stared in amazement as a long, thin tongue—or something resembling some kind of tube—sluggishly stretched out from the center of what was more reminiscent of a cylindrical intake port than a mouth.

"*That's one of Chrome Disaster's abilities, Drain,*" Kuroyukihime uttered sharply. "*He steals the HP gauge of his opponent in battle.*"

As she spoke, the long tube slithered out, trying to circumvent the Green King's cross shield to approach his head.

"*Watch out!*" Haruyuki cried out involuntarily.

Black Lotus, who until that point had stayed hidden, not joining in the battle in any way, flew out from the background of the image like a flash of black lightning. She brought the sword of her right arm down at a speed that made it impossible to see, and Chrome Disaster's tongue was severed at the root.

"Gah! Gahgahgahgahgah!!" The enormous avatar threw his head back, cries of clear distress and a murky darkness coming from the round mouth.

Black Lotus applied the sword of her left hand to a large wound carved into his chest and plunged through mercilessly, right up to the base.

The long blade, piercing through his back, suddenly shone a blinding violet. The Black King yanked her limb upward, ever higher, as she somersaulted magnificently backward. Before the glittering, ink-black avatar could land again, Chrome Disaster's head was ripped in two.

And the slide bar displaying the play time in the bottom right of the screen reached its end.

Returning from the full dive with the "link out" command, Haruyuki realized the palms of his real hands were damp with cold sweat. Takumu, sitting straight across from him, was also pale. Looking to his left, he saw that even the Red King Yuniko kept her lips silently pursed.

"He continued to fight in that state for another two minutes before finally perishing," Kuroyukihime murmured, removing the two cables plugged into her Neurolinker.

Haruyuki followed suit. "That...Was that really a Burst Linker?" he asked hoarsely, while bundling up the cables with stiff hands. "There was really a real player inside just like us...?"

"For sure. I mean, there's no real difference from the way The Fifth fights now...and that is that, Black King." Yuniko spoke in a low voice as she stood. She threw a glance at Kuroyukihime, who wore an unusually stormy look on her face. "I guess it's a fact you guys worked your butts off to take down The Fourth, since you have the replay. But, okay, if that's the case, why didn't the armor there, the Enhanced Armament, why didn't it disappear?!"

"It did!" Kuroyukihime shouted back, leaping to her feet. Lips pressed tightly together, she threw herself into a chair at the table. She waited for the other three to do the same before continuing in a strained voice. "Immediately after the owner of the Armor—the fourth Chrome Disaster—left the Accelerated World forever, the Green King and I rejoined the other five and checked our status windows then and there. We all confirmed it then: that we did not have the Armor in our storage. Meaning it was annihilated. The curse of continual transfer to the opponent defeating its host was severed at that time. And, in fact, Chrome Disaster stopped appearing after that!"

Abruptly cutting off the declaration that had practically become a shout by the end, Kuroyukihime glared at Yuniko as if challenging her.

The second Red King squarely accepted the pressure of those ink-black eyes. "If that's true, how do you explain what's going on now?!" she demanded sharply. "How do you explain the fact that The Fifth is definitely out there and running wild just like the old days?"

"What is The Fifth called? If whoever it is equipped the Armor, had their mind contaminated, and became the fifth Chrome Disaster, there's no reason their name in the system would change. If you duel them, you should be able to find out the name of the avatar inside the armor. Exactly which King was it who was possessed by this armor?!"

This time, Yuniko lowered her gaze and dropped into silence. A few seconds later, she heaved a long, deep sigh and shook her head from side to side.

"...It's not a King. The Fifth one is one of our...a member of the Red Legion, Prominence. Originally named Cherry Rook. But that guy's not in there anymore. He's been eaten up by the Armor; he's gone." Her voice, in contrast with her tendency toward aggressive words, was unusually hoarse and shaky.

"It's not...a King? A member of the Red Legion? But..."

Kuroyukihime's eyes narrowed swiftly, and she stroked her pale lips with her right index finger.

As she furrowed her brow, sinking into thought, Takumu raised a hand lightly and began to speak. "Perhaps it's something like this, Master. If they connect directly, perhaps through the shop, Enhanced Armament can be transferred between Burst Linkers. I can't really speak to this personally, but considering that backdoor program incident, I can't believe all the Kings are pacifists with perfectly clean hands. Perhaps some King with an ax to grind made a false promise two and a half years ago, secretly carried the Armor away, and then handed it off to Cherry Rook?"

"Could something like that...have happened? But it's as I said before, the Kings—level-nine players—no longer have any reason to desire large quantities of points. No matter how many we collect, we still can't reach level ten. So if this King did hand the armor over...the only reason could be to strengthen their own Legion and weaken the others. But the risk of setting the uncontrollable Chrome Disaster loose is too great. Moreover, if a Red Legion member has it, then the originator would have to be the Red King. But the Red King who took part in the subjugation two and a half years ago..."

Most likely, Haruyuki was the only one who noticed Kuroyukihime's voice stiffen for an instant.

Her cool hand suddenly touched his under the table. As if gaining strength from his warmth, she continued speaking, the tremor in her tone under control.

"The Red King of the time is no longer in the Accelerated World. He was also killed a mere three months after the subjugation of Chrome Disaster. So it's not possible for him to have been the originator."

"I don't actually know the details since I had only just become a Burst Linker and was just chirping away back then," the Red King interjected gloomily, seemingly having failed to notice

Kuroyukihime's momentary trouble. "Obviously, I didn't inherit any Armor or anything from my predecessor. And even if I had, I wouldn't dream of making a member equip it. Why would I? Just seeing that demonic fighting style…"

"I-is The Fifth…that incredible?"

Yuniko glanced up at Haruyuki's question. "More than in that replay, in some ways," she spit out. "He's no Burst Linker anymore, and the way he fights is no duel. I…I saw him pluck the arm off a fallen opponent and chomp down on it."

"Geh," he groaned, imagining the scene involuntarily. Overpowering the sour, bitter taste of his coffee with plenty of milk and sugar, Haruyuki asked the two Kings before him, "B-but… before you said stuff like 'possessed' and 'contaminated mind.' The Enhanced Armament…Does that mean it's not just an ordinary weapon? Does it actually interfere with the thoughts of the Burst Linker themselves?"

"It does. And it's certainly possible," Kuroyukihime asserted immediately. "Do you remember? I explained it to you when you became a Burst Linker, Haruyuki. Brain Burst reads the user's feelings of inferiority and obsessions, condenses them, and creates the duel avatar."

"R-right."

"That means that it has the ability to access not only the sensory areas of the brain through the Neurolinker, but also the domains of thought and memory, although general applications are strictly regulated. All of which is to say—the Enhanced Armament is stained with the awareness of losing the Burst Linker who produced it. When someone else equips it, it's quite possible that that awareness flows back into them."

"That's…I can't…" A shiver ran up Haruyuki's spine. He often found his own negative thoughts too much to handle; he was sure he would be instantly crushed at having to bear another person's. "I-I'm fine. No Enhanced Armament for me."

"Good," Kuroyukihime agreed, laughing briefly. "Although,

well, it's most likely only Chrome Disaster that would contaminate your mind to the point where your entire personality changes. Just what kind of person was the first Chrome Disaster—"

"I don't know. And I don't care!" Yuniko shouted, standing suddenly, chair clattering. "He was a stupid bastard ruining everything! He was an idiot for making it! Same goes for the idiot who picked it up and hid it and then gave it to Cherry Rook! Cherry was...He was a good guy. Didn't have any incredible abilities or anything, but he kept plodding ahead and made it to level six. Things were supposed to be fun for him from now on! And now...Shit! Goddammit!!"

As she turned away with incredible swiftness, Haruyuki saw something slightly damp in the Red King's large eyes.

Staring out at the group of skyscrapers on the other side of the balcony, Yuniko squeezed out a trembling murmur. "He's still a member of the Red Legion, and he's going through the other members and attacking them systematically. Breaking the non-aggression pact. I...I have to clean house."

"I see." Kuroyukihime broke the profoundly heavy silence that descended briefly with a quiet observation. "Although this is *the* infamous Chrome Disaster. Even if you set out to defeat him normally...that is while he remains a member of the Legion...being Legion Master, you could expel him forever from the Accelerated World with a single move, with the Judgment Blow."

Holding her silence a few seconds longer, Yuniko nodded slowly before shaking her head from side to side. "Ten days ago—he had just gotten to level seven—I challenged him to a one-on-one. To clean house, right? But—Get this, Black Lotus. He—Chrome Disaster managed to dodge every single one of my long-range attacks."

"What?"

"Doesn't matter which Legion Master you are, the Judgment Blow is a close-range technique, basically point-blank. To land that blow, you gotta slam 'em with a normal attack to cut their legs out from under them. But no matter how much I fired my main weapons or my missiles, I couldn't even scratch him. The opposite, actually. His sword chipped away at my HP until finally...I lost in a time-up."

"You lost?! You're telling me that even with the Judgment Blow, you, a King, lost?!"

"Don't go acting all surprised. You fought him; you get it. That kind of mobility, no one but monsters can move like that. Incredible long-distance jumps, control of his trajectory in the air, it's almost like he's flying."

"Fly...ing..." Swallowing back a murmur, Kuroyukihime stared first at Yuniko, standing on the other side of the table, and then at Haruyuki, sitting next to her. Then she nodded, slowly, deeply. "I see. We finally come to your objective. I understand why you spent such an incredible amount of time cracking Haruyuki in the real and going on this suicidal social engineering mission."

At that point, Takumu seemed to arrive at the same conclusion, and scrutinized by the other three, Haruyuki squirmed, swinging his gaze from side to side.

"Wh-what? This objective...What is it?"

"Isn't it obvious, big brother?" Yuniko said sweetly, abruptly adopting the pure demeanor of her angel mode. "You capture Chrome Disaster for me."

Nearly five seconds passed with Haruyuki in a slack-jawed daze.

No way. Too scary. You've gotta be kidding.

Haruyuki shouted, fell off his chair, and tried to hide behind Kuroyukihime. But the Black King dropped her head thoughtfully, grabbed the back of the collar of his school uniform, and yanked upward mercilessly.

"Haruyuki, all things are experiences," she whispered, the gentle smile of a saint on her face. "I don't think there's any harm in trying."

"Wh-what?!"

"I'm not saying go in there and fight one-on-one. However, this problem involves not only the Red Legion, but the entire Accelerated World, including those of us in Nega Nebulus. In which case, perhaps this is a situation where you need to stand up as a man, as a Burst Linker."

When she gets that look on her face and starts talking like this, she's generally plotting something, Haruyuki groaned in his heart, but unable to guess what that something might be, he groped frantically for a decent excuse.

"B-but...even a King, I mean, a level-nine Burst Linker, was no match for this guy! A level-four Linker like me, he'll send me flying instantly, and the whole thing'll be over! And I don't want to have my head or arms or anything yanked off!!"

"I would not let that happen to you, would I?" Once again: that smile like the finest gelato melting. "All you need to do is follow Chrome Disaster with your speed and flying ability, and prevent him from moving for a brief while. Myself and the little girl here will then steal from the enemy the power of movement."

"Y-you say that, but—" Not knowing when to give up, Haruyuki dialed up his escape skills to full and somehow managed to come up with a final argument. "That means, then, that you're assuming you'll bring him into a team battle? But that'll put Chrome Disaster up against at minimum me, you, and Scarlet Rain all by himself. There's no way he'll accept a duel with that kind of handicap!"

As long as a Burst Linker's Neurolinker was connected to the net, they couldn't refuse a challenge to a normal one-on-one duel from another Burst Linker. But it was a different story when the duel mode was "team" or "battle royale." They would be challenging the person inside Chrome Disaster to an extremely disadvantageous three-against-one fight, and he couldn't possibly agree to that.

Wait a minute. Wasn't I just wondering about that?

Speechless, Haruyuki dipped his head lightly, and Kuroyukihime said, glancing over at Yuniko as if to confirm, "If Chrome Disaster were running wild in normal duels, news of that should have already reached my ears. However, I haven't heard a single rumor. Which means…"

"Right." The Red King stuffed both hands in the pockets of her cut-off jeans, leaned her slim body back, and nodded decisively. "His hunting ground isn't the Normal Duel Field…it's the Unlimited Neutral Field."

What the hell is that? Haruyuki once again had a question mark hanging above his head, but it was Takumu to his right who cried out sharply.

"I-it's too dangerous, Master!" Leaning forward in his chair hard enough to make it clatter, he proceeded to argue even more vehemently. "Diving with our battle array is too reckless! Forget Haru and me; you're constrained by special rules! If by chance another level-nine Burst Linker launches a surprise attack on you, if you're defeated even once, you'll lose Brain Burst instantly…and in the worst-case scenario—"

Takumu glanced at Yuniko standing to his right and seemed to hesitate slightly, but as he touched a finger to the bridge of his blue glasses, he said, "It's my duty to say this. So I will go ahead and say it. In the worst-case scenario, it's even possible that this entire spectacle—cracking Haruyuki in the real, telling us this story about Chrome Disaster, all of it—is just a trap set by the Red King. It's possible she's planning to lure you into the Unlimited Field, ambush you with a large force, and take your head."

"Welp, thanks for saying it, Cyan Pile." Yuniko, returning once again to tiny demon mode, jerked her slender chin out, hands still in her pockets, and glared at Takumu. "This whole time, you've been the one saying all the smart stuff. What's your deal? You the glasses guy? Your nickname 'Professor'?"

After looking slightly injured momentarily, Takumu quickly regained his composure. "I'm saying, show us some proof, Red

King," he replied. "We're a legion of just three people; if you'd have us brave danger and dive in, you should have come with some kind of collateral for asking that!"

"Isn't the collateral right here?" Yuniko quickly jerked her right hand, freed from her pocket, around her virtual desktop; bringing three fingertips together, she flicked. A semitransparent name tag again appeared in Haruyuki's field of view. But this one was a little larger. Because it didn't just have her real name; her address was displayed below that.

Haruyuki stared dumbfounded at the row of letters that started with "Tokyo, Nerima Ward" and ended with the name of a school and dorm he'd never heard of. She had exposed enough about her true identity just by telling them her real name and showing them her face; revealing her current address went beyond bold and into reckless.

Takumu and Kuroyukihime also appeared surprised by this, and under the wordless scrutiny of the three junior high school students, Yuniko jabbed at her own thin chest with the thumb on the right hand she pulled away from her desktop.

"Don't you get it yet, why I contacted you in person? On the real side, I'm just an elementary school kid with no strength, no money, no organization. If I was attacked here, I'd be helpless. If I betray you, you can come and make me pay anytime," Yuniko said, and Haruyuki watched as her eyes caught the afterglow of the midwinter sun streaming in the window and burned a radiant red.

She was fiercely determined, to the point where it was almost desperation. And it was true that a member of your own Legion breaking the nonaggression pact and going after other Legions was a problem you couldn't shut your eyes to. But the major premise here was that at the end of the day, Brain Burst was a fighting game, a thing that existed to play, to enjoy, to thrill.

Which is why Haruyuki thought it was a mistake to sacrifice your real-world self to Brain Burst. He was sure this was the issue that had confused Takumu three months earlier, a problem that probably made him suffer even now.

"Yu-Yuni," Haruyuki called out unconsciously on Takumu's behalf, silent as if overawed, groping for what to say next.

"I know what you wanna say." The Red King smiled self-deprecatingly as she lowered her right hand, as if guessing Haruyuki's feelings from that single word. "But you know…You'll probably realize this if you get up here one day, but when you get this game, the real is just so incredibly weak. Because of this 'acceleration' technology. If you knew exactly how much time me and that girl there had spent in the Accelerated World up to now, it'd knock you flat on your butt."

"Huh…so your total play time…?" Haruyuki cocked his head and did a back-of-the-envelope calculation. Break it down to about ten duels a day. If the average time for one fight is twenty minutes, that's a total of two hundred minutes—just over three hours. That was a lot of game play for someone in junior high, but it wasn't unreasonable.

Over three hours a day, that would be a hundred hours a month. Twelve hundred hours in a year. And Yuniko said it had been about two and a half years since she became a Burst Linker, so…

"About…three thousand hours?"

That seemed huge, but compared with full-blown VRM-MORPG (virtual reality massive multiplayer online role-playing game) addicts, it was practically nothing. Those guys easily dove ten consecutive hours in a single day.

But Yuniko started cackling the instant she heard the results of Haruyuki's earnest mental arithmetic, and even Kuroyukihime was roused to a faint, wry smile.

"Huh? That's not it? Then how how many hours in total, Yuni…?"

"Not telling. You decide the answer yourself. And—" The expression on the Red King's face was suddenly scary as she continued darkly, "Quit with the 'Yuni.' Makes me itch all over. Niko's good. Call me 'Niko,' and don't you dare add any cutesy flourishes or anything."

Feeling like he'd been let off the hook somehow, Haruyuki bobbed his head up and down and ran his eyes over the room. "Umm...then does this mean we can help Yuni—the Red King after all, as Nega Nebulus?"

"Mmm. There are many risks, but for the present, let's accept this thing at face value. And it's not as if there aren't benefits."

"B-benefits?" Haruyuki asked in response, and Kuroyukihime shifted her gaze to glance at the Red King.

"Exactly. Because for the incomparable Prominence to come to us with such a significant request, they've naturally prepared some bargaining points. For instance...they won't lay a hand on our modest Territory in the future. Things like that."

"Tch!" Clicking her tongue softly, the Red King—Niko—waved her right hand lightly. "Got it. If verbal's good, we can make an agreement right now. I'll tell my guys not to touch Suginami for the time being."

Kuroyukihime dipped her head and from crossed arms lifted a single finger on her right hand. "However, that is just one point. Scarlet Rain...exactly how are you intending to ambush Chrome Disaster in the Unlimited Field? I'm sure you know it's very nearly impossible to target and confront someone there."

"I won't make any trouble for you guys. I'll take responsibility for this, set the time and place. Right now, all I can say is...it'll probably be tomorrow evening."

"My. Can you do that?"

Yuniko nodded her assent to Kuroyukihime's question and its implications.

"In that case, I'll let you handle it. We'll meet again here after school tomorrow and dive into the Unlimited Neutral Field. Acceptable, yes? Haruyuki, Takumu?"

What exactly is this Unlimited Field, though?

But even before the desire to pose that question, Haruyuki couldn't help but feel his heart lurch. *What? My place again?!* It might be okay because his mother wouldn't be back from Shanghai until the following day, but if he came home tomorrow and this time Niko was in the middle of appreciatively sampling the "other kind" of M-rated games in the living room—if that happened, he'd be doomed forever.

He had to defend it. This time for sure, he would defend his room!

Making this vow, Haruyuki bobbed his head as Takumu slowly nodded.

"Well, then let's leave off there for today. Haruyuki, thank you for the coffee." Kuroyukihime stood as she spoke and stared again at the collection of vintage Western games from several dozen years earlier scattered around the living room. "I'd like to come over and play sometime. You have a lot of titles I've never even heard of."

"S-sure, that'd be great." *One of the ones that doesn't have too much blood and guts*, he added in his head as he saw Kuroyukihime and Takumu to the door.

"Okay, Haru, see you at school tomorrow. Whoa! It's already so late!"

First Takumu, too impatient to even take the time to wave a hand, ran off toward the skyway connecting to a separate wing, and then Kuroyukihime slipped on her loafers and turned around.

"U-um...I'll walk you home. It's already late—" Haruyuki offered, but a dismissive wave of her hand interrupted him.

"No need to worry. It's common for me to be even later with student council business. And my house is surprisingly close."

"Oh...is it? But be careful."

"Mmm-hmm. All right, then, thanks for having me over. See

you tomorrow." Kuroyukihime smiled, raised her right hand, and started out the door.

"'Kay then, Blackie," Niko drawled at her back from behind Haruyuki. "Don't be late tomorrow, y'hear? Now then, back to what I was doing…"

"Hold up!" Kuroyukihime whirled at top speed and shouted after the Red King who had started trotting back off into the living room. "Hold on a sec, Red!"

"Whut?"

"You can't possibly be intending to stay here again tonight?" She glared at Niko, throwing her neck back, eyes shining from deep within, and demanded an explanation.

"Totes. Too much hassle to go all the way home and stuff."

"Quit fooling around and go home! Children should go home, do their homework, brush their teeth, and go to bed!!"

Niko guffawed, and let the heat roll right off her. "It's just, I go to a boarding school. And I got a three-day pass to leave, so even if I do go back, there won't be anything for me to eat. So! Biiiig brother, what am I gonna make for supper tonight?" Uttering the last bit in angel mode, Niko disappeared into the living room.

"Wh-wha—" Kuroyukihime, on the verge of a massive explosion, both fists clenched and shaking, glared sideways at Haruyuki, who was standing stock-still in mute amazement. "I take back my 'see you tomorrow.' I'll stay here tonight as well."

After giving voice to this terrifying announcement/declaration of war, she shut the door forcefully, removed her shoes, and stomped down the hallway, returning to the living room.

His brain completely frozen, Haruyuki needed a full minute to reboot.

What's going on?

What's going on how is this happening is this actually real? Or is it, A to Z, all of it, fake and made of polygons?

Haruyuki sat down on the living room sofa, clutched a cushion, and let his gaze wander in space.

Maybe all of it right from the start—meeting Kuroyukihime, getting Brain Burst, becoming the Burst Linker Silver Crow— every little bit of it was a dream. He was probably running some kind of app to escape reality by constantly viewing a lengthy simulation.

Although Haruyuki tried seriously to doubt what was happening, the aftertaste of the slightly burnt hamburger he had eaten just half an hour earlier, the happy sensation in his stomach, and the sounds of water and girls' voices as they played around, echoing from the bathroom and separated from him by a mere hallway, were just too real.

After Kuroyukihime's sudden declaration, the three went shopping together in the shopping center at the bottom of the condo, made supper together, and did the cleanup. Ending the night with Niko and Kuroyukihime using the bath together first. But...

The situation and the sudden and precipitous turn it had taken was just too unrealistic, and Haruyuki was, wastefully, left running on automatic. His consciousness simply could not adjust to the scenario "home alone," "two girls come to stay over," and "make dinner, get in the bath." Exactly what was the optimal solution to the problem of how to act now? What choices would be normal at a time like this, for a boy?

Smoke coming out of his ears in puffs, Haruyuki kept the excessive load of his thoughts scraping round and round. In anime and games of this type, this sort of scene generally had the boy going to ask about the temperature of the water, after which some crazy accident happens, and he ends up tumbling into the bath. Resulting in bath buckets and shampoo bottles being thrown at him until he beats a hasty retreat.

In which case, me doing that is really the optimal solution.

Haruyuki bounced to his feet and started staggering toward the bathroom. Already in his mind, he could see nothing other than a cut scene of Kuroyukihime and Niko covered in bubbles, washing each other.

However, unfortunately—or perhaps fortunately—just before he could open the living room door, he heard two sets of footsteps heading his way down the hall. Haruyuki teleported to the sofa at light speed.

The knob turned with a violent clack, and Niko sprang through first, shouting, "Ice cream!" as she ran into the kitchen. When he instinctively averted his eyes from her, roughing it in a loose sweatshirt and shorts, his gaze fell upon Kuroyukihime.

She was wearing thin pink pajamas, likely bought at the shopping center that evening. From the slightly doubtful-looking figure, towel over damp, shining hair, came the scent of a touchingly defenseless loveliness, an impression he would never have even imagined given her usual black accoutrement, which separated her from other people. All Haruyuki could do was gaze at her, jaw dropped.

"Don't stare at me like that. This color was all they had in my size," Kuroyukihime said, turning away, and Haruyuki finally came back to his senses, shaking his head violently from side to side.

"N-n-n-n-no, it's fine! Th-th-they look good on you! Really good!"

"D-do they? They're not a bit childish?"

"No! Not at all! They're perfect. Just right. Critical hit." He had desperately, frantically gotten that much out, still kneeling, spine straight, when Niko popped her head in from the side and waved a popsicle in her right hand.

"Hey! Silver Crow! Know what?"

"Wh-what?"

"This girl might look like this now, but take her clothes off and she's surprising*loof*—"

The ending was courtesy of Kuroyukihime landing a merciless blow to her solar plexus.

"Now." Squeezing the Red King's throat from behind, Kuroyukihime smiled coolly. "You hurry and use the bath, too. The water will get cold."

He looked at Niko dangling there and flew off the sofa, giving a little scream in his head. "R-right! Okay, I'll leave you two and take a quick jump in the tub! There's barley tea in the fridge, so please help yourself!"

The evening ended with an M-rated retro game tournament that lasted until the middle of the night.

As they sat on the floor around the massive game console from forty years earlier, chattering and laughing, slaughtering the flat images of creatures, Haruyuki could not stop wondering if the whole thing was actually real.

Me and these people, we're basically only connected through the VR game Brain Burst. So I should recognize that the foundation of our relationship is online—the Net.

I do love Kuroyukihime, and she says she likes me, too. But the intermediary for those feelings up to now has basically been the quantum signals exchanged nonstop between our Neurolinkers. And I thought I was okay with a relationship that could be widely recorded and captured by vector data.

But today we made supper together, we ate it together, we took turns in the bath, and now we're sitting here separated by only a few dozen centimeters; we can even feel each other's body heat.

In this world where the border between real and virtual is endlessly blurred and we can't even tell how much of the information our senses receive is analog and how much is digital—is this something that can happen in this world? How am I supposed to grasp and process off-line human relationships? After all, off-line—in the real world—all I've done is run away, hide, and shrink from everything.

The showy scream erupting from the enormous boss monster on-screen interrupted his rambling, whirling thoughts. At the same time, Niko dropped her controller and flopped over backward.

"Aah...I'm can't go anymore. I'm tired. Tired!"

"Well, I did tell you. Children should—Naaah." Kuroyukihime put her left hand to her mouth and yawned elegantly.

Looking up at the clock on the wall since he had already removed his Neurolinker for the night, Haruyuki saw the time creeping up on midnight. "O-okay, I guess we should head for bed already? Umm...Yuni—I mean, Niko—maybe the sofa here is good for tonight. And Kuroyukihime, please use my mom's bedroom. Oh, but maybe it'll be cold in there if I don't turn the heater on for a bit—" Haruyuki had gotten that far when Niko interrupted loudly.

"Whatever. Such a hassle! Bring out a blanket, I can just sleep... here..." She buried her head in an enormous cushion and soon closed her eyes.

"Mmm. That's good for me, too. Sleeping together in a pile, surrounded by games, a historic experience...actually..." And then she, too, was flat on her back.

Although he wondered at this, there was no way to do anything like valiantly pick them up and carry them to bed, so Haruyuki did as he was told and brought out whatever blankets they had. He gently covered Niko and Kuroyukihime, who were already asleep, and thought to himself, *Now, then. I guess I should go sleep in my room?*

But isn't it kind of jerky to leave my guests to sleep on the floor while just I go sleep in a bed? Shouldn't I sleep on the floor, too, in the interest of fairness? Isn't that what a gentleman would do?

After persuading himself with this rationalization, Haruyuki turned the ceiling light to its lowest setting and curled up in a ball on the spot. The floor, embedded with heat-circulating pipes, was slightly warm, and the large, malleable cushions were fluffy and soft. And from so close he could reach out and touch it, he could smell the most amazingly pleasant scent.

Haruyuki closed his eyes tightly beneath his blanket thinking that there was no way he'd be able to sleep in a situation like this. But oddly, rather than nervous tension, a strange serenity descended on him, and his consciousness immediately dropped into a gentle darkness.

Haruyuki woke just once in the middle of the night.

When he stood to go to the washroom and casually shifted his gaze, an unexpected scene popped into view in the dim illumination of blue-white moonlight.

Niko and Kuroyukihime, who had been a meter or more apart, were glued together, sleeping deeply, as if they had at some point been squeezed down the valley of the two cushions. More than that, Niko had her head buried in Kuroyukihime's chest and was tightly gripping the fabric of her pajamas with her right hand. And Kuroyukihime had both of her arms around her, as if wrapping up Niko's red hair.

Rather than surprise at this sight, he felt something hit his chest and make him gasp, and Haruyuki opened his eyes wide.

The Red King and the Black King. Level-nine Burst Linkers bound by the special rule of sudden death.

Haruyuki couldn't even imagine how many hours these two had passed in the Accelerated World, engaging in mortal combat over and over each time they went, or what lay ahead for them. But he could say this at least. If they both had their sights set on level ten, then one day, they would have to fight. Because the only way a King could move forward was by defeating another King.

But...

Tonight the two of them, through a coincidence brought about by a complicated entanglement of circumstances, were sleeping alongside each other like this in the real world. Almost as if both had wished for this moment deep in their hearts.

Was this scene the illusion of a single night? An accidental miracle never to happen again?

Or...

Haruyuki was seized with the premonition that he was on the verge of arriving now at a very important something. But the unnameable feelings cutting through his chest and the tears blurring his eyes would not allow him to put his thoughts into actual words.

So Haruyuki just stood there and stared, as if he could stand and stare forever at the girls slumbering soundly in the pale blue moonlight.

4

"All right, we're off."

"W-we're off!"

"Yup, have a good 'un." Niko waved a hand beside her face in response to Kuroyukihime and Haruyuki, then furrowed her eyebrows. "Hey. Isn't this kinda weird?"

"Hmm? What?"

"Nah...When you ask, I can't really..." Niko crossed her arms as she stood on the step of the entryway, deep in thought.

Kuroyukihime shrugged easily. "You're a strange one. In any case, I'm leaving the particulars of today's strategy to you. You won't have any problems with specifying the position and time of Chrome Disaster's appearance, yes?"

"N-no...Leave it to me."

"Mmm. All right, we're off."

"Yup, have a good 'un."

Closing the door with a *clack*, Kuroyukihime turned around and took a step down.

January 23, Friday, 7:30 AM.

It was time to begin that shifting of coordinates known as "going to school" that Haruyuki had executed countless times up to that point. The gray light shining into the shared hallway of the condo, the exhalations colored white by the cold air—all of it was the same as the day before.

However, one thing was different: a female student dressed neatly in the Umesato uniform walking alongside him. Her blue ribbon tied, school-designated bag in her right hand, and shopping bag in her left.

"Apparently, it's going to be cloudy all day," Kuroyukihime said to him casually after turning on her Neurolinker and running her gaze over empty space. "I hope it doesn't rain. Well, shall we go?"

"R-right." Dipping his head, Haruyuki started walking after her, assuming his home position behind her to the left and wondering vaguely. *Huh...so is she like my big sister? And the other's the little one?*

No, forget that. That kind of setup would never exist in reality. Going to school with your big sister, this isn't some ancient visual novel or something.

He shook his head fast like a wet dog and climbed into the empty elevator car arriving before them.

Normally, if this were a game, there'd never be just two girls, the big sister and the little sister. Right?

As he toyed with this idea in his head (which wouldn't quite get up to speed, possibly due to a minor lack of sleep) the elevator stopped a mere two floors down, on the twenty-first floor. Haruyuki automatically took a step back, opening up a space for someone to get on.

As the door slid open, his gaze crashed into a girl wearing the same color uniform who jumped in with a spritely, bouncing movement—his childhood friend, Chiyuri Kurashima.

No... he screamed in his heart.

Seeing him, Chiyuri blinked her large, catlike eyes rapidly before breaking into a broad grin. "Oh, Haru! Morning! What happened? You were superearly yester—What...wh-what?!"

Once she noticed the person to Haruyuki's right, Chiyuri's

voice and expression evolved rapidly. From distracted, passing through stunned, and then arriving at the critical point: the calm before the storm.

"...Haru? What is this?" Chiyuri murmured, eye twitching.

"Oh, morning, Kurashima!" Rather than Haruyuki, who was frozen solid, it was Kuroyukihime who greeted his friend with a carefree salute.

"G-g-good morning." Chiyuri lowered her head instinctively, then grabbed Haruyuki's necktie and shouted, "What's going on?!"

"I-it's not what you think!" Shaking his head back and forth, Haruyuki launched his mail with a hand behind his back, seeking help from the only person with a chance of managing this situation; i.e., *"Taku, in trouble. Help."*

"And how is it not what I think?!"

Just when it seemed like she was getting serious about grilling him, the elevator finally arrived at the first floor, and the door opened. Haruyuki grabbed Chiyuri's shoulders and spun her halfway around saying, "C-come on. First, we gotta get to school! We'll go to class first, then come home, and by the weekend, we'll forget all about this."

"Don't try to weasel out of this!"

Shoving Chiyuri's shoulders as she shrieked, he cut through the residents and their widened eyes in the lobby and managed to get her out into the courtyard when he heard the sound of his rescue from behind.

"M-morning, Chi! Morning, Haru! Mor...ning..." Here, Takumu pulled his glasses down slightly and stared questioningly at Kuroyukihime's composed face. "Good morning, Master."

His partner, somehow having read his mail and rushed down, muttered to Haruyuki, expelling large puffs of white breath in the chill morning air, "Haru. You sure like to live dangerously."

"I don't like it. I don't like it at all," he returned, before turning Chiyuri who was still shrieking, "Explain yourself!" toward Takumu and letting go.

And Takumu, being Takumu, took the bullet and calmly reassured her: "Chi, I was at Haru's place yesterday, too."

"What? What do you mean?"

"Just had a little problem with that application." Faced with the extremely doubtful look on the face of his childhood friend, Taku offered up smooth explanation. Haruyuki could never even hope to imitate his effortless eloquence. "We used Haru's place as a meeting room. But it ended up running late, and if the social cameras caught some junior high kid out walking alone at that time of night, it'd turn into a whole big thing, so Kuroyukihime was basically forced to stay at Haru's. Right?"

Fortunately, Kuroyukihime accepted the question lobbed at her and nodded obediently. "That's essentially the case. No need for any strange suspicions, Kurashima."

Chiyuri was silent for a few seconds, the expression on her face becoming complicated. "That again? Brain...Burst?" she asked finally in a hushed tone.

She puffed her cheeks up as she looked around at the three of them nodding in unison. "I am not okay with this! I mean, it's just a game, right? So what is there that you need to spend hours talking about?"

"I-it is a game, but it's not just a game." Haruyuki glanced around the wide condo courtyard and confirmed that no one was around before continuing. "We talked about this before...It creates another world by accelerating your thoughts. So just like the real world, all kinds of problems happen—"

"Hmph!" Chiyuri pursed her lips and made a dissatisfied noise. "And I don't believe a word of that. I mean, you say you 'accelerate,' but I don't even know what that means...Okay, fine. If you show me, I'll shut up about it."

"Huh?"

"You can copy and install this game, right?" Chiyuri asked Haruyuki, eyes like saucers, as if it was no big deal. "I'll load it up, too. And then I'll be, what did you call it, a, uh...'Burst Linker,' too."

"Wh-what?!" The shout came not just from Haruyuki but from the mouths of Takumu and Kuroyukihime as well.

All three immediately brought hands up in front of their faces, waving them fluidly back and forth.

"I-impossible, no way. Absolutely no way." Haruyuki accidentally let his true feelings slip, and Chiyuri pinched his round cheek.

"What do you mean?! Just hand it over!"

"No, it's just—You need an aptitude for the ga—"

"And if I don't try, we won't know, will we?!"

"But I mean, you're...superslow and everything." The moment the words left his mouth, Chiyuri's cat-shaped eyes glinted.

"Oh ho! You've got some nerve. I get it, you just watch! I'll practice and get so good I can beat you and Taku at video games!"

"Wh-what?!" Haruyuki's jaw dropped, and he stared at the challenging glitter growing in her eyes. It was her "Once I say it, there's no turning back" face, often seen when they used to play together way back in the day.

She yanked Haruyuki's cheek out as far as it would go, like a sticky mochi rice cake. "And then you're gonna copy that whatchamacallit Burst to me, too!!" Having said that, his childhood friend, this girl who was the same age as he was, dropped her hand, stuck out her tongue, and ran off at a blistering pace.

"'Practice,'" Haruyuki muttered, rubbing his cheek. He turned again to Takumu beside him and bowed deeply. "Sorry, Taku. I made you lie to Chiyu."

The explanation Takumu had given Chiyuri before was not 100 percent accurate. At the time Kuroyukihime declared that she was staying over, the meeting had already ended.

Takumu smiled and shook his head slowly. "It's fine." His expression was calm, but Haruyuki felt like it held something somehow self-deprecating, and he bit his lip.

"Takumu," Kuroyukihime said, sounding concerned. "Perhaps I'm intruding by asking, but...are you and Kurashima still... well..."

"We're a long ways from the way we were." Shrugging his shoulders, Takumu turned his gaze to the tops of the trees lining the road, completely bereft of leaves. "Because of what I did. And it might be that we can never go back to boyfriend-girlfriend. But...if I can be with Chi in a way that makes her happy, then I feel like that's enough for me."

"Taku..." Haruyuki fumbled for what he should say, but his throat always got plugged up at the critical moments.

Kuroyukihime spoke softly instead. "If...you feel like it's too much of a burden, or it's interfering with your relationship with Kurashima, you can delete it, you know... Brain Burst."

Takumu's eyes flew open. But he was quick to shake his head firmly from side to side. "No. I still have to repay you for...and Haru, too."

"Y-you don't. There's nothing to repay us for, Taku." This time, Haruyuki managed to speak, albeit mechanically. "I've never thought you had anything to repay me for. And Kuroyukihime's the same. That's not why Brain Burst exists. That, that game..." But again, Haruyuki's meager lexicon was exhausted.

"Don't worry." Takumu returned Haruyuki's gaze with sad eyes and patted his shoulder. "I mean, I definitely have fun in duels. Anyway, Master, I wanted to talk to you about something." Turning his entire body toward Kuroyukihime, he continued in a serious tone. "Do you really think there's no possibility of Chi becoming a Burst Linker?"

Kuroyukihime tilted her head thoughtfully, her expression essentially unchanged as opposed to Haruyuki's bug eyes. "To begin with, does she meet the first requirement?"

"Yes, she should," Takumu assented immediately.

The first requirement for Burst Linkers was to have been wearing a Neurolinker since birth. Takumu met the requirement due to the educational policy of his overly enthusiastic parents; Haruyuki because his parents, who both worked, had used it as a remote monitor.

Chiyuri was raised by deeply loving and broad-minded parents, and they had placed a Neurolinker on her from the time she was a newborn for different reasons. Chiyuri's father had once been treated for pharyngeal cancer, and it was difficult for him to speak naturally. Thus, Chiyuri had grown up listening to her father's neuro voice via the network.

Takumu didn't go so far as to explain all that, and Kuroyuki-hime didn't ask.

"I see." Nodding, she turned her gaze in the direction in which Chiyuri had run off. "The truth is, the second requirement... It's not as though there are strict standards for cerebral reaction speed. Some people who are terrible at VR games have been able to install Brain Burst. However, I have to say, trying to make someone you're not sure of into a Burst Linker is an enormous gamble."

"G-gamble...?" Haruyuki asked in response, and Kuroyuki-hime shifted her gaze in a way that seemed meaningful and nodded.

"Currently, a Brain Burst copy license—that is, the right to make a 'child' of someone as a 'guardian'—is limited to just one. That right is exercised even if the install fails and can never be recovered."

"O-one time?!" Haruyuki stammered involuntarily and hurriedly clapped his mouth shut. He lowered his voice and continued, still flustered. "B-but that—the number of Burst Linkers basically isn't gonna go up at all, then. I mean, the number of people losing all their points and leaving and the number of new people joining... They'll just barely be balanced?"

"In other words, Haru," Takumu said, pushing up his glasses, apparently already aware of this "one-time rule." "I think that the mystery administrator who runs Brain Burst wants the current number of people—about a thousand—to be the upper limit. That means that's probably the threshold for keeping the acceleration technology hidden."

"O-okay, that's probably true, but...but come on, even if it keeps going like this, at some point, the day is going to come when the secret gets out, right? I mean, Chiyu already knows pretty much everything and all. I-if this admin or developer or whoever is running this whole show with the understanding that the existence of Brain Burst will someday be revealed to the world, and when that happens, we won't be be able to use our Neurolinkers to accelerate anymore, then…what's this guy's objective?"

Haruyuki spread out both hands and looked at Takumu and Kuroyukihime in turn. "It's just, we…we haven't paid the price of entry to play this game. And we never see any ads or anything."

There were two general types of profit structures for the many net games in the world: either charge the gamer with a monthly fee or via item sales, or flood the user with in-game ads from contracting companies.

Brain Burst was definitely a net game, and more than that, it gave its users an extraordinary privilege with the acceleration technology. No matter how he looked at it, a price of zero didn't make it worth anyone's while.

Kuroyukihime listened to Haruyuki's fundamental and very belated question, a faint and wry smile crossing her lips. "Think about that all you want, but there's no answer to be had, Haruyuki. If you want to know, your only choice is to reach level ten and ask the developer yourself. But I can say just two things with certainty. The first is, as you said before, the Accelerated World likely can't continue forever given the way things stand currently. The time will inevitably come when the curtain will be lifted and every last Burst Linker annihilated. And the second is…the day will also definitely come when we are made to pay a price in line with the privilege of acceleration. Or…" Her voice became uncertain, and her lips moved very slightly.

But Haruyuki felt like he could see the tiny letters in his exhaled breaths, colored white in the morning chill.

Or we're already paying it.

"But I digress." Kuroyukihime laughed briefly and looked at Takumu. "Back to Kurashima. I believe that the possibility of her becoming a Burst Linker is extremely low, but there is value in trying."

"R-really, Master?"

Kuroyukihime nodded slowly at Takumu and his wide eyes. "Physically, her potential is certainly not low. That sprint of hers earlier was wonderfully quick."

"Oh, that's 'cos she's on the track team," Haruyuki interjected.

"Hmm. I see," Kuroyukihime murmured. "In your brain, the circuits that move your physical body and those that move your virtual avatar are basically one and the same. Which is to say, in Kurashima's case, it's possible she meets the necessary conditions for the performance of those circuits. The problem is her affinity with the Neurolinker, although there's nothing to do about that but jump right in and test it."

"Oookay. But she can't even neuro-speak."

"You, on the other hand, are too specialized on the Neurolinker side. Move your real body a little more."

Haruyuki was slammed into silence, and Kuroyukihime shifted her attention from him to Takumu.

"Takumu. If Kurashima is able to install Brain Burst successfully, a strong connection between the two of you will be created. That of guardian and child. But remember, that does not necessarily mean that there are only positives there."

Haruyuki couldn't understand the meaning of these words, uttered quietly and forcefully, right away.

Not positives...Negatives? Between a Burst Linker "guardian" and "child"? What could they be? The guardian leads, the child adores. There's no dark side or anything there; that's true, right? It's different from parent-child relationships in the real world. Totally and completely different from my dad—who shook off weepy, clingy me and left us, and my mom—who doesn't bother to even look at me, much less talk to me in any real kind of way. Between guardian and child in the Accelerated World—between Kuroyukihime and me—there's definitely a strong bond.

A thrill ran through Haruyuki, and he stared into Kuroyukihime's obsidian eyes as she stood next to him. They were filled with the same gentle glow as always.

No. Beyond that, though, something kind of sad. Or maybe it's just my imagination. I thought I saw a flash of something like fear.

In an instant, a doubt he'd never once given thought to since becoming a Burst Linker under Kuroyukihime's guidance flickered to life in the back of Haruyuki's mind.

The question of who Kuroyukihime's guardian was.

"...U-um."

"Now we've done it," Kuroyukihime said, as if cutting him off the moment he ever-so-timidly spoke up. "We got too caught up standing here talking. And now we'll be late if we don't hurry."

"Huh..."

Quickly glancing up at the horizon, Haruyuki noted that the sky on the other side of the low clouds had grown much brighter.

"Whoa, you're right! Maybe we should run a bit, Haru."

"Ugh! Give me a break."

Even as Takumu clapped him on the shoulder and he shook his head, Haruyuki couldn't forget his unasked question. Chasing after Kuroyukihime, who had already started walking briskly, he tried again to pose it to that black back, but for some reason, the words wouldn't come out.

They managed somehow to fly through the school gates just before the first morning bell rang. After checking that their Neurolinkers were connected to the Umesato local net and that they hadn't been counted as tardy, Haruyuki split off from the other two.

But even during his morning classes, a single thought swirled persistently through his brain.

Why did Kuroyukihime say that stuff about negative aspects of the relationship between Burst Linker guardians and children? And why did she look a little sad? I want to know. I have to know.

As soon as the virtual blackboard disappeared from his field of view at the end of second period, Haruyuki brushed away his hesitation and launched his text. Keeping it short, he typed and sent, CAN WE TALK NOW? in a mere two seconds.

The reply arrived eight seconds later, a single line: LET'S MEET IN THE VIRTUAL SQUASH CORNER ON THE LOCAL NET. He settled deeper into his chair, closed his eyes, and called out the "direct link" command.

Since there were only fifteen minutes between second and third periods, the fairy-tale forest that made up the Umesato local net was deserted. The short legs of his avatar had barely touched the virtual ground before he was dashing toward a single, large tree towering on the outskirts.

The ringleader of the group of bullies who had forced Haruyuki to use this ridiculous pink pig avatar was no longer around, and his underlings were keeping to themselves, so Haruyuki could have changed to a cooler design anytime, but he missed the window of opportunity, dragging it out so that he was still using this one. This might also have been Kuroyukihime's influence, telling him she liked it.

In this form, he bounded up the stairs cut into the trunk of the tree and leapt onto the squash court set up on the top floor, his eyes falling on a slender avatar standing quietly in the center of the court.

A jet-black dress with silver edging. A parasol of the same in her hand, the wings of a black spangled butterfly run through with deep crimson lines.

Kuroyukihime, disguised in this form as a fairy princess of darkness, turned her essentially colorless face toward Haruyuki and smiled slightly. "Hey. It's been a while since I saw you in that form. I suppose because we're always talking in the real world lately."

"You almost never come to the local net. The fans of your avatar are sad," he replied in a voice 30 percent smoother than in the real world.

Kuroyukihime's smile grew wry, and she shrugged lightly. "Goodness. And here I was thinking I should go ahead and get a black pig avatar to match you. Anyway, what is it? You wanted to talk."

"Oh...umm...um, well..." This time Haruyuki stammered as usual and fumbled for words.

If he thought about it, the number of personal questions he'd asked Kuroyukihime up to this point was essentially zero. So was it okay for him now to suddenly be acting like she owed him explanations?

For a while, Kuroyukihime looked down at him with a bemused smile, flustering him even though he was the one who had asked her here, but eventually, she rippled the wings on her back and lightly stepped away from him. The bells adorning her parasol rang clearly.

"Haruyuki. You want to hear about my 'guardian,' don't you?" Kuroyukihime spoke softly in her silky tone, somehow even more mysterious than her real-world voice.

Haruyuki gasped and, without waiting for his response, the young woman lowered her long eyelashes. "Sorry. I can't tell you that name just yet. Because I don't want you to have any contact with that person, just in case. As a Legion Master...and as a girl. Perhaps it's an ugly jealousy."

Freezing and opening his eyes wide, Haruyuki was aware of several thoughts flashing through his mind.

From what she'd just said, he learned two things. First, Kuroyukihime's "guardian" was still alive and well as a Burst Linker in the Accelerated World. And second, it was probably a girl.

Moving soundlessly along the squash court, Kuroyukihime continued, playing her voice as if plucking the low string on a harp. "That person was once...the person closest to me. I believed this Linker would shine brightly forever at the center of my world and keep all kinds of darkness and cold at bay."

Almost the way you are for me, Haruyuki thought suddenly.

"However, one day...one incident, one instant, I realized that this was an ephemeral illusion. Now you could go so far as to say that, for me, this person is my archenemy. So much so that I could almost believe that this inexhaustible hatred existed inside me from the moment we first met." Her voice was calm and controlled, but the passion of her words was incongruous with the usual Kuroyukihime.

As her downcast eyes briefly caressed Haruyuki's stationary figure, the raven fairy princess brought a hollow smile to her lips.

"If it were possible, I would fight this person right now, this second. After a delightful match spent severing the avatar's limbs with my sword and making the Linker crawl before me to beg pathetically for its life, I would offer no amnesty and lop off the avatar's head. However, I will never realize that dream...Haruyuki. Do you understand where the relationship between Burst Linker guardian and child is fundamentally different from, say, the relationship between partners, or lovers, for instance?"

After a moment's confusion, Haruyuki remembered the thing glittering in Kuroyukihime's proffered hand that fateful day three months earlier. The silver direct cable. "It's...Guardian and child know each other in the real, without exception."

"Yes, exactly." Nodding, Kuroyukihime tapped the court with the tip of her parasol. "Because to install Brain Burst, the two Neurolinkers must be directly connected. When that happens, guardian and child are most certainly looking at each other's real faces and have a relationship such that directing is permitted. Because of this, the relationship between Burst Linker guardian and child is the strongest bond in the Accelerated World, having the potential to become its greatest curse at the same time."

"C-curse?"

"Yes. Because if guardian and child were to part ways, when their relationship becomes acrimonious, that hatred is intensely amplified in the real world. I...I can't fight my guardian, not with this much hatred. My guardian exerts overwhelming influence on me in the real world. The only proof of a Burst Linker's existence is the duel, after all. We carry the duel avatars in our minds in order to fight each other. And yet only guardian and child cannot fight. If you don't call that a curse, then what is it?"

"Kuroyukihime," Haruyuki murmured, groping for something to follow that with. But he felt it was impossible to say anything; his voice would be too clogged by the emotions swirling around in his heart.

So he took one, then two steps forward and cradled Kuroyukihime's limply hanging left hand tightly in his own plump hooves. Although their avatars should not have been different temperatures, her hand was as cold as ice.

"Haruyuki..." Her quiet voice echoed his.

Kuroyukihime probably still agonized over the fact that she had hunted the former Red King and chased him away forever. And to martyr herself for that act, she would push herself to turn her sword against any and all Burst Linkers. Even if, for instance, it was her own guardian—or her child.

Trying to bring her white hand to his mouth but in fact pressing it into his large nose, Haruyuki thought, *This is the only thing I can say.*

"I said this yesterday, too," he murmured earnestly. "I absolutely will not fight you. I won't become your enemy. If a time like that comes for some unavoidable reason...I will uninstall Brain Burst before I fight you."

A long silence filled the space in the virtual sunlight, which drew a diagonal line interrupted by the treetops.

Finally, Kuroyukihime, a bit of her warmth returning, spoke as she tapped Haruyuki's round head with the handle of her parasol. "Fool, I'd be the one to step down. You fight. You have much more fun with Brain Burst, with the duels, than I do; you should be the one to stay in the Accelerated World."

"No. I definitely don't want that!"

And then the parasol rolled onto the carpet of fallen green leaves, causing a soft rustling. Haruyuki was half carrying on like a spoiled child when a soft, smooth hand caressed his right cheek.

Raising his face, he met Kuroyukihime's eyes, discovering

she had dropped to her knees at some point. Her pale red lips, extremely close by, moved subtly.

"No matter what future comes for us, I will at least not regret choosing you." As she spoke, her hands stretched out to embrace Haruyuki's head tightly.

Despite the fact that he should have been in heaven right then and there, mingled amongst beautiful sensory signals that were almost too overwhelming to process, Haruyuki felt an indescribable sadness.

After school.

Kuroyukihime and Takumu had said they would come over after dropping stuff off at their respective places, so Haruyuki went home by himself.

Bracing himself to a certain extent, he opened the door but heard neither the sound of a game blaring nor an eager greeting today, and when he peeked in the living room after saying, "I'm home," very quietly, he saw Niko from behind seated on the sofa.

It was so ridiculously quiet Haruyuki thought she might be sleeping, but her small hand soon waved briefly at him. Going around to face her, he saw that she was staring off into space with eyes wide-open. He supposed this meant she was taking in the virtual desktop visible only to her.

"I'm home."

When he said it again, Niko responded with a curt "Hey" and flicked her gaze at him for an instant. "The other two?"

"They said they were going to stop at home and then come over. They'll probably be here in twenty minutes or so."

"Good. We should make it in time. Chrome Disaster's not moving yet."

Haruyuki blinked with surprise. Apparently, Niko was somehow monitoring the movements of Cherry Rook, the member of the Red Legion who had inherited by means unknown Chrome Disaster's Enhanced Armament, the Armor of Catastrophe—but to do that, she would naturally have had to connect her Neuro-linker to the external net.

"I-is it okay for you to connect to the global net? Even though you're outside Red Legion Territory here?" he asked spontane-ously, which elicited a bold smile from Niko.

"Well, I ran into just one foolish intrusion earlier. Knocked that kid flying in ten seconds, told her to tell everyone else not to bug me, so I'm prob'ly good now."

"O-oh, I see..."

Within a Territory, members of the controlling Legion were given the right to refuse challenges by other Burst Linkers unless they had their settings otherwise.

Because of this, Haruyuki and his friends could now safely connect globally at home and around the school, but obviously, that right did not extend to Niko. But when he thought about it rationally, the only one who could win one-on-one against Niko, a King, was another King, and they had negotiated a mutual nonaggression pact, so there was no way any of them would sud-denly provoke a fight. Presently, the traitor Kuroyukihime was the only King who absolutely had to terminate her global con-nection when leaving her territory.

Trailing his thoughts this far, Haruyuki realized with a start that the redheaded girl before him was also someone who could potentially vanquish Kuroyukihime. He decided to try to con-firm this at least, taking the opportunity of it being just the two of them there.

He cleared his throat and opened his mouth. "U-um, Yuni—Niko. Can I ask you something?"

"Nope...or at least don't start with a pointless intro that lets me just say 'nope.' What?"

As she glared at him, Haruyuki, still standing next to the sofa, asked as simply and straightforwardly as he could, "Y-you don't hate Kuroyukihime?"

"Huh? Why?"

Seeing the look of genuine surprise on her face, Haruyuki, not to be outdone, was also dumbfounded.

"Why? Because she has the biggest bounty on her head. And not only that, it's on her head because she took down the former Red King, i.e., the person who was the Prominence Legion Master before you."

"Oh, that." Sniffing slightly, Niko stretched the slim legs poking out of her cutoffs. Twirling a red pigtail with a finger, she let her eyes wander toward the window. "Yeah, well, he might have been the master. But I never spoke directly with my predecessor, with Red Rider."

"R-really?" Haruyuki leaned forward unconsciously; he'd supposed Niko's "guardian" might be this Red Rider.

"I mean, I became a Burst Linker two and a half years ago, and then my predecessor was retired a few months after that. I was still level three back then, or four maybe, and we hadn't even dived in the same field or anything. When I heard the Master had been struck down in a surprise attack by Black Lotus and lost all his points, the only thing I thought was how tough level nine must be. And anyway…" Niko raised a single eyebrow deftly. "The main reason I could fly through the ranks all booster-powered and become the next king was because Lotus took out the old king, temporarily dismantling the Red Legion for me. Back then, it was a real 'warring states' kind of deal for Nakano and Nerima. Every day, new fight groups were being formed, so you just racked up the points. Doesn't matter if I'm the strongest, if that hadn't happened, it would have taken me another two years to get to level nine."

A stiff smile broached Haruyuki's face as Niko cackled. "O-okay. So then, you and the Red Legion aren't interested in any kind of vengeance on the Black King?"

"Hmmmmm. Well, to be honest, there're probably some old-timers who would be. But the ones burning up with a hate-on for Black Lotus transferred to other Legions pretty quick when

Prominence disappeared back then. Honestly, doesn't make any sense. The whole idea of picking up where the last guy left off makes me laugh, but if that's where their heads are at, fighting to bring back Promi would've been the easiest way."

She cut herself off there, stared up at Haruyuki, and muttered a threatening, "What?"

He shook his head hurriedly and turned away.

After a brief silence, Niko opened her mouth once again. "And—you totes can't tell that girl this..."

"O-okay."

"The truth is, I think she's—Black Lotus is pretty amazing. Kinda motivates me."

"Huh?! Th-that's—what do you—"

"No telling. For reals, no telling." After giving him a sharp glare, Niko kept going in a quiet voice that didn't match her rough tone. "Because she's the only one of all the Kings who said she was serious about getting to level ten. Meanwhile, the other Kings, me included, are running around playing at duels under the lukewarm pretext of the stupid territorial nonaggression pact. The worst part is that some of the other Kings secretly have their sights set on level ten, too. Small-minded bastards looking for a chance to get the jump on the others, all the while singing their little song of the status quo 'for the continued existence of the Accelerated World.'"

"And you?" Haruyuki asked, reflexively, the moment Niko's monologue was done. "Which are you, Niko?"

"Dunno." Her response was short and contained the ring of truth.

The young King rolled her too-slender frame over onto the sofa with a *thump* and folded her arms behind her head. The toes of her bare feet, thrust nearly into Haruyuki's face, tapped the air rhythmically.

"The other Kings—especially Purple and Yellow—are pushing this theory that the moment even one Burst Linker makes it to level ten, that'll be the end of Brain Burst. There'll be some doo-

doo-doo trumpeting and fanfare, the developer'll appear, say congratulations or something, and roll end credits. And then all the Burst Linkers get Brain Burst forcefully uninstalled."

"Tha…"

That can't be. There's no way a net game would end for everyone all at once. He almost laughed, but then his mouth froze.

He remembered what had come up when he was talking with Kuroyukihime and Takumu that morning. At some point, there will come a day when the Accelerated World is no longer hidden, and the game is destroyed. Haruyuki himself had said it.

Niko nodded lightly, almost as if reading Haruyuki's thoughts. "And I don't think what they're saying is totally impossible. To be honest, I don't want to think about what it'd be like after Brain Burst's gone. I mean, for me, that over there's basically the real world. But… I wonder if it's really okay for us to cling to it like this just 'cos of that. The Seven Kings—no, the Six Kings—and their nonaggression pact distort what the Accelerated World should be, and we're paying the price for that all over the place now."

"D-distort…?"

"Chrome Disaster, for example," Niko muttered abruptly, closing her deep green eyes. "Cherry Rook gave in to the temptation of the Armor of Catastrophe because of his despair at the wall between him and the higher levels. I mean, prob'ly. Because of the pact now, the Accelerated World's stagnating, and no matter how hard you fight in the Normal Duel Field, getting to level nine—no, even level eight—is crazy-hard. There's no one to fight. I got to nine, like I said before, because I managed to sort of surf the total chaos Black Lotus caused. But that kinda thing's not gonna happen again. So these days, if you've got your sights set on a high level, all you can do is take the risk and fight in the Unlimited Field. The thought of it tormented Cherry, and he reached for the Armor. And in a way, what pushed him to it was a single King, me…"

Niko suddenly blinked hard and clenched her teeth.

Haruyuki watched her flat chest heave twice, three times, and he held his breath and whispered unconsciously, "N-Niko..."

"Shut up! Don't say anything! Don't look at me! Go away!" she shrieked, still flopped atop the sofa, pumping her legs in the air, and rubbing her eyes hard with her right arm. Then they flew open abruptly, and she cried out as if surprised, "Anyway!!"

"Huh?"

"Anyway, why am I telling you all this stuff?! Just forget it, all of it!! All this now was lies!! If you don't forget it right here and now, I will knock your face in!!" she ranted and raved only half audibly.

Haruyuki automatically reached out with both hands to stop her legs, which flailed as if trying to kick him down to the ground. Then he squeezed those tiny bare feet, almost clutching them to his chest.

"Aaah! Wh-what are you doing, you perv?!"

"Niko." Not flinching at the blatant name-calling, Haruyuki put even more strength into his grip. What he really wanted was to hold her hand, but if he did that, it probably wouldn't end just with her punching him.

"Niko, you're not wrong."

The moment Haruyuki gave voice to those words, Niko's violent struggle to free her legs stopped. He stared right into her large eyes and continued earnestly.

"It's totally natural that you wouldn't want the game to stop, that you'd want to stay in that world forever. But...I've played a ton of net games now, so I get it. There's nothing sadder and lonelier than the 'end' of a game with no ending. Net games that stop making money because the users get bored and move on to some other game, there's a quiet announcement that it's shutting down, and then the servers get turned off and no one really even says anything about it. I've experienced the 'middle' of that moment countless times. I've watched the familiar old man at the weapons shop or the girl at the inn 'die,' smiling forever, and after I've linked out, back in my own room, I've cried countless times. That kind of ending is wrong. It's completely wrong."

Not moving a muscle, feet still in the care of Haruyuki's chest, Niko opened both eyes wide.

Feeling the thin skin on the palms of his hands and the blood flowing beneath it, Haruyuki continued speaking, his voice slightly hoarse. "If…if there is an ending to Brain Burst, we should be trying to get there. Even if, say, we lose the ability to accelerate because of that, compared with the world just fizzling out pathetically, it's way, way…It's the *right* way."

Because that effort itself is probably the price we have to pay for all the things this game Brain Burst has given us. Because melancholy me being able to talk this long in my real-life voice with a girl I only recently met is probably thanks to the program.

Hiding only this last thought in his heart, Haruyuki closed his mouth.

Silence fell, and Niko stayed quiet for a long time, not moving a muscle.

Aah! Did I say something totally nuts again?

Just when Haruyuki was becoming utterly discouraged, the young King finally muttered grudgingly, "The right way, huh? So there actually are Burst Linkers who talk like that."

Eyes turned straight up at Haruyuki, Niko flashed him a smile, a bit like the one she gave him in angel mode. "You're a weird one. To be honest, I was really wondering why the one and only flying ability would go to a lazy pudgeball like you, but…I kinda feel like I maybe get it a bit. But, that said…" Here the look on her face turned stormy, and Haruyuki stood up straighter. "Exactly how long are you gonna fool around with my feet, you perv? I'll kill you!!"

At the same time, her left foot shot out at the bridge of his nose, and Haruyuki fell helplessly backward.

The sound of the door chime danced cheerfully over the thud of his body.

"And then I ran into Master. Oh, here, treats. I nicked some we had at my place," Takumu said, lifting what looked like a cake box, then tilting his head to the side after his gaze had made the return trip between Haruyuki sitting on the floor and rubbing his nose and Niko looking the other way on the sofa. "What are you doing?"

"Perhaps they were fighting. No matter, no matter!" Kuroyuki-hime smiled faintly, hand on her uniformed hip, and Niko sniffed derisively.

"Weeell. You know what they say, the more you fight, the closer you are."

Haruyuki hurriedly inserted himself between the two, certain to send sparks flying if left to themselves. "W-welcome, both of you! Thanks for the treats, Taku! So okay, let's eat! I get the one with a strawberry on top!!"

As he stood swiftly and headed toward the kitchen, two voices sounded off simultaneously behind him.

"The strawberry's for me!"

"The strawberry's mine!"

"...Right." He dipped his head grimly and prepared plates and tea.

Fortunately, the box contained two pieces of strawberry shortcake and two of chocolate cake, so no further fighting was provoked—although there was the exchange: "You don't have to have black cake, too?" "Chocolate isn't black; it's a burnt brown." Once the four of them had concurrently taken their first bites of cake and sips of tea, the look on Kuroyukihime's face changed.

"Are you able to track Chrome Disaster?"

At the question, Niko quickly ran her eyes over her virtual desktop and gave a slight nod. "Yeah. He should be moving pretty soon."

This steady reply made Haruyuki feel slightly uncomfortable.

How was remote tracking of a Burst Linker even possible? You could tell a Burst Linker's current position if the target started a duel and you dove into the field as a spectator, but Niko hadn't had the look of accelerating. Or maybe the Legion Masters had some kind of crazy privileges that let them check in on the whereabouts of members in the real world?

He opened his mouth to casually inquire along these lines.

"There he is!" Niko shouted sharply, stabbing the almost circular strawberry she had set aside for last with a fork and tossing it in her mouth. "Cherry's on a train on the Seibu Ikebukuro line. Given his pattern up to now, today's hunting ground's gonna be the Bukes."

"Ikebukuro? Annoying." Kuroyukihime clicked her tongue lightly. She placed her fork on her now-empty plate with a clatter. "How will we move? Are we going to use a train, too, or a cab in the real? Or shall we cut through inside?"

Unable to understand the meaning of her words, Haruyuki furrowed his brow.

"Inside," which was to say the duel field, had the appearance of continuing endlessly, but movement limit lines were set up along the borders. Without them, it would've been possible, as a battle strategy, to run desperately in a straight line until time ran out after landing a blow.

So for example, diving from this place, from Haruyuki's house into the field, the northern edge of Suginami Ward would be the farthest they could go; they definitely shouldn't have been able to get all the way to Ikebukuro in Toshima Ward.

However, Niko answered readily after only a moment's thought. "We'll go from inside. With this setup, we shouldn't get tripped up by any Enemies."

"If we're lucky," Kuroyukihime assented, looking severe.

No longer knowing which way was even up, Haruyuki was caught by Kuroyukihime's serious gaze head-on.

"Now, then. Haruyuki. I'll teach you the command to dive into the true battlefield of the Burst Linkers. It will use ten of your burst points, but that's not a problem, is it?"

"N-no, not if it's only ten points. But more important...the true battlefield...?"

"Exactly what it sounds like. The true nature of what we call the Accelerated World is there. Shout the command after me, just like I say it. Here we go. Fifth Chrome Disaster Subjugation, mission start!"

There, she took a deep breath, straightened her back, and—

As she touched the button to connect her Neurolinker to the global net, the jet-black, beautiful princess shouted in a commanding voice, "Unlimited burst!"

5

"Unlimited burst!"

At the same time he shouted, lost in himself, an acceleration noise twice as loud as normal slammed Haruyuki's consciousness. His vision blacked out momentarily.

But a silver light soon cut through the darkness: the effect light transforming his entire body into metallic steel.

In normal acceleration—with the "burst link" command— he would first become his pink pig avatar, but that phase was skipped here, and Haruyuki transformed directly into his pure silver duel avatar, Silver Crow.

The surrounding darkness was then blown away by a rainbow-colored light. From the other side of the radiating aura, there appeared the glittering of blue-black steel.

The place that should have been his living room had been metamorphosed into a cold, metallic corridor, almost like the castle of the king of hell in some fantasy film. The windows that opened to the south had disappeared, and several light blue flames flickered on walls and pillars sporting the design of several steel plates pulled together in the shape of radiating fins. A thick fog coiled around his feet, and the high ceiling was sunken in darkness, leaving him unable to really make it out.

The leaden place closely resembled a purgatory stage, but there was absolutely nothing organic about it. Haruyuki briefly surveyed that cold and linear scene that extended as far as the eye could see.

Reducing his focus, he saw three duel avatars standing very close to him:

Cyan Pile, dark blue armor on sturdy limbs, right hand equipped with its enormous Pile Driver.

Scarlet Rain, a lone handgun hanging from her slender, crimson-red frame.

And Black Lotus, shrouded in semitransparent, pure black armor, her four sharp, sword-shaped limbs glittering.

Haruyuki secretly swallowed back the feelings of inferiority welling up in him standing alongside Cyan Pile—Takumu, who was the same level as him—much less the two Kings, as he muttered, "This is the Unlimited Neutral Field…"

"It is," Kuroyukihime affirmed in a voice distorted by a metallic effect as she turned around lightly. The tips of her toes essentially sharp sword points, Black Lotus did not walk normally, but rather hovered slightly above the floor.

Raising her right hand, the same elongated blade shape as her legs, Kuroyukihime indicated the end of the corridor. "That's likely the exit. It would be faster to actually look."

"Yeah. Let's go." Scarlet Rain—Niko—nodded, making her antennae-like pigtails bounce.

After walking a minute or so, an external white light started to shine in their path along the steel passageway, sinking into the heavy fog. Unconsciously quickening his pace, Haruyuki overtook the other three, cut around the bend to the left, and stared.

The place that had originally been the eastern wall facing the main street had changed into an open terrace, the entire area opened up to the outside. Their current location was still at a height equivalent to the twenty-third floor of his building, so the terrace offered an unbroken view of the outside world.

Tremendous. There was no other word.

In the sky, piles of thick gray clouds twisted, bluish-purple lightning frequently piercing the gaps between them. On the ground, like Haruyuki's condo, the buildings were covered in a design of layered, sharp steel plates. The heart of Shinjuku, faint and hazy directly ahead of him, was now more jostling strongholds of evil armies than a group of skyscrapers. No matter how much he rubbed his eyes, he saw nothing moving. It was absolutely deserted.

The words "city of evil" lingering in the back of his mind, Haruyuki whispered to Kuroyukihime advancing to his side, "I've never seen a field like this before. What are its attributes…?"

"Chaos." After giving this brief response, she turned eyes glowing violet toward Haruyuki and added, "You'll understand what that means sooner or later. Anyway, Haruyuki. It's all well and good to take in the view, but there's something else you should have noticed first."

"Huh…?" Haruyuki hurriedly swiveled his head through his surroundings before finally spotting what should have been the focus of his attention.

In the duel fields he'd visited up to now, his own and his enemy's HP bars had always appeared in a fixed location in an upper portion of his field of vision, separated by a timer that started at 1,800 seconds and counted down the time remaining. Now, however, the only HP bar was his, and there was no sign of the count numbers.

Although the technical aspects of Brain Burst were the ultimate of the game apps Haruyuki had used so far, feeding back to players fields so detailed and apparently tangible to the senses that they were indistinguishable from actual sensory input, the game itself was the ancient and hoary one-on-one fighter. Despite the fact that the image before him had changed only slightly when he came to the Unlimited Neutral Field, it made him feel like the game had suddenly gotten a face-lift into a cutting-edge, large-scale net game, and Haruyuki shouted involuntarily, "Th-the time remaining's gone?! What's going on…?"

"*That's* what going on." It was Niko to his left who replied.

"There's no upper time limit for dives set here. That's why it's 'Unlimited.'"

"What?!" At a loss for words yet again, Haruyuki considered seriously the implications of what he had just heard. "Uh, um. We are accelerated, right?"

"Yes, of course." Kuroyukihime's response set his thoughts whirling full speed again.

Brain Burst accelerated the consciousness of its users a thousand times and caused a full dive into a virtual field. So even if you used the full thirty minutes that was the usual upper limit for acceleration, a mere 1.8 seconds passed in the real world.

However, without that upper limit...

Spending just ten real-world minutes in this Unlimited Neutral Field, that would end up being ten thousand minutes—i.e., about 160 hours, i.e., about seven days. And if that was the case, what about spending the equivalent of a full day in the real world in this field?

After counting on his fingers, Haruyuki muttered in a hoarse voice, "Th-three years..."

What did that even mean? That was basically an eternity. Which meant, if you used this "unlimited burst," no matter how much homework you had piled up, no matter how much you skipped out on studying for exams—

"You'd be better off giving up on that, Haru," Takumu said from behind him, as if perfectly sussing out Haruyuki's miscreant thoughts.

When he turned around, his friend shrugged the solid shoulders of his avatar and continued in a voice sporting a laugh, "I came here exactly once before. I got excited that time just like you. I even thought going home right away would be a waste. I mean, I had spent those ten burst points, so I just hung around for three days, inside time. When I got back to the real world, I had forgotten everything I was planning to do right before I accelerated. It totally sucked."

"That's right, Haruyuki. In just three days, you'll simply forget what you were going to do, but if you spend, say, a month or six months here..." Kuroyukihime's tone grew serious. "*People are changed* when they return. It's only natural; in the worst-case scenario, the you you were and the soul you have are different ages. If you don't want your family and friends eyeing you suspiciously, you should avoid coming here too often."

The moment he heard that admonishment, a voice revived in the back of Haruyuki's brain.

If you knew exactly how much time me and that girl there had spent in the Accelerated World up to now...

The words Niko had said smilingly the day before. So what made it meaningful was—

But before he could pursue that thought, the girl herself patted his shoulder lightly. "Anyway, let's get moving already. Although we do have time to spare. When we accelerated, there were still two minutes real time before the train Cherry's on gets to Ikebukuro."

"R-right. So, moving...you mean, to Ikebukuro?"

Two minutes in the real world was more than thirty-three hours in the Accelerated World. Thinking that this was rather more than "time to spare," Haruyuki turned his gaze to the northeast.

On the far side of the blue-black steel city that seemed to stretch on to infinity, he could make out an enormous structure dimly rising. If that was the massive shopping center Sunshine City in Ikebukuro, then the distance from here to there should have been the same as it was in the real world, six kilometers.

"Umm. Are we walking? Or running? Or?"

"Why would we do that? Why do you think you're here?"

"Huh? What..."

The adorable crimson duel avatar at the other end of Haruyuki's dumbfounded gaze clasped both hands tightly in front of her chest and tilted her head to one side.

"You'll give us a big hug and carry us, right, big brother?"

*   *   *

After using Punch and Kick to destroy the obstacles—strangely shaped statues and iron lattices set on the open terrace—and building his special-attack gauge up to the maximum, Haruyuki turned around, muttering, "Let's see."

He saw the two Kings shoot dangerous looks at each other.

"I have no choice but to be held, not with these arms. You hang from Silver Crow's legs."

"You gotta be kidding! Why would I do something as humiliating as that? Your design's the problem here. Take the train by yourself!"

Takumu pushed in between the two squaring off with each other and sending actual, not just metaphorical, sparks flying and sighed. "Okay, how about we do it like this? Master, Haru holds you with his right arm and the Red King with his left. And then I'll hang from his legs. Can you do that, Haru?"

"Oh. Y-yeah, prob'ly. Although I probably won't be able to go too fast."

Stepping out in front of Niko and Kuroyukihime still looking dissatisfied, Haruyuki stretched out his right hand first.

"E-excuse me." He got a firm hold on the slim waist above Black Lotus's armor skirt with its black lotus flower design and then wrapped his left arm around Scarlet Rain's even more slender torso.

Without a scrap of mental energy to spare on the excitement of having flowers in both arms, Haruyuki nervously focused his power in his shoulder blades and deployed the metal fins folded up on his back.

The wings, spreading with a cold shuffling sound, soon began to emit a light vibrating noise. The virtual lift power generated brought the tips of his toes up off the floor. After ascending very slowly to a height of 1.5 meters, Haruyuki went into hover mode.

"Climb on, Taku."

"Thanks, Haru." Soon enough, Cyan Pile's sturdy arms were wrapped tightly around his calves.

"Okay, then...Here we go!" Haruyuki declared, oscillating his wings as hard as he could.

Although a load of three people was definitely appreciable, he still reliably ascended into the sky. The steel terrace immediately receded, and the deserted, strangely shaped city sprawled in all directions beneath their eyes.

"O-oh, wow!" Niko cried out from under his left arm. "We're seriously flying! That's Kannana Street...Is that the Chuo Line? Maybe I can see my school!"

For Haruyuki, the view from the sky was a familiar sight. Even with the restricted movement of a Normal Duel Field, visually, the whole of the Kanto region, not just Tokyo, could be taken in.

But no matter how many times he saw it, the deep emotion that pierced the depths of his heart showed no sign of abating. And this Unlimited Neutral Field, according to Kuroyukihime's explanation, continued on without bounds to every nook and cranny the social camera net covered—in other words, the whole of Japan.

This was not on the scale of a game map anymore. It was a *world*.

"Right...so this...," Haruyuki mumbled unthinkingly. "This right here is the Accelerated World. Always existing right next to the real world. Not momentarily, but a permanent world."

"Exactly." It was Kuroyukihime, whose body was entrusted to his right arm, who replied briefly. Sharp, shining eyes were turned on Haruyuki, and her voice flowed both severe and gentle at the same time. "And this is the Burst Linkers' true battlefield. If you are aiming for level nine, one day you will have to fight in this place and come out victorious. Although now is not yet that time."

Did that mean that his level wasn't high enough yet, or that his own abilities weren't enough?

Aware of a faint impatience biting into his heart, Haruyuki nodded slightly. "Right...a-anyway..."

"Hmm? What?"

"If this is the permanent map, then that means that Burst Linkers other than us are diving at this moment, right?"

"Totes." It was Niko who responded.

"B-but the ratio—It doesn't feel like there's anyone at all here," he said querulously, turning his face.

The strange city below him was replete with a cold silence; he couldn't see a single thing moving. Haruyuki had thought there would definitely be duel avatars everywhere like in the usual duel field, so he couldn't help but wonder at the quiet.

A laugh came quickly from Takumu, who dangled from his legs. "Ha-ha! Of course, Haru. Given the fact that there's a grand total of only a thousand or so Burst Linkers, the number diving in the Unlimited Neutral Field at any given time is supposedly just barely a hundred. Put simply, it's totally natural that you wouldn't see anyone in a place like Suginami, where there's nothing at all."

"O-okay, then. So if we go more into the center of town?"

"That's how it works. Which is exactly why we, and Cherry Rook, are headed for the Bukes." Niko hit Haruyuki's helmeted head lightly as she spoke. "But you keep floating like this without moving, and your gauge'll run out."

"Oh! R-right." Haruyuki checked the blue special-attack gauge shining thinly below his HP gauge. Hovering didn't use up much, but it was already down nearly 10 percent.

"Okay, I'll head out on a direct course," he announced, increasing his wings' oscillation again.

They moved ahead, gliding directly below the twisting clouds. Soon enough, they crossed the deserted Kannana and entered Nakano Ward.

Haruyuki caught sight of the Chuo Line Bridge, supported by pillars with a ridiculously tapered design, and casually followed it to the end where he saw something unexpected and muttered quietly, "Ah! Th-the train's moving?!"

Although it was a mere two-car configuration, a train-like, long, thin shadow was definitely moving in the direction of Shinjuku on the blackly lustrous rails, echoing solemnly.

"You can get on as well. Although it costs you points," Kuroyukihime explained, somewhat delightedly, and his eyes popped unconsciously beneath his silver armor.

"What?! Wh-who's driving it?!"

"Heh-heh, you should check yourself, one day."

Even while they were having this conversation, the tracks quickly passed into the distance behind them, and the Yamanote Line appeared, as if to replace it. Once they got past that, they'd be in Mejiro, and Ikebukuro would soon follow.

In the real world, Haruyuki often went to buy older-generation games and used paper-media books, but access from Suginami was surprisingly poor. He either had to go out to Shinjuku by train or get a bus from Koenji, but either way, he was moving at right angles, so it took a while.

Carefree thoughts about how much easier it would be if he could fly there like this were spinning around in his head when Kuroyukihime, riding on his right arm, indicated the east side with the point of her sharp sword.

"See, Haruyuki? Take a look at that."

Turning his gaze lazily in that general direction, Haruyuki was so shocked he nearly dropped the two Kings. He hurriedly strengthened his grip.

"Whoa! Wh-wha—?!"

An enormous shadow moved densely down Yamate Street—which was covered in a thick fog—a shadow that could only be described as strange. Its overall form was like a four-legged beast, but its torso was flat like a stingray, and from the place where its head should have been, countless feelers drooped down toward the ground. At the ends of its long, sturdy limbs, two sharp talons like those of an insect stretched out to the point of heinousness.

And its size...it had to have been at least as big as a three-story building. It completely occupied the three lanes into the city and was moving leisurely toward the south.

Feeling a heavy, low crunch shake the air each time its legs came into contact with the road, Haruyuki mumbled, dazed, "What...is that?"

"An Enemy. The inhabitants of this world, created and moved by the system."

Picking up where Kuroyukihime left off, Niko whistled briefly, "You're pretty lucky, you know, getting to see one that big right off the bat. But don't get too close. We get targeted by that thing and even a group like this is gonna get slowed down."

"Targeted...You mean, attacked?!"

"You do learn the meaning of the word 'Enemy' in junior high, right?"

With nothing to spare to react to Niko's spiteful style, Haruyuki hurriedly gained altitude. The strange, enormous beast seemed not to notice the spectators in the sky and continued lumbering along.

"Wh-why would something so dangerous be part of the game?"

"Why? Well, that is..." Kuroyukihime started to answer and faltered. Niko and Takumu also appeared similarly pressed for a response, and Haruyuki cocked his head to one side.

"Oh!" Takumu, dangling from his legs, cried in a strained voice. "Look, it's just starting. The hunt."

"H-hunt...?"

The enormous beast suddenly roared as below their eyes it moved farther. Haruyuki abruptly flew up several meters.

"Whoa?!"

The beast stood on its hind legs and howled again, violently swinging its bundle of tentacles. But Haruyuki quickly realized that he and his companions had not incited this roaring.

There were several small shadows farther south on Yamanote Street.

At first, he thought they were other Enemies, but he soon gathered that this was not the case. The silhouettes were human shaped in various colors of armor—they were Burst Linkers.

A large one standing in front lifted its right hand swiftly and swung it downward. Immediately, a firing line of several beams and live ammunition surged from the roofs of the buildings lining both sides of the street and exploded against the monster's skull.

Instantly, the Enemy, massive bulk reeling, emitted a strange howl of a war cry and turned its head toward one of the buildings. Scratching the air with its forelimb, it started advancing with a subterranean rumbling.

However, before its enormous bulk slammed into the building, the Burst Linkers who had taken up positions on the road launched a midrange attack. The beast, peppered by explosions, changed targets with an angry cry and plunged toward the Linkers exposed on the road.

"Ah! Watch out!" Haruyuki shouted automatically.

The beast brought its forelimb down from high in the air, smashing without the slightest resistance into the leader. Or at least that's what it looked like, but the duel avatar, with its bluish-silver heavy armor, stopped the huge talons with crossed arms.

The idea was apparently not to stop and fight head-on then and there. The Linkers gradually retreated, all the while guarding against the fierce attacks of the rampaging beast. When they had drawn it sufficiently far away from the two buildings, another simultaneous launch came from the rooftops, hitting the base of the creature's tail. The monstrosity changed directions on heavy feet and plunged toward the building on the east side, and this time, the ground troops chased after it to initiate a close-range attack.

"Fairly decent party. Good hate control. Who's the leader?"

Niko responded to Kuroyukihime's admiring tone. "Pretty sure it's a senior member of the Green Legion. Although the party looks mixed."

At this conversation, Haruyuki finally grasped the facts of the battle spreading out below his eyes. "I-Is that it…Those Burst Linkers aren't being attacked by that huge monster. They're targeting it and trying to bring it down, right?"

"Yes. It's a hunt."

"So then if they defeat it, they get experience poi—I mean, burst points?"

"Mmm-hmm. That's the idea."

Following the assenting Kuroyukihime's lead, Niko patted Haruyuki on the head. "Even you should get it by now. The reason Enemies exist in the Unlimited Neutral Field is, ultimately, the reason the field exists at all. Burst Linkers can level up not just with regular duels, but by hunting and stuff here. But, you know—"

"It's remarkably inefficient compared with duels. Even if you're willing to risk the annihilation of your points to hunt a large monster at that level, you might, if you're lucky, get what you'd get for winning a duel at the same level. Ten points." Having picked up the explanation, Kuroyukihime paused there for a moment and lightly shook the mask of her elegant form. "There's no avoiding that. Hunting Enemies in this world is essentially an act of generating burst points from nothing. Which is to say, in Brain Burst, which is at best a one-on-one fighting game, hunting in the Unlimited Field is basically nothing more than a supplementary means of point supply. However, currently, it has essentially become the lone road to a higher level. The reason being—"

"The mutual nonaggression pact, right?" Haruyuki murmured.

"Even if high-level Burst Linkers want to fight, they can't just go invading another Legion's Territory. And given that, the weekend Territory Battles aren't functioning because of the pact…"

"But, Master," Takumu said thoughtfully from Haruyuki's feet as Silver Crow started to fly north again, moving them away from the fierce battle unfolding far beneath them, "if I'm correct, there's just one more, isn't there? A means of earning points to swiftly gain the higher levels with great efficiency, even given the current situation?"

"What? Taku, what do you...?"

"The thing is, in this world, there are things besides Enemies you can hunt. Prey with way, way more points."

After sinking into thought for a moment, Haruyuki inhaled sharply. "R-really? Not the huge creature back there, but the Linkers...?" Glancing back, he could see the ongoing battle fire making the heavy fog sparkle even now far to the south.

Kuroyukihime's quiet voice broke the slight silence. "That's it. In this place, you can attack to your heart's content those high-level Burst Linkers you can't challenge otherwise. Even if you would like to challenge them to regular duels, it's impossible due to the fact that they almost never leave their Legion Territories. And anything is possible here: ambushes, surprise attacks."

"And we're about to do exactly that to Cherry Rook—I mean, Chrome Disaster," Niko whispered while directing both eyes, covered by round, cute crimson lenses, abruptly forward.

They had already passed Mejiro Street, aka Ring Road No. 7, and the center of Ikebukuro was dead ahead of them. So Haruyuki supposed that the palace surrounded by a group of strange steel spires piercing the sky from where the inky road was swallowed up was JR Ikebukuro Station. From there, an enormous skyway stretched out to the south and connected with a highrise fortress a little distance off—Sunshine City. At the foot of the passageway was a jumble of tiny buildings, looking like multicolored lights twinkling.

Are those just plain old light effects? Or is there actually a shopping district down there, just like the real Ikebukuro? Which reminds me, Takumu and Kuroyukihime didn't say what that shop thing was all about before. Maybe down there—

As he drifted on to other things, unconsciously forgetting about the current situation, Haruyuki's head was yanked back to reality by Niko's right hand.

"Heyo, not stopping here. We should still have a fair bit of time before Cherry gets here, but let's keep an eye out on the ground. Flying like this, we're totes exposed."

"Well, that's true, but Ikebukuro *is* quite large. Do you know where he'll appear?"

She sniffed at Kuroyukihime's question. "Given his pattern 'til now, somewhere around Sunshine City. Just come from the south and land on the roof of whatever building there is."

Haruyuki prepared to do as he was told, angling his body toward the east. He could see the sky-impaling fortress diagonally to the left in front of him. To its right was something like a basin gaping open. That was probably South Ikebukuro Park in the real world, but with nothing treelike to speak of, it gave off an air of desolation like a crater where a giant meteorite had violently collided with the earth.

"Okay, I'll come down in front of the empty lot." Haruyuki checked his special-attack gauge, which had only a little left in it, judged that he could just barely make it, and flapped his wings. Bearing the weight of four people, he began his slow advance—

"Haru!!" Takumu, at his feet, cried.

Snapping his head down, Haruyuki caught the dazzling orange of a firing line, stretching upward from a gap between the buildings on the ground.

"Ngh!!" Without even the time to scream, Haruyuki instinctively put all his power into a forward dash, diagonally to the right.

The air burned around him, and he felt an enormous amount of heat scraping very close to his back. It felt like the tips of his wings, which should not have had the sensation of pain, were splitting into tiny bits.

Regardless, Haruyuki once again slid through the sky, this time tacking left. His eyes perceived a second launch from the ground—and the color was different from the first round.

After he just barely dodged a blue-white beam of light, Kuroyukihime cried in a low voice, "Impossible. Chrome Disaster?!"

"It can't be," Niko replied in a voice echoing with tense amazement. "It's too soon. We should still have an entire day in this time before he shows! And this kind of technique, he doesn't—"

Haruyuki interrupted their conversation with a desperate cry. "We're going down!!"

This due to the fact that on one side of the buildings below, he could see the third volley—and multiple points of light blinking. Those weren't linear laser attacks, but rather the lights of real projectiles firing, probably missiles equipped with a tracking function.

Haruyuki stopped the lift force of his wings temporarily and went into a sudden descent equivalent to falling. However, if they fell straight down, they would be immediately captured by the mysterious foe coming to meet them. Spreading his wings out to their fullest and drifting along like a glider, he aimed for the enormous crater in front of him.

"Here they come! Missiles!" Clucking her tongue and twisting her body in Haruyuki's arm, Niko unholstered the gun at her hip.

The staccato sound of repeated fire followed, and several small-scale explosions roared. However, she obviously couldn't intercept every missile with a single gun, and a few of them pierced the flames and closed in.

"Yah!" Kuroyukihime ripped through them in a single swipe of her left arm.

A second passed before the explosion. Using the pressure of the blast, Haruyuki cut through the last few dozen meters and stepped hard on the brakes in the center of the round crater.

First, Takumu separated from Haruyuki's legs, digging into the ground as he impacted. The two Kings then leapt out from his arms to land delicately on the ground. After crashing clumsily in the middle, Haruyuki hurried back to his feet and saw, checking his HP bar with a glance, that fortunately it hadn't dipped even 3 percent. Kuroyukihime and the others shouldn't have taken any direct hits at all.

In the center of the enormous hole, countless cracks radiating outward, Haruyuki and the others held their breath.

The world returned to silence, almost as if the attacks of only a few seconds earlier had never happened. All that could be heard was the lightning flashing in the distant black clouds above them and the sound of the wind blowing past.

Then…

The quiet crunching of footsteps broke the silence, and a lone shadow appeared on the western edge of the crater. A Burst Linker. No doubt their assailant moments earlier. But it was nothing more than a silhouette, and Haruyuki couldn't make out details like its color.

"That's…our attacker from before…?" Haruyuki muttered in a croak that didn't quite constitute a voice.

However, seconds later, a second shadow rose up soundlessly to the right of the first. And then a third and a fourth.

"Wh-what the…" Takumu cursed under his breath at the same time countless heavy footsteps echoed around them.

Shadows of avatars lined the circumference of the crater in every direction. Big, small, long-distance, close range, their characteristics ran the gamut, but there was just one thing they all had in common: their aura. The eyes Haruyuki felt on him conveyed a thirst for battle that practically overflowed from the assemblage as they stared intently and silently at their prey. The aura of a hunter.

The number of Burst Linkers quickly reached thirty. And finally, the center of the group encircling the outer edge of the crater parted, and an avatar with remarkable presence appeared.

Long and thin, it was probably taller than Cyan Pile, but the slenderness of its limbs was on par with Silver Crow's. On this body, a skeletal insinuation of a human, only the shoulders and hips were rounded and filled out. Atop its head, it sported a hat shaped like thick horns, curving long and thin to both sides. Large spheres stuck onto the ends of the horns wobbled soundlessly. The face was covered by a mask in the pattern of a smile.

"A clown?" Haruyuki whispered. The avatar's silhouette eerily resembled the joker from a deck of cards. But there wasn't a hint of humor in the mask. The long, thin eyes—nothing more than upended talons—shone dimly white with a cruel glimmer in the backlit shadow.

Abruptly, the clouds in the sky above parted, and beams of ashen sunlight weakly trickled across the landscape, illuminating the avatars tightly encircling the crater. They represented a rainbow of colors, but if anything, the majority were red and yellow. Shining conspicuously vividly among them was the armor of the clown avatar standing lanky in their nucleus.

The armor was a garish yellow like uranium ore, without even a trace of dullness to muddy it. The instant he saw it, a fierce shudder ran down Haruyuki's spine. Duel avatars with that kind of vivid color saturation just didn't exist. He'd seen this sort of color personally only twice: obsidian darkness and crimson fire. Which meant... Which meant, this clown...

As if to give credence Haruyuki's speculation, the crimson avatar next to him emitted a hoarse acknowledgment. "Yellow Radio. The Yellow King. Why is he—"

A King. A level-nine Burst Linker, one of only seven in existence in the Accelerated World.

Up to now, Haruyuki hadn't had any contact with members of the Yellow Legion, much less the Yellow King himself. This was because the Territory the Yellow Legion controlled was the opposite side of Tokyo as seen from Suginami—the area from Ueno to Akihabara. Although he occasionally went to Akihabara to buy old computer parts and such, Haruyuki made sure to cut off his global connection when he did.

Put another way, it was highly unnatural that the Yellow Legion would be here in Ikebukuro at this moment and accompanied by such numbers. Obviously, it wasn't a coincidence. Because the four of them had used the "unlimited burst" command at Haruyuki's condo to dive into the Unlimited Neutral Field, only something like a few seconds would have passed in real time. Definitely not enough time for a member of the Legion to discover them, contact the outside, get other members together, and meet up in Ikebukuro.

Which meant they were also monitoring Cherry Rook's movements, had predicted that Haruyuki and the others would turn up here, and laid an ambush.

If that was true, then there was only one reason for it. All of it. Every little thing leading to this situation was their—

"Bastard!!" Niko howled suddenly.

The Red King, likely having reaching the same conclusion with similar rapidity, jumped a step forward, clenched her fists, threw her head back, and roared in an accusation that was at once both childish and menacing, "You're behind this whole thing, Yellow Radio!!"

Right. That was the only answer.

The raging flames of her blame flared at him, but the Yellow King's slim figure didn't flinch. Unexpectedly, he took his time raising his bone-like arm. He waved it out broadly to the right and flipped his palm up.

"Well, well, when the little bug fluttering in the sky comes falling to earth, he brings a surprising guest. Hello, Red King." Emanating from the grinning mask was the clear, fluid voice of a boy. However, a distortion effect, almost as if it had been encoded at an incredible compression ratio, added a certain odiousness to it.

"What're you talking about? You're the one who ambushed us!"

"You don't understand what I'm saying? I only came out this way to have the Red Legion take responsibility one way or the other for violating the nonaggression pact and attacking my precious subordinates and hounding them into total point loss. This duel avatar running so insolently wild in our Territory recently is a real problem, hmm?"

Countless layers of metal rings that comprised the horns of his hat wobbled lazily. Almost as if he was trying to suppress a smile.

Niko jabbed her index finger at him and cried, flames leaping forward, "And you're the one who made him like that! You gave Cherry Rook the Armor of Catastrophe, which you had concealed, to lure me out to this place...You were the one who laid

the temptation in front of him and sent him on a rampage in violation of the pact!!"

"'Concealed'? 'Gave'? That's no way to talk to a person. The
Armor disappeared ages ago, hmm? Didn't your subordinate
simply make it again?" he asked throatily. This time he stretched
out his left arm before continuing, tracing a line in the air with
an abnormally long and sharp finger.

"In the sacred pact formerly consecrated among the Kings, we
have this clause: 'Should a member of a given Legion be pushed
to the forced uninstallation of Brain Burst due to an attack in
violation of the pact, the aggrieved Legion may select one from
the ranks of the Legion to which the transgressor belongs, con-
signing that person the same fate.' An eye for an eye, a tooth for
a tooth...In truth, it's an uncivilized method of revenge, hmm?"

Heh. Heh-heh-heh.

This time an unmistakable laugh leaked out from beneath the
acute angles of the inverted triangle of the mask. The upward-
arching eyes flickered faintly in time with the laughter.

"However, rules are rules. Isn't that so? If I, a King, were to
ignore the pact here, we can't say for certain that there wouldn't
follow a string of similarly insolent fellows, one after the other.
Thus, I had no choice but to come all the way out to the boonies
of Ikebukuro. To find one person affiliated with the Red Legion
and have them pay for their comrade's sins, yes? However...per-
haps this is yet another cruel trick of fate?"

Placing both hands on his hips and bending over abruptly, the
Yellow King uttered coolly, obscenely, "That this person *coin-
cidentally* turns out to be none other than the head of the Red
Legion, Scarlet Rain herself."

It's no coincidence! Haruyuki screamed in his heart, grinding
his teeth.

The duel avatars lined up outside the crater had topped out
at about thirty. It might have been a King's Legion, but this was
probably about the maximum that could be mobilized on a week-

day evening. It was impossible that their objective was anything other than hunting a King, the strongest prey in the world.

The Yellow King had predicted that Scarlet Rain—Niko—would pursue this course of action. That, given Niko's personality, she would show up like this in the Unlimited Neutral Field to punish the crimes committed by her subordinate, Cherry Rook, with her Judgment Blow.

No, it wasn't just that. Luring Niko into this situation and *legally hunting one of the five heads he needed to elevate himself to level ten*—for this purpose, the Yellow King had slipped the Enhanced Armament Chrome Disaster to a Red Legion member. That was the only thing that made sense. In which case, that meant...

"It was the Yellow King who hid the fact that the Armor dropped two and a half years ago when The Fourth was defeated," Haruyuki whispered to himself, unaware that he was speaking aloud. But there wasn't a shred of evidence supporting this. If he started hollering about his hypothesis here, it would just be an endless argument.

Likely understanding this, too, Niko stayed silent, her clenched fists shaking violently. Finally, her hands opened and dropped to her sides. A controlled, level voice flowed up from the bottom of the crater.

"It should also say this in the pact: 'It is permitted to select any one person and exact vengeance, but this shall not be the case in the event that the Legion Master personally judges and sentences the offender to total point loss.' I'll judge him; I'll judge Cherry Rook. You got no problem with that, right?"

"Go right ahead!" Spreading his hands smoothly, the Yellow King, Yellow Radio, said amusedly. "If you're capable! I heard the rumors on the wind. The other day, you certainly made an attempt, and you lost spectacularly. And you suffered the further shame of a crude time-out loss! Isn't that so? If you are going to challenge him again, you are free to do so. However, where exactly is this Cherry so-and-so?" He swiveled his enormous hat-accesorized head from side to side theatrically.

"We are busy, too, you know. You don't plan to make us wait here for days when you don't know when he'll make an appearance, do you? If you can't deal with him right away, then it seems our only choice will be to make do with you here, hmm?"

"Hngh!" Niko grunted, vexed.

They had verified that Cherry Rook was moving in the real world with Niko's remote monitoring before accelerating, but there was a time lag before their opponent actually appeared in the Unlimited Neutral Field. For instance, even with a lag of a few minutes in the real world, in this world, where time was accelerated by a factor of a thousand, in the worst case, the difference could end up being a day or more. Just as the Yellow King said, it would be impossible to capture Cherry Rook right away.

Bracing himself, Haruyuki took a step forward and murmured very quietly at Niko's back. "It's hopeless, Niko. Right from the start, he was trying to trap you. There's no way he'll let you go. Let's retreat temporarily. Log out and then the next chance—"

"We can't." Her reply was immediate and concise. "System-wise, we can't do that. In the Unlimited Neutral Field, immediate log out's not possible."

"Wha—" Speechless, Haruyuki heard Takumu, who'd moved alongside him, murmuring in his ear.

"It's true, Haru. The only way to get out of here is to go to one of the leave points set up in the area. Even if you commit suicide, you can't log out. You'll just be resurrected an hour later in the same spot you died. Of course, if someone on the real-world side yanks your Neurolinker off for you, that's a different story. But, right now at your place..."

There was no one. His mother didn't get back from her business trip until tomorrow, and three years would pass before then in this world.

"The closest leave point is either Ikebukuro Station or Sunshine City," Niko whispered quickly, glancing backward. "We can't get to either of them fast. And even if we did head for one, we'd have to fight at least once just to bust through this circle."

She cut herself off momentarily, both eyes glinting sharply like rubies. "But y'know, this Radio Jackhole's made a miscalculation of his own."

"M-miscalculation?"

"Yeah. This is how many people he got together to take me down, to take down a King. But, uh, we got another one here right now, don't we?"

Haruyuki's eyes flew open.

On the color wheel that determined the attributes of a duel avatar, yellow excelled at midrange attacks. Although it was particularly good at unpleasant, back-stabbing kind of maneuvers, it was inferior to the other colors in terms of direct attack power. Meanwhile, Red King Niko was a demon with long-range heat powers, and although he could count on one hand the number of times he'd seen her fight, from her form alone, he could see the Black King Kuroyukihime specialized in close-range attacks.

If the two of them worked to cover each other, they might have a chance at winning, even up against thirty people, one of whom was a King.

Having thought this far, Haruyuki was suddenly gripped by a physical unease. Why had Kuroyukihime been silent this whole time? Normally, she would have been flaring up at the Yellow King the second he showed his face even more aggressively than Niko.

Turning abruptly, Haruyuki saw the jet-black avatar, sword hands dangling at her sides, head hanging, almost as if she was afraid. "Ku—"

Just as he was about to instinctively shout her name, the Yellow King's clear voice rang out once again.

"As long as Cherry-whatever doesn't show up, it seems the only thing to do is have you take responsibility, hmm, Red King? And that being the case…" A long finger on his leisurely raised arm aimed straight at a black spot at the bottom of the crater. "You'll just sit back and watch the thrilling, wonderful carnival about to commence without interference, hmm, Black King?"

Even slapped with the Yellow King's overly self-righteous manner of speaking, Kuroyukihime showed no reaction whatsoever, head still hanging. After a full five seconds had passed, she finally lifted her face in an almost rusty motion and pointed the sword of her right hand at the Yellow King.

"You've got to be kidding, Radio." The words slipping out from under her mask were combative, but her voice didn't contain its usual severity. Almost as if talking to herself rather than her opponent, Kuroyukihime went on spitting out words. "Even you don't believe you'll actually be able to bring down two Kings with this strike force. If you think I'm just going to sit back and watch, you've made an enormous mistake."

"Oh? So you're saying you'll fight? That you'll turn that bloodstained sword on me as well? And here I was trying to give you a front-row seat to the show. But you're saying you'd rather deliberately meet with a bad end?"

Despite the fact that the situation could not in any way be said to be to his party's advantage as Kuroyukihime had indicated, the Yellow King laughed from deep in his throat. "It is true that I hadn't considered that you might join Scarlet Rain in appearing in the Unlimited Field here today. But, well...a wrinkle like this won't put a stop to our Legion Crypt Cosmic Circus's exciting carnival. You see, I have been waiting all this time, aaaaaall this time in my heart of hearts, to meet you like this one day, Lotus. So that I can give you this wonderful present I've been carrying around in my pocket for so very long!"

Haruyuki saw something square glittering at the end of the Yellow King's fingers as he stretched them out with a performer's grace. It was about the same size as a playing card, but he couldn't make out the pattern on it.

The clown avatar twirled the card around deftly with his fingertips before flicking it out. It reflected the sunlight trickling through the gaps in the thick clouds and danced several dozen meters into the air, shimmering and glistening before striking the ground soundlessly a short distance from Haruyuki and the others.

It didn't seem to be anything dangerous. Haruyuki stared absently at the sideways triangle, which popped up on the card surface and blinked. Immediately, Niko next to him warned in a low voice, "A replay file."

The card's surface sparkled dazzlingly and emitted an inverted cone of light straight up. Countless horizontal lines ran through the sky like noise, soon coming together in a single image. The semitransparent 3-D projection was of a duel avatar that Haruyuki had never seen before.

Red. The figure was an orthodox human shape, but the balanced armor it bore shone a red so pure it seemed impossible for it to be any more so. It was different from the flaming crimson of Scarlet Rain—the color of passion, as it were.

Once again, a hoarse voice slipped out of Niko. "My predecessor...Red Rider."

Kuroyukihime took a step back and said, almost shouted, "Stop...stop it!"

It was then that the semitransparent 3-D image suddenly started to move.

The bright red avatar projected large in the sky clenched his right fist in front of his body and waved his left directly to the side. The crisp voice of a boy broadcast loudly, echoing clearly in Haruyuki's ears.

"This...this ridiculous goal is what we've been fighting for up to now?! Hating each other, stealing from each other, killing each other...Did we keep fighting however many thousands of duels for however many years because we wanted to see an ending like this?! No, even if this is the scenario the developer of Brain Burst wrote...we're not NPCs made to dance by the game master! The heroes of this game are us, all of us here! Right, Lotus?"

Here, the screen pulled back, and as the red avatar grew smaller, another avatar sitting in front of him came into the frame. A jet-black avatar equipped with four long, daunting swords. Black Lotus.

The first Red King continued tossing out harsh words, accompanied by even harsher gestures, at the Black King, who quietly hung her head.

"It's true we all control our respective Legions, and we've fought hard up to now. But that's definitely not because we're enemies! It's because we're rivals, isn't it?! I...I like your fighting style, Lotus. If we ever met in the real world, I could be buds with you. Totally. Actually, I want to be! Which is why I don't want us to try to kill each other in sudden death! It's gotta be the same for you!"

At that moment, the slightly sharp voice of a girl came from offscreen. *"Hey, Rider! You think I'm just gonna let that go?!"*

The red avatar turned to the left as if flustered and held a hand up. *"N-no, that's not it. I didn't mean it like that...Ah, crap."*

Background laughter could be heard above this exchange.

The Black Lotus, hanging her head on-screen, abruptly relaxed her shoulders. Raising her face, in a calm voice, she said: *"Mmm... I suppose so. It's just like you say, Rider. I like you, too. Naturally, I mean, I respect you."*

Standing smoothly and taking a step up, the Black King extended her right sword hand to the Red King.

"I knew you'd get it, Lotus!" the Red King shouted gleefully, and when he reached out to shake hands, he stopped as if confused.

The Black King shrugged and said, her voice tipped with laughter, *"Oops! Apologies. Well, then...how about this?"* In a smooth, unreserved motion, the Black King thrust herself against the Red King's chest, bringing both arms up around his neck and hugging tightly.

Something like a blush sprang up on the Red King's cheeks before he wrapped both hands around Black Lotus's waist.

Once again, the girl from before cried out offscreen, *"Hey! Come on!"*

"Don't get mad. It's just instead of a handshake." The Red King

excused himself impatiently, and several voices rang out in laughter.

And then.

Black Lotus's eyes lit up with an icy, bluish-white light behind her sable goggles. The swords of her arms intersecting behind the Red King's neck glittered an intense violet.

"Death by Embrace."

She uttered the name of the special attack quietly as the two crossed blades swiftly intersected, like a pair of enormous scissors.

Red Rider's body went limp and crumpled at Black Lotus's feet, a broken doll. His head alone remained on the crossed arms of the Black King. She brought the freshly severed head, dripping copious bright red sparks from the cross section, gently to her cheek.

The thick, full silence was shredded by a high-pitched, despairing scream.

"N-noooooooooo!!"

The replay video ended there, and the figure of Black Lotus cradling her rival's head faded back into the noise of the scan lines.

Only the thin wail did not cut out, continuing to ring in Haruyuki's ears. He finally realized it was being ripped from Kuroyukihime's throat next to him.

"Stop! Stop, stop!"

"K-Kuro—" Haruyuki gasped at how violently his own voice shook as he called out to her.

Kuroyukihime glanced at Haruyuki but quickly turned her face away and shook her head from side to side, over and over. "Haruyuki...I...I'm..."

No other words followed.

Suddenly, her eyes, shining a bluish purple behind the mirrored surface of Kuroyukihime's goggles, became narrow lines of light and flowed from left to right before disappearing abruptly. At the same time, almost like a robot with its power cut, the obsidian avatar's whole body went limp, and the Black King crumbled to the floor of the blue-black crater with a dry crunching sound.

"Kuroyuki...Kuroyukihime?" Uncomprehending, Haruyuki could only, quavering, call out, kneel down, and gently shake the slender avatar. But she did not react in any way.

"Zero Fill! Lotus, you...to go that far..." Niko cried in a low voice from behind.

Unable to grasp the meaning of her words, Haruyuki started to turn to her when there came a high-pitched laugh, and he froze.

"Hmm-hmm-hmm! Ha-ha-ha! Wah-ha-ha-ha-ha-ha-ha!!"

The cackle belonged to Yellow Radio, looking down from on high as a king onto his kingdom. "Heh-heh-heh-heh-heh! Of course. I thought you might still be strongly affected by this betrayal. That you would live up to my expectations and zero for me is actually almost disappointing...simply going quietly and hiding yourself in a hole, and so willingly! What of all your big talk about wanting to get to level ten, hmm, Black Lotus?"

"Y-you..." The stammer leaked from Haruyuki's throat like a groan.

The Yellow King's tone changed abruptly and filled the crater, colored with a whiplike sharpness. "Now, then, let us enjoy the final program of our carnival! Ready attacks! Target: Scarlet Rain! Destroy without mercy any bit players who get in the way!!"

"Dammit!" Niko cursed and spread out the hands of her cute avatar. "Come! Enhanced Arm—"

However, Takumu's arm snaked out to grab her shoulder. "You can't, Red King! If you deploy your weapons, you'll lose your mobility and won't be able to withdraw! Even if you are a King, a fight with this many people is impossible for one person. Leave subjugating Chrome Disaster for the moment, break through the circle behind us, and retreat to the leave point in Sunshine City!"

His eyes, glittering pale blue from under the mask's narrow slits, turned to Haruyuki next. "Haru, take care of Master! I'll hold them off, so you just get her to Sunshine somehow!"

"B-but—If we do that, you'll—"

"I don't matter! Once these guys take down the Red King, they'll definitely go for Master! We can't let that happen!"

Haruyuki could only nod at Takumu's voice, clear and yet tense.

"G-got it! Do what you can!" he shouted, grabbing Kuroyuki-hime's body with his left hand.

"Commence attack!!"

The Yellow King dropped the right arm he had raised.

6

The first to come pouring down was, naturally, the torrential rain of the distance attacks.

It might have been the Yellow Legion, but that didn't mean that all its members were in the yellow family—that the legion was made exclusively of Burst Linkers whose affinity was midrange attacks. The group of thirty foes encircling the crater looked like it included at least ten in the red family, and the number of beams and explosive rounds could more aptly be called concentrated fire.

The majority of it was aimed at Niko, but the Red King dashed backward and avoided the rounds admirably, with a nimbleness that was a far cry from her fortress mode. However, one blue light beam, whether targeted or a misfire, came straight for Haruyuki, who was holding on to Kuroyukihime and unable to get his feet to move.

"Ngh!" Although he tried twisting his body to avoid it, the beam grazed his shoulder. Playing at being tough, he was laughing it off in his heart—*Can't even call that a scratch*—when:

"Hnngh!"

Haruyuki's back arched at the scorching heat suddenly generated in his shoulder.

When players took damage in a duel in Brain Burst, they were given a pain stimulus on a level that was not possible with normal Neurolinker apps. But the pain Haruyuki felt was twice that of a normal duel.

Which meant something like: In addition to features like "no time limit" and "can't instantly withdraw," this place, the Unlimited Neutral Field, increased the sensation of pain by an order of magnitude when struck, as a risk to counterbalance the advantage of being able to earn points outside of duels.

After a slight lag, a number of small missiles rushed in above Haruyuki's head as he stood there.

"Heeey!" Howling, Cyan Pile came to stand before them, blocking Haruyuki and Kuroyukihime with the Pile Driver device in his right arm, aimed at the missiles.

The sharp iron spike launched with a metallic rasp, and the majority of the enemy rounds exploded from the impact wave. However, a few survived and struck the body sheathed in blue armor. Flashes of light. Sounds of explosions.

"Gaaah!" he cried out and reeled back, but Takumu did not fall. Instead, he turned his enormous body around, plumes of smoke rising from it, and barked, "Haru! Run!"

"G-got it!"

Apologizing in his heart, Haruyuki started running, practically dragging Kuroyukihime's avatar along with him. In his path, Niko had already drawn the gun on her hip and was firing blindly at the enemies in position on the east side of the crater.

If they didn't get out of this siege first, retreating or fighting back would be impossible. Fortunately, because their foes had spread themselves out along the entire hundred-meter-diameter crater, the wall, as it were, was thin. If they could break through in a single hit and get out onto Green Street, Sunshine City and its leave point were right there.

Haruyuki, still holding Kuroyukihime under his arm, opened the wings on his back. Thanks to that hit earlier, his special attack gauge had increased, albeit by just a tiny bit. But it was enough to make a sliding dash to the edge of the crater possible.

One point in the eastern circle was starting to come apart thanks to Niko's steady fire. Staring right at it, Haruyuki kicked the ground with everything he had.

Then the voice of the Yellow King, smooth and cool while also somehow discordant, echoed remarkably high behind him. "Silly Go Round!!"

A special attack!

But it was too late! The edge of the crater was right in front of his eyes—

"Waaah?!" Haruyuki reared at the phenomenon that abruptly unfolded.

The world had started to turn. No, the truth was the inside and outside of the crater were rotating in opposite directions, with the edge as the border. The buildings in the background, and the enemy duel avatars standing there, flowed from left to right at high speed.

Around them, several toy horses had popped up at some point, a transparent, hazy yellow, and were moving up and down together in a happy-go-lucky way. He even heard a sunny country tune, but that, too, was eerie.

Immediately, Haruyuki lost his sense of balance and dropped to one knee. He saw that Niko, right ahead of him, and Takumu, at his side, were also bracing fiercely, their bodies swaying.

"Th-the field's rotating?!" Haruyuki blurted, dazed, to which the Red King replied sharply.

"It just looks like it's rotating! The truth is, nothing's moving! Close your eyes and run!"

"But...which way?!" He already had absolutely no idea which way was east, which was what he'd been aiming for. It would all be for nothing if he charged forward blindly and ended up farther away from the leave point.

"That way!"

"This way!"

Niko and Takumu simultaneously pointed in completely opposite directions.

Instantly, as if aiming to strike while they were frozen in place, the surging wave of a volley spiraled in from the outer edge of the crater and converged on them.

As he looked up at the multicolored line of fire, Haruyuki knew in his gut that he wouldn't be able to dodge. That trajectory of the volley only looked like it was deeply arching. It only felt curved because of Yellow Radio's hallucination attack.

Thinking that at the very least he had to protect Kuroyukihime, he tried to cover the slim avatar beneath his outspread wings.

But before he could, Takumu cried out, "Get down!!" Scooping the three of them up in his strong arms, he covered them, as if falling.

"Ta—" Haruyuki's words as he opened his eyes wide were erased by the fierce instrumental ensemble of explosions. His field of view was painted white, and heat scorched his cheeks. The stifled scream of his friend popped next to his ear.

"Ngaaaaaaah!!"

At that moment, every single kind of long-distance attack was raining down in a fierce barrage on Takumu's broad back. With the pain from just one round scraping Silver Crow's shoulder being that intense, exactly what was the sum total of the agony hammering Takumu's nerves? Given the circumstances, it would have to be even greater than what Haruyuki inflicted on himself in his training room.

"Stop...Taku, stop already!" Haruyuki cried, trying to crawl out from under his friend.

But the young man's essentially steel arms held him even tighter, locking him in place, while at the same time, he gasped. "I-it's okay, Haru. I have to...do this much...to pay you..."

"You don't! You don't have to! How many times do I have to tell you that, Taku?!" Haruyuki shouted desperately, but the answer he got was more anguish. Each time he felt the shudder of a direct hit, a cracking groan slipped out from the slits dividing Cyan Pile's mask.

Mixed with the sound of countless shots firing, the Yellow

King's detestable voice just barely reached him. "Monstrous... Burn that little puppet up already."

The sound of several shots in concert came in response, but Takumu did not fall.

The red Burst Linkers in this enemy group probably weren't very high level. And although Cyan Pile was still level four, he was blue, a type emphasizing endurance. Thus, even taking this kind of concentrated fire, he could keep going without falling. But that also meant the agony Takumu himself was experiencing would be drawn out until who knew when.

There was nothing left for Haruyuki to say. Takumu was prepared to continue protecting the three of them until the effectiveness of the Yellow King's special attack wore off.

Likely having already guessed this, next to Haruyuki, Niko said clearly, "Retreat in your mind at least, Cyan Pile. Thirty more seconds."

"Under...stood..."

An unpleasant rasp nearby erased Takumu's voice, and Haruyuki stared, dumbfounded, at three glittering chunks of metal protruding slightly from the thick chest sheltering him.

At some point, the enemy fire around them stopped. In the midst of the sunny and strange music of the merry-go-round, Cyan Pile's enormous body was lifted in a movement not of his own volition.

Standing behind him was a blue-green duel avatar with basically the same physique. A remarkably massive right arm in the middle of its unrefined form caught Haruyuki's eye, reminding him of heavy machinery used for public works projects. At the end were three fiendish claws, which had pierced Cyan Pile's chest from behind.

One close-range type who'd been put on standby had probably gotten exasperated and come flying down. Its goggles, the shape of which reminded Haruyuki of the CRT monitors of the previous century, blinked, and the avatar emitted a thick voice.

"I'd heard you do reasonably well among the young blues.

Was that just bravado, Cyan Pile, nothing more than empty boasting?"

The heavy machinery avatar yanked the skewered Takumu up and sneered. "Heh-heh! Before you drop dead, listen good. The one who defeated you was me, Saxe—"

"Not interested…in the name of an idiot," Takumu rasped. Raising his right arm, he pressed the launcher to the center of his own chest.

"Lightning Cyan Spike!!"

With a weak but resolute cry, a bluish-white flash of light surged from of the end of the cylinder. At the same time, a bolt of lightning pierced Cyan Pile's chest, to the heavy avatar's right arm, and then, by extension, its square head. Saxe so-and-so's right arm and goggles went flying with a crack, and both avatars were tossed into the air before collapsing in a thunderous roar.

Because of the merry-go-round hallucination, they couldn't accurately target their enemies, even close-up. But when the enemy's arm had you, it was a different story: a body had to be at the other end of that arm.

"T-Taku!!" Haruyuki shouted.

Amazing, you really are amazing. Way stronger than me, way smarter. I'm proud to be your friend. But he didn't get the chance to put the feelings rushing through his chest into words.

"Unh…Aaaaaugh!!" With his remaining strength, Takumu leaned against the enemy avatar, which was pressing its left hand to its face and writhing on the ground as it screamed.

A hoarse voice came Cyan Pile's mask as he turned briefly toward Haruyuki. "The rest…is up to you, Haru." And then, firmly pinning the enemy down with both arms:

"Splash Stinger!!"

From the gap between the two bodies pressed together came the sound of rapid fire, like a machine gun, and successive flashes of light. The enemy's thrashing ceased abruptly, and innumerable fissures pitted the pair of avatars.

A moment later, two pillars of blue light in differing shades soared high upward from the bottom of the crater. Takumu and the enemy burst and scattered, fragments of polygons flying, and then they were nowhere to be seen.

Meanwhile, the merry-go-round hallucination attack ended, and the world took on its original aspect.

A moment's silence filled the crater in what was once South Ikebukuro Park.

The shots from the outer edge had stopped as well, with just the distant lightning and howling wind resounding heavily once more.

There were limits to the duel avatars' long-distance attacks—overheating in the case of light beams, number of bullets for live rounds. It wasn't as if they could keep shooting forever. Even making allowances for that, this silence was strange. They were likely caught up in it, too. In the dreadful theater of the simultaneous deaths of Cyan Pile and the other one.

This is our chance to escape, Haruyuki thought. This was the time Takumu literally laid down his life to create for them. But for some reason, his feet didn't move. Still raised up on one knee, his thin avatar trembled all over.

A feeling he couldn't explain swirled in the depths of his chest. A sense of helplessness due to his inability to act while his friend protected him. Rage at the Yellow King and this cowardly plan that toyed with other people's emotions. And more than either of those, directed at the pitch-black avatar hanging limp, as if its power had been severed, still clutched in his right arm—

"Kuroyukihime...Kuroyukihime." Haruyuki squeezed a voice like a groan from the depths of his throat. "Kuroyukihime. Why... why won't you stand up...?"

"It's pointless, Silver Crow," Niko muttered. Making her footsteps resound loudly, the Red King came to stand directly over the petite figure.

"Zero fill. Right now, the signal output by the girl's soul, which is supposed to be communicating with the avatar, is at zero, so the system's overwhelmed. Without a Burst Linker with the will to fight, the avatar can't move. The duel avatar's power source is the heat of the heart of the person inside it. If you don't have the strength to face your own wounds, you can't even stand up. That's what this Brain Burst game's about. And this girl understands that, so much that she hates it. Even if you get it, it's a problem you can't do anything about."

Once she had explained all this in hushed tones, Niko glanced back at Haruyuki. "Sorry. I know Cyan Pile sacrificed himself to buy us time, but...I can't run. I didn't train all that time just to go running all helter-skelter here. You're good. You take the girl and get out of here."

The girl's crimson avatar looked like it was burning up. It wasn't an illusion. Around the foot that had stepped forward, Haruyuki actually saw faint flames rising.

It was reckless. The enemy battalion was still essentially unharmed. There was no way she could win.

Even as he told himself he should do as reason dictated and run, he couldn't move. He felt like something would be decisively lost from him and from Kuroyukihime if he ran off and left Niko here, and, still crouching on the spot, Haruyuki whispered in return, "I won't run. I'm not going to run off and leave a friend behind!"

"Friend... You're really a hardcore idiot. Well, you do what you want," Niko muttered after a brief moment of speechlessness, as if dazed, and then took another step forward.

The Red King stretched her right arm out straight ahead, jabbed a fingertip at the Yellow King standing at the western edge of the crater, and shouted, "Yellow Radio! That special-attack gauge you so diligently charged up before making your awesome appearance is totally empty! Now it's my turn to pay you back. Don't forget, if I take you out, you get banished forever, right there on the spot!!"

As if overawed, the Yellow King's clown avatar retreated a half step.

Niko responded with another step forward and threw her arms open. "Come! Enhanced Armament!!"

An inferno raged suddenly, and the avatar engulfed by it floated up gently. From the surrounding sky, armament containers covered in flames sprang up one after another and began converging on the girl from all sides. The shoulder missile pods, the thick armor skirt, the thrusters on her back—and the terrifyingly huge main weapons in place of her arms.

Finally displaying the true form implied by her second name, Immobile Fortress, the Red King Scarlet Rain struck the center of the crater with a heavy, rumbling shock, and white gas plumed from her entire body.

The collective discomposure of the thirty avatars surrounding them was clear even to Haruyuki. Because the Yellow Legion had their headquarters on the east side of Tokyo, they didn't have many chances for contact with the Red Legion, which ruled Nerima and Nakano in the west. The majority had never even watched a battle with Niko in the gallery, much less fought her directly themselves. The enormity of Scarlet Rain's true form, so large that she could barely be called a duel avatar, struck them dumb. The same way it had struck Haruyuki the day before yesterday.

The sound of Niko's quiet voice, with strong effects applied, reached Haruyuki, who was holding his breath anxiously. "Hey, Silver Crow. Sorry, but you just take care of any close-range opponents sticking to my butt."

"G-got it. But…Kuroyukihime…"

"These jerks won't touch the girl. Not until they take me down, anyway. If I get done in, don't sweat it, fly out of here with Lotus."

Done in—In this situation, that meant the forced uninstallation of Niko's Brain Burst.

Before Haruyuki could say anything in response, the Yellow King looked down on them from on high and cried out even more venomously, "There is no need to fear! That thing is just a fixed fort; if you glue yourself to her, she's simply a lump of steel!"

He threw his right hand up. "Close-range team, you're up! Long-distance team, support! Now go!!"

His arm flashed with yellow reflections as he brought it down, and the roar of a war cry rang out as fifteen or so duel avatars surged forward as one from the outer edge of the crater.

As if acting in concert, the missile pods on Niko's shoulders deployed with a crisp metallic *clack*. Dozens of seeker heads poking out shone red and fired, leaving a trail of white smoke.

Fanning out into a semicircle, the missiles flew straight up before spreading out and raining down on the enemy duel avatars on the ground. Some pulled up in a dash, others tried to drop into defensive postures, and the force of the charge slackened.

Scarlet Rain immediately sighted two standing frozen with the main weapons of her arms. The ruby-colored heat beam these weapons released with shrill resonance swallowed the unfortunate Burst Linkers whole. The lump of energy briefly swelled into a sphere before quickly destabilizing into a fierce explosion.

The denotation erupted into a pillar of fire, and light the same color as each of the avatar's armors rose into the sky. Their HP gauges were blown away, disassembled, annihilated.

One shot! Haruyuki shuddered. At the same time, he thought, *If that's how this is...then maybe.*

However, the long-distance avatars had finished recharging and launched a bombardment from outside the crater. Given Scarlet Rain's enormous size and immobility, there was no way they could miss, and every shot was absorbed by the crimson fortress.

Explosions bloomed all over her body, but the Red King didn't even flinch. In response, she turned toward the crest of the crater and began unloading on them with her four machine guns.

Her only answer to the long-distance attacks at the moment was to endure. Haruyuki clenched his teeth tightly and laid Kuroyukihime's avatar down.

Niko had said that a Burst Linker couldn't move until she

healed the wounds in her heart. This was something Haruyuki was familiar with.

Three months earlier, back around the time when he had just learned about the existence of the Accelerated World, Haruyuki had fought his good friend Takumu—Cyan Pile—to protect Kuroyukihime. And he had been beaten horribly, swallowed up by his own insignificance and helplessness, and ended up not even being able to stand next to the unconscious Kuroyukihime's avatar.

If, at that time, he hadn't heard Kuroyukihime's voice—either a hallucination or she had actually communicated with him—Haruyuki probably wouldn't have been able to fight again. The hidden potential of Silver Crow—the ability to fly—would not have awakened, and he would have lost everything.

So now, Haruyuki did not feel despair or even anger at Kuroyukihime's inability to move.

He was sad. He didn't know why, but he couldn't help feeling sad.

Closing his eyes tightly, Haruyuki removed his hand from the ebon avatar and stood up. He started running in a straight line. In his sights was a close-range avatar trying to get onto Niko's back. It was olive green in color, and the tips of its ridiculously long and thick arms were U-shaped metal.

Seeing Haruyuki en route, his opponent gave a guttural howl. "Shoo, small fry!" It turned the U of its left arm toward Haruyuki and continued shouting.

"Magnetron Waaaaave!"

As the avatar uttered its technique, purple lightning gushed out and captured Haruyuki. However, rather than being damaged, Silver Crow's slim avatar was yanked up by an incredible force and snapped onto the U with a harsh clanking.

"Hee-hee! Metal colors get sucked in so nicely!" Olive Green shouted and started pummeling him with his right hand.

Guard against these blows with both arms, Haruyuki thought calmly. From the name, this special attack probably pulled in opponents with magnetism. In which case, there should be a time limit. And given that the technique completely immobilized an opponent, that was at most maybe ten seconds.

Haruyuki abruptly stretched his arms out to cover his opponent's scope-shaped eyes. Then he spread his wings and took off in one go.

"Hey! You! Let me go!"

Pulling airborne both the magnet affixed to his chest and his struggling opponent, Haruyuki quickly flew up to a height of a few dozen meters. The surge of purple emitted by the magnet disappeared abruptly, and his opponent knocked Haruyuki's arm away with his free right hand.

"You trying to blind me? That's not gonna damage—Aaaah?!"

His challenger shrieked as he realized his situation—plummeting from a ridiculous altitude without a handhold in sight—but Haruyuki paid no attention and dove at full speed. Overtaking the magnetic avatar in the sky, he pointed his legs into his best approximation of a cylinder and charged.

"Yaaaaah!!" With a yell, he pierced the back of a drill-equipped avatar that had tried to jump Niko. He slashed a left overhand into the seams of his target's neck armor, punching him into the surface of the ground with a thunderous slam.

"Ah! Gah! Aaaah!"

Just as he leapt away from his enemy, who was screeching at having had two vertebrae gouged out, the magnet avatar crashed out of the sky in front of him. This one was also unable to move, convulsing from the shock that had slammed its entire body.

But a sudden blow caught Haruyuki's right cheek as he was about to take off to finish the the two. Sent flying spectacularly, he ended up tumbling along the ground. A fierce pain ripped through his mouth as if his molars were shattering, and sparks flew before him.

This third enemy closed on Haruyuki, who forced himself to ignore the pain and sparks and jump to his feet. A pale blue karate uniform covered a body as square as if carved from stone. The mask, which closely resembled an Easter Island statue, was funny, but the threat hidden in the avatar's rocklike fists could be seen at a glance. It was a weaponless, extremely close-range type, and this sort of orthodox avatar was actually terrifying.

Likely experienced in a crisis, the karate master avatar came after him following a suitable pause. Without wasting its breath on pointless chatter, it suddenly delivered a right front kick.

Silver Crow's extremely slender body proved fortunate in that he managed to dodge the direct impact. But sparks scattered where the blow clipped his left flank, and his HP bar dropped. He launched a left Punch in counterattack, but this was blocked by a massive right arm, like hitting a tree trunk.

In the event that a metal color ends up in close combat with a type specialized in blows, against which metals are weak... Unexpectedly, a lecture from Kuroyukihime he had heard at some point resurfaced in Haruyuki's brain. *Do not panic and guard or try to hit back; instead, turn aside the enemy's attacks and use that power. With your reaction speed, it's possible. Understand? Don't forget that no matter how mighty the fist, it is slower than a bullet.*

"Hiyaaah!!" The karate avatar let fly a thick battle cry and thrust forward the face of his fist.

Haruyuki squashed his terror and stared at the mitt, which was encased in a blue aura and approaching fast. Falling backward, he would apply his left hand below his enemy's fist and his right foot to the enemy's stomach.

"Hah!" As he shouted, he flapped the wings on his back as hard as he could for an instant. Using the thrust generated as a catapult, the force of Haruyuki's right foot and his counterpunch sent the clumsy karate master soaring into the air.

"Niko! Above you!" Haruyuki cried, and instantly, the missiles on Scarlet Rain's shoulders were brought together and launched, every one of them seizing on the karate avatar in the sky. It crashed to earth, swallowed in multiple, reddish-black explosions and trailing a tail of smoke before turning into a light blue pillar of light and vanishing.

"Ooh, for as weak as you look, you do reasonably well, Silver Crow."

"Well, thanks!" he called back at Niko's insult, and bracing himself to face the next enemy without letting his guard down, Haruyuki stared at the jet-black avatar still lying a slight distance away.

She's—Kuroyukihime's definitely not some flawless superhero. She's a teenager like me, a girl who's easily hurt. Haruyuki had never once forgotten this, ever since the time he saw Kuroyukihime shed tears at his own thoughtlessness. However, that said, the admiration and adoration inside of Haruyuki was not diminished in the least.

It wasn't her strength.

It was the determination to be strong itself. Haruyuki was absolutely drawn to her spirit and the way it shone, trying to fight back against any and all adversity.

Which is why you'll stand up again. I don't know what your relationship with the former Red King was, but you'll get over that memory and stand up for me. Right?!

When he uttered this soundless cry beneath his silver mask, the enemy legion's attack, which had temporarily slackened, started up again, even fiercer than before. The remaining close-range types didn't even number ten, but they were charging from all directions. The long-range barrage to support them fell like heavy rain.

"Is that all you got?!" Niko roared, deploying with a *crack* both main weapons on her sides, the missile pods, and the machine guns.

They erupted in fire all at once. Before they did, though, a strange noise disturbed Haruyuki's hearing. A high-frequency grating sound, like static, shook the air. At the same time, he saw double, triple.

The missiles launched by Scarlet Rain abruptly went into a tailspin and struck the wrong places. The main weapon beams targeting the long-range types on the outside of the crater also turned away from their intended targets and hit a building in the distance, causing a faint explosive rumbling.

"Dammit! They're jamming me!" Niko cried in a low voice. "It's not Radio...It's one of his yellow subordinates! Find them!"

"R-right!" Haruyuki spread his wings, kicked hard on the ground, and flew up.

However...

Two wires snaking up from the ground wrapped themselves around his ankles. Immediately yanked back down, he slammed into the ground hard. The impact knocked the breath out of him, but Haruyuki moved to bring his hand down sharply like a sword to free himself of the wires.

"Shock Therapy!!"

"Ngh...!!"

Together with a voice calling out the name of someone's attack, bluish-white lightning suddenly surged through Haruyuki's body, assailing him with an intense shock. When he looked, he saw a mechanical avatar at a distance from him. Wires stretched from both arms, sparking energetically from a device it carried that looked like an old electrical transformer.

The stun effect seemed to be the main attack. Haruyuki took almost no damage, but, unable to make his body do what he wanted, he couldn't get free of the wires around his ankles.

"Unngh!"

The electricity-generating avatar showered the groaning Haruyuki with a high-pitched, scornful laugh. "Hee-hee-hee-hee! You just sleep there for a while, brat! Until we've peeled away every bit of the Red King!!"

Just like the avatar said, he could see several close-range types flying toward Niko's fortress avatar. They started attaching themselves to her guns' blind spots and peppering the joints of her

Enhanced Armament with punches and kicks. Orange sparks flew, bolts popped, and first one and then another thick armor plate was ripped off.

Desperately fighting to roll over against the current numbing his entire body, Haruyuki tried to turn toward the electricity-generating avatar and inch in its direction. But the current didn't seem to be weakening in the slightest, and he couldn't even turn his head.

What can I do? What am I going to do? What am I supposed to do at a time like this, Kuroyukihime? If I don't... If I don't hurry, Niko will—

As he raised a despairing voice in his head, Haruyuki heard a laugh rich with inflection ringing out from high on the distant outer edge of the crater.

"Ha-ha-ha! Ha-ha-ha-ha-ha!!"

The Yellow King, Yellow Radio. Long, thin body and double-pointed hat shaking, he expressed his joy with pantomimes. "How! How uncouth! How funny you look! The dignity of a King and all that... Not a shred of that here, is there?! You two were unfit to call yourselves Kings after all, that's what this is!! Because the Red is an upstart and an imposter!! And the Black, well, she is a cowardly traitor, isn't she?!"

Over his merciless contempt, Haruyuki heard a metallic creaking. And then the thin voice of a girl in pain.

"Ah... Ah!"

Quickly turning his gaze, Haruyuki saw a large, close-range avatar standing on Scarlet Rain's missile launcher, holding her left main weapon. The avatar was using its entire body to forcefully twist the enormous armament. Sparks flew like flames magnificently from the joint, almost like fresh blood. Finally, with a remarkably fierce wrenching sound, the main armament was torn off.

At the base, the left arm of Niko's real body dangled, snapped off at the elbow. Niko's scream poured out unchecked, and the roar of the elated enemy avatar raising the weapon high blended together with it.

"Yesssss! This is what the Red King is! Guys, peel back every bit of skin and drag that kid out!! We'll humiliate her plenty, right up until her gauge runs out!!"

Haruyuki clenched his teeth until they almost cracked and scratched desperately at the earth with the outstretched fingers of his right arm. Ahead of them, the Black Lotus avatar lay covered in dust, the light completely gone from her eyes.

"Kuroyukihime…Kuroyukihime." Haruyuki pushed a hoarse voice from a throat tingling at the stun effect.

Behind him, the sound of her remaining weapons fired continually, likely Niko's final push. Feeling the vibration of the empty explosions, Haruyuki called out once more.

"You…Is this what you want? Is this how your game ends?"

In the back of his mind, he faintly saw the image of the real-life Kuroyukihime and Niko sleeping against each other as he'd seen them the night before. Haruyuki couldn't even guess at what that scene symbolized, what these two girls really wanted. But the one thing he was sure of was that everything was about to end. That the faint bond accidentally created one night was about to be cruelly severed.

"Kuroyukihime…Black King!!" Haruyuki screamed, mustering every last bit of strength remaining to him.

The mental wounds Kuroyukihime was confronting now were no doubt so deep Haruyuki couldn't begin to understand them. She had almost certainly continued all this time to regret from the bottom of her heart the impulsive act of betrayal that had banished the first Red King—her companion, her friend—forever from the Accelerated World.

Or maybe she and Red Rider were something more than companions or friends. Maybe she had attacked someone like *that*.

But…

Even if that were so…

"What acceleration is to you!! What Brain Burst is!!" Fighting the charge to bring his clenched fist down violently on the ground, Haruyuki howled passionately. "Is this all it was, all your ambition to reach the untrodden ground of level ten and see the future of this world?! Was it such a cheap thing that it can be replaced by the memory of one guy?! You were trying to go beyond your human shell…and now you're just going to be paralyzed by past regrets and crawl around forever like a bug?! You don't have time for this! I thought you decided that you were going to cut down every obstacle, mow them all down, and keep charging forward until you were the last one standing! Black Lotus!!"

Clink.

He was probably hallucinating that he saw the obsidian tip of her splayed right arm twitch.

No, he wasn't—he could see a violet light blinking faintly in the depths of the goggles of the ink black form, like a very distant, fixed star. It pulsed—*throb, throb*—with a weak flicker that made him think of the glowing ember of a soul.

"Kuro…yu…" Haruyuki whispered.

Bzz!

A strong vibration detonated. It was the sound of two eyes glittering fiercely beneath those goggles.

A light of the same color filled the crease lines of the semi-transparent armor from head to toe, like carved onyx. As it did, the dust covering her body blew away, restoring a fresh reflective sheen. Finally, the swords of her arms and legs chimed loudly.

Haruyuki could only stare, lump in his throat, at the jet-black avatar rising, as if gently pulled by an invisible thread. Standing straight, Black Lotus flicked the tips of her legs, floating slightly above the ground, and started moving in a leisurely hover. Still gripped by the electric shocks and lying on his side, she drew close to Silver Crow and stopped abruptly.

"Haruyuki." Her voice was the usual, gentle and severe.

"Yes," Haruyuki replied, suppressing a sob, and she started murmuring with her familiar, bitter smile.

"Look. The way you spoke before, it was almost as if Rider and I had been in love, yes?"

"Y-you weren't?"

"We absolutely were not. I told you, you're the first. And... don't just keep rolling around. Thrust a hand into the ground."

"Huh?...O-okay."

Haruyuki did as he was told and brought together his sharp fingertips, thrusting them into the dry earth before him. The instant he did, he could feel the sparks binding his body seep quickly into the ground, and he cried out, "O-of course! Earth..."

"If you think about the technique affinity and characteristics, you should be able to handle them even on a first encounter. It seems I still have a lot to teach you."

He heard a pathetic sniffle from behind, and Haruyuki turned his face back to see the electricity-generating avatar gradually retreating, white smoke rising up from the transformer on its back.

"You can handle the rest, yes? I'm going to go look after the little girl who got caught in a trap." She had barely even finished the nonchalant remark when the sky boomed and her raven-like avatar disappeared.

A dash with absolutely no preparation, so swift it was terrifying. Kuroyukihime, plunging ahead several dozen meters like a beam of darkness, appeared the next instant beside the enemy's close-combat leader, striking a pose on top of Niko.

"Whoa!" A startled cry slipping out, the enemy avatar abandoned the red artillery he'd been holding, unfurled hands with abnormally tough fingers, and danced toward Kuroyukihime. Just from the fact that it had ripped Niko's main armament off through brute strength alone, it was likely not a pugilist type, but rather a grappling-technique duel avatar.

Despite this, Kuroyukihime inexplicably stuck her right arm

straight out, practically asking to be grabbed. The enemy's eyes blazed fiercely, and arms struck out like snakes to take hold of Black Lotus's arm in two places.

"Gotcha! One Way Thr—" Shouting the technique as it angled its body around, the avatar hoisted the captive arm against its right shoulder and took on a posture for a one-armed throw.

And with that motion, something spilled down, falling in pieces.

Ten thick, curved cylinders: Fingers. The fingers the enemy used to clench the swords that were Kuroyukihime's arms were severed against the blades by virtue of their own strength.

"Sorry, but grappling techniques basically have no effect on me," she said to the frozen enemy as she started bearing down, arching the arm still braced against the avatar's shoulder in a downward diagonal.

A thin ray of light escaped from the right shoulder to the left flank. From there, the enemy avatar's muscular torso slid smoothly away and dropped to the ground, leaving 70 percent of its body behind.

"Ah! Ga—Gaaaaaah!!" Although it apparently still had HP since it didn't disappear, given its situation, disappearing would no doubt have been preferable.

No longer interested in the enemy shrieking at the pain of having been bisected and bouncing around on the ground with its remaining arm, Kuroyukihime glared in turn at the seven or eight close-range combatants still surrounding her.

"It's nothing personal, but anyone who engages me must inevitably experience amputation." Her tone was calm, but its violent undertones made everyone on the battlefield hold their breath.

"So…don't go telling me now you don't want it!" she called out sonorously, and she leapt to attack the first unfortunate avatar like a bird of prey. The high-pitched sound of metal endlessly screeching and the desperate, angry voices of the surrounding Burst Linkers immediately filled the air.

Deciding that she would be fine if he left her to that for the time being, Haruyuki turned again toward the electricity-generating avatar that still had him ensnared in its wires.

The instant their eyes met, the enemy reared back. His face resembled an old gauge, and he held a single hand out. "Hey, hold on. The battery's recharging now—"

"As if I'm going to wait!!" Haruyuki yelled, grabbing the two wires tied to his ankles with both hands and pulling before kicking off the earth and ascending in one fluid motion.

"Aaah!"

He gained altitude, still dangling the struggling enemy, and started turning in circles while hovering.

"Wah! Aah! Aaah!"

After adding sufficient centrifugal force to his opponent so that its prolonged scream rose and fell with the doppler effect, Haruyuki released the wires. The bulky robotic avatar flew toward the south with incredible force, and a small crash echoed somewhere amidst a group of buildings there.

Somewhat dizzy himself, Haruyuki shook his head hard before looking down and gazing in wonder at the aspect of the battle unfolding. Perhaps it would have been more accurate at that point to call it a "massacre" rather than a "duel."

The blue close-range avatars mostly fought with their own fists and feet, or hand-to-hand weapons like swords and hammers. So if two blue avatars went up against each other, the basic strategy would be to exchange attacks and guard while aiming for any gaps that appeared in their opponent's defenses.

But although Kuroyukihime—Black Lotus—was at first glance an extremely close-range type, given that her limbs were actual swords, every single motion was an attack.

Obviously, this included purposeful action like cutting and thrusting, but if an opponent's fist caught her arm, that fist was severed, and the movement of her legs could shred her opponent if she simply chased them down. She brooked no contact at all; everything that touched her was dissected—she was, without doubt, the water lily of black death.

Her figure, fighting as if dancing, was absurdly beautiful and so cold it was almost sad.

In the span of a mere minute or two, the majority of the enemy's infantry had either been annihilated or rendered helpless by the intense pain of severed limbs that left them rolling around on the ground.

"Aauuugh!!" The enormous Burst Linker that was the last of the close-range types howled thickly, abruptly. Brandishing a long sword with a fat blade over its head, it moved to strike Kuroyuki-hime headlong.

Its speed and timing were impressive. Unable to avoid the blade, a steel-colored bolt of lightning thundering down— Kuroyukihime stopped it on the intersecting swords of her arms.

Skreeee!

A high-frequency, ear-piercing screech rang out. Dazzling sparks flew from the point of contact, and movement on both sides stopped. Followed by successive, high-pitched metallic creaks. The silver and black swords increased the depths at which they bit into each other with each second.

Haruyuki couldn't determine in that moment which carved into which. But the warrior avatar with the sword contorted its grinning, demonic mask into a sneer.

"Ha!" The warrior's low voice cried out at the same instant that Kuroyukihime's arms, directly beneath his sword, disengaged themselves and immediately sliced out to the sides.

Falling soundlessly were the warrior avatar's head and the top half of the enormous sword. Kuroyukihime ruthlessly pierced the head tumbling to the ground with the tip of her left leg, its eyes still wide-open, as if unable to comprehend what was happening. A pillar of light soared up, and the enemy avatar shattered like glasswork and disappeared.

Once again, a few seconds of silence.

Breaking that silence came a short voice issuing from the distant edge of the crater. "Why?"

In a tone so flat it made Haruyuki wonder if he had finally

lost the composure that had kept him going up to now, the Yellow King whined, as if moaning, "Why do you appear *now* and obstruct the circus carnival I've been preparing all these years? After curling up and hiding in some little hole somewhere for two years, *why*?"

The upturned eyes carved into the clown's laughing face filled with a white phosphorescence. He spread arms like dead twigs out to his sides, jumped up onto one leg, and shook his head from left to right. Suddenly from beneath the mask, there slipped the short, staccato beats of laughter. The Yellow King pointed accusingly at Kuroyukihime with his right hand, muttering in a voice swiftly regaining its derisive color.

"Does this mean you've already forgotten? The friend of ours you betrayed and beheaded? I wonder where he is and what he's doing now. I don't suppose he's dwelling on the fact that he can never return to the Accelerated World... or the certain someone responsible for that, hmm? I, for one, certainly cannot forget it. A straightforward duel is one thing, but that sort of surprise attack... Hmm?"

Listening to the sneering, throaty chuckle, Haruyuki screamed in his heart. *You can't listen to him. He's just trying to incapacitate you again.*

However, Haruyuki couldn't bring himself to actually utter the words. He could see that these two—the Black King and the Yellow King—shared a history that no one could come between, a history training together since the early days of the Accelerated World and of friendship until the incident two years before.

Haruyuki descended gently and stood directly behind the half-demolished, silent Scarlet Rain and Black Lotus standing next to her. He prayed fervently, somewhere deep inside, that they not lose.

Suddenly, Kuroyukihime's right arm came up without a sound. She turned its obsidian edge, unblemished by even a single scratch despite the fierce battle, straight at the Yellow King.

"You've got one thing wrong, Yellow Radio," the Black King declared, her voice crystalline and clear.

"Oh? And what's that? You can't possibly mean to say that that wasn't a cowardly ambush?"

"No. That you think your head carries the same weight for me as Red Rider's. Shall I tell you something else? You see, I..." Kuroyukihime brandished her right arm to the side with a clink and said, "I have hated you from the very moment we first met!"

The Yellow King threw his upper body back with a start.

Kuroyukihime glanced back quickly and yelled, "Rain, your remaining weapons have finished charging, yes?! Crow, protect her!! I'm going!!"

She set off a savage dash, carving a rut into the bottom of the crater.

"Hey! Rest a little longer!"

It was Niko who cursed at her. She made her remaining weapon—the right-hand one—and the half-destroyed missile pods click into place and pointed them at what was left of the enemy's long-range battalion, which was arrayed on the edge of the crater.

Neither had Haruyuki just been standing idly and listening to the exchange between Kuroyukihime and Yellow Radio. Taking advantage of the dozen seconds of cease-fire, he'd been looking for something: the enemy's midrange avatar that was the source of the signal for the jamming attack.

There! Haruyuki's heart cried when he spotted a yellow type on the northern face of the crater, lurking behind a red type as if hiding. The pods mounted on either of its shoulders were deployed, and a light effect of concentric circles was being generated from the parabolic antenna protruding from the center.

No sooner had he spied this figure, which practically screamed *radio attack in progress*, than Haruyuki was springboarding off the ground.

However, it was a full thirty meters from the center of the crater to its outer edge. No matter how speedy Silver Crow might have been, he wouldn't be able to cover that distance in an instant; there'd be just enough time for the big gun of the red bodyguard to get him in its sights.

Something chillingly cold ran up Haruyuki's spine. He was being targeted by a gun on an open plane with no cover. This was the exact scenario responsible for his winning slump these last few months.

He would just have to dodge it. If he didn't take down that jamming avatar, Niko's firepower would stay locked up. In which case, the gunfire of the red avatars still going strong in the enemy array would focus on Kuroyukihime, necessarily impeding her showdown with the Yellow King.

The tide of this battle likely hinged with whether or not Haruyuki could dodge this one bullet.

His hands and feet chilled to numbness at this overwhelming pressure. His vision narrowed, and only the darkness of the gun barrel grew larger. It was hopeless. There was no way he could dodge in this situation. In the stillness of his virtual training room, he could only barely avoid the projectile 30 percent of the time.

No. This situation is different from that white room.

Because this gun was attached to the avatar holding it. A sniper-type duel avatar, large-lensed eyes glittering on a brown, camouflage-patterned body. Instead of the gun, he should watch the guy. He should watch for a sign telegraphing the pull of the trigger.

Instantly, everything but the enemy avatar disappeared from Haruyuki's field of view. He forgot even the battlefield, his wide eyes capturing only the figure of his opponent readying its rifle.

The back of the enemy's neck stiffened abruptly, its right shoulder went up a few millimeters, and its right arm shook—

Here it comes!

—and its right finger squeezed the trigger, the muzzle flickering white.

By that time, his body was already twisting, barreling left.

The air whizzed past his ears, and the heat beam skimmed his chest and right shoulder before flowing off behind him. Ignoring the gouge of scorching heat, Haruyuki plunged ahead the final ten meters, slipped close past the side of the enemy sniper, and sprang at the midrange type behind it.

With hands flat, he chopped at the antennas stationed on the shoulders of the radio-wave avatar, who looked profoundly stunned. The moment the delicate device was smashed, Haruyuki crouched, only to fly straight up.

Niko!!

He wasn't certain whether or not this shout in his mind reached her, but the instant the jamming ceased, Scarlet Rain's remaining weapons fired all at once.

Assailants on her right flank were mowed down by the heat beam of her main cannon, and missiles rained down on her left, launching a curtain of flames as if tracing the outer edge of the crater. Naturally, the enemy army was not completely destroyed with this one volley, but the long-distance attacks that had been targeting Black Lotus and fired at random dropped en masse into silence.

The sound of explosions died down, but the quiet that was briefly born was pierced by a howl, a raging fire from Kuroyukihime.

"Radio!!"

The sword of her right arm drew a black arc. Split soundlessly in two, dancing in the air, was the right corner of Yellow Radio's enormous hat.

"Lotus!!" the Yellow King answered back angrily in a voice lacking even the slightest hint of the teasing lilt it had held up to that point. He offered a counterblow with a long, large, baton-shaped weapon he had produced from somewhere. With her left arm-sword, Kuroyukihime knocked aside the thrust launched at her, drawing out a yellow line. The sparks that flew lit up the pair brilliantly.

Haruyuki landed on the stabilizer extending prominently

from Niko's back, the Red King continuing to launch intermittent cover fire, and he stared, half-stunned, at the fierce fight beginning on the western end of the crater.

It went without saying that this was the first fight between Kings—level-nine Burst Linkers—he had seen.

It was likely that could have been said about anyone there—including the two participants themselves.

The current Kings of Pure Color, except for Niko, had reached level nine at basically same time two and some years earlier. They had then learned of the harsh sudden-death rule to advance to level ten and had held a roundtable meeting to avoid fighting to the death.

At that meeting, Black King Black Lotus had killed the first Red King, Red Rider, with a surprise critical hit. That was the first and last time a King had defeated a King. The Black King, hunted ever since as a traitor, had hidden herself for two years in the Umesato local net, and the other Kings had concluded a mutual nonaggression pact and no longer ventured out of their respective territories.

Which is why this was the first time since the founding of the Accelerated World that two level nines had crossed blades in so natural a duel.

Haruyuki. And Niko. And the dozen or so remaining Yellow Legion members who had at some point stopped their attacks, held their breath, and watched the tide of the fight.

They're so fast! Haruyuki let a sigh of admiration slip out in his heart.

If he didn't concentrate, all he could see were mysterious bolts of lightning popping off in succession in the area where the pair faced off. The Black King slashed out four, five times in a row; the Yellow King admirably stopped the blows with his baton, twirling in a frenzy; and then he kicked out a long leg, not missing the slight opening she left. Each time Kuroyukihime blocked one of these Kicks with her leg, shock waves spread out like ripples on the water and distorted the background.

Perhaps because of these successive and incredibly high-powered attacks, cracks started to radiate out from beneath the feet of both fighters, and pieces of rubble began flying. As the air filled with a colorless pressure, the light emitted by their armor seemed to increase in strength.

"…Nearly there," Niko muttered, and Haruyuki replied reflexively with a question.

"Wh-where?"

"Their special-attack gauges should be just about full. The real show starts now."

Before the last word had faded from his ears, a remarkable crash exploded, and both fighters moved away from each other, as if propelled by it.

Instead of springing back into the fight, Kuroyukihime leisurely lowered her hips and set her left arm sideways in front of her body, notching the sword of her right arm perpendicularly at the peak of the first. A pulsing violet light engulfed the long blade in tandem with a low-frequency vibration shaking the air.

Facing her, Yellow Radio crossed both arms in front of his body and inserted the yellow baton between his fingertips. The spheres attached to either end of the wand also emitted a cyclic light.

Haruyuki felt the rapidly increasing pressure touch his cheek, as if it were shooting out in bits and pieces. He had witnessed a glimpse of the power of a King's special attack during his duel with Niko. The enormous beam that shot out from one of her main weapons had casually blown the uppermost part of the Shinjuku Government Office onto the other side of the duel field.

What would happen if you got hit by an attack with that level of potential at such close range?

"…It's not power that decides this. It's speed." Niko's murmuring reached Haruyuki's ears again as he kept his eyes wide-open and forgot to breathe.

"Huh? Wh-what do you mean?"

"No matter how you slice it, Lotus's special attack is direct. Against that, Radio's prob'ly got a hallucination. Which means the whole thing hangs on whether or not Lotus can deliver her blow before Radio's attack is effective."

Haruyuki gulped hard.

The steeply inclined sun dropped a single ray of red light through a gap in black clouds, red light that glinted off the obsidian sword.

Black Lotus called in a clear voice, "Death by Pier—"

At the same time, Yellow Radio shouted, "Futile Fortune Wa—"

However...

The two voices, simultaneously calling out their two attacks, failed to utter their final syllables.

Thuk.

This dry sound, quite small and yet carrying an overwhelming presence, silenced the voices of the two Kings.

It was the sound of something piercing the vibrant yellow chest armor of Yellow Radio from behind.

Kuroyukihime halted her attack midway. Haruyuki, Niko, the other Burst Linkers, and the Yellow King himself all simply stared at the silver-gray metal protruding neatly from the armor and extending out about fifteen centimeters.

7

"Wh-who is—?" Haruyuki croaked in something that couldn't rightly be called a voice.

Approaching the hypervigilant Yellow King from behind unnoticed, and on top of that piercing his armor like it was made of paper, without even using a special attack. But even more importantly, who on earth would think to jump into a direct clash between Kings?

Almost as if it had heard Haruyuki speak, a shadow oozed out from behind the Yellow King. A dark gray silhouette essentially assimilating every nightfall everywhere. The instant the faintest afterglow caressed its surface, it shone as if the reflected light were leaking out.

The entire body of the mysterious intruder was wrapped in blackened silver armor with a mirrored surface. Although this aspect did bear some resemblance to Silver Crow, the figure was completely different. Heavyweight like a knight from the Middle Ages, voluminous shoulders, chest, elbows. Its right hand, wrapped in an enormous gauntlet, held a double-edged sword that looked nearly as long as its owner was tall, the tip of which, tapering off into essentially nothing, lanced the Yellow King from behind.

What drew the eye even more sharply than this sword was the knight's head.

It wore a hood-shaped helmet with long horns, stretching toward the back from both sides. However, in the place where there usually should have been some type of face, there was nothing. Given the angle of the sun, the interior of the hood should have been illuminated, and yet it was simply painted a lone black, looking very like the darkness itself had taken on physical form and was lurking there. If Haruyuki really, really strained his eyes, he could see some kind of pitch-black something wriggling on the surface like a living creature.

A blackened silver knight with a mask of darkness.

Immediately before its name slid from Niko's mouth at his feet, Haruyuki made the same connection. That was probably...It had to be—

"The Armor of Catastrophe. Chrome Disaster." After these hoarse words, Niko continued in a whisper, "How? It's too soon. We should have had an entire day to spare."

Haruyuki soon guessed the reason for her shock. They had dived into the Unlimited Neutral Field two minutes before the train carrying Chrome Disaster's real self, the Red Legion's level-six Burst Linker Cherry Rook, would arrive in Ikebukuro. Since time here flowed one thousand times faster than in the real world, those two minutes were equivalent to thirty-three hours.

There was only one answer. Cherry Rook, the resident of that armor, had accelerated while still on the train and appeared in this world.

This was understandable in a Normal Duel, which lasted at most 1.8 seconds in the real. But they were in a higher-order world that could not be escaped once a player dived in, unless they made it to a withdrawal point. Leaving your real-life body behind pressed up against other people in the train, on public transport no less, was an act that surpassed daring and went right into recklessness.

"Cherry...are you so crazed now you can't even hold on for two minutes?" Niko murmured in a stifled voice.

However, Haruyuki couldn't read that kind of insanity in

the Fifth Chrome Disaster, standing on the western edge of the crater.

His physique was not particularly powerful. Just barely 170 centimeters and much smaller than the Fourth Chrome Disaster they had seen in the replay file Kuroyukihime had showed them the previous day. Its form was an orthodox human shape. It stood quietly, almost vacantly, still gripping the sword piercing the Yellow King but doing nothing more.

Why didn't the Yellow King break free? Why did he just stare silently at Chrome Disaster, his face turned as far to the rear as it could go?

A second later, Haruyuki got his answer.

"Yuroooooo!" A strange scream abruptly gushed forth. It was neither a human voice nor a beast's. Not an alarm. It was an alien howl the likes of which he had never heard before.

Its source was the darkness lurking on the knight's face. A darkness with actual substance erupted together with this cry from beneath the tossed-back hood of the helmet, immediately solidifying into a particular shape: a row of sharp triangles biting into each other, above and below the hood. Fangs. Inky black fangs protruded from the edge of the hood, almost as if the entirety of the cowl made up a mouth.

With a wet sound, the "mouth" opened.

In the rich darkness of the interior, two small, perfectly round eyes shone a faint red.

The instant he saw this, Yellow Radio finally snapped into motion. More throwing than reaching both hands around his back, he grabbed the sword piercing him and tried to pull it out.

He hadn't moved sooner because he'd been frozen. Constricted with terror.

Even Kuroyukihime, a short distance away, remained silent, still striking her pose. She didn't have the look of fear to her, but Haruyuki could sense a faint hesitation. Although it was a chance for her to attack, this wasn't the kind of situation that facilitated quick decisions about which one of the avatars to target.

Chrome Disaster, the Armor of Catastrophe, brought the Yellow King, struggling to break free of the sword, to his enormous mouth, almost like a piece of food stabbed with a fork. As the jaw, opening even farther, drew nearer the round, puffy shoulder of the clown avatar, a clear, viscous liquid hung from its fangs.

"Deceit Firecracker!!" Yellow Radio cried out in a high voice, on the verge of having his shoulder eaten.

In a puff of vile yellow smoke, the skewered avatar exploded and disappeared.

Self-destruction?! Haruyuki opened his eyes wide, but he soon saw the same yellow smoke rise up about five meters away with the clown flying out from inside the cloud. It was probably a special attack of the glamour/escape type.

Fine sparks scattering from the razor-edged hole in his chest armor, the Yellow King back dashed another several meters. After ordering his subordinate avatars to draw near, he finally spoke.

"Pathetic dog, have you forgotten your master and now you're here to get in the way of the program? Well, fine. If you're as hungry as all that, go ahead and eat Blackie there in front of you! Although it's not a color that stimulates the appetite, is it?! Ha-ha-ha-ha-ha!" He laughed, but in his voice was a tension he didn't try to hide.

Opening and closing his black maw with a clang, Chrome Disaster looked in turn at the Black King and the Yellow King, each standing an equal distance away. There was nothing remotely like a player struggling to decide who to fight in this gesture.

This was the look of a creature assessing which prey to attack.

That face which was not a face casually turned toward the bottom of the crater. Its gaze rested momentarily on the Red King, silent and covered in wounds, but it showed no sign of emotion even at the sight of its own Legion Master. It turned its face up at Haruyuki, standing atop the stabilizer on her back.

Suddenly.

He felt like the strange voice was delivered directly to the core of his brain. Inflectionless, like an animal—or a machine.

Get eaten.

Be eaten, be meat.

What was more terrifying than anything else was that the tone of the voice itself was most certainly that of a boy the same age as he was, before his voice changed. Haruyuki felt a species of dread run up his spine, one he had never before felt in the Accelerated World.

Setting aside the alien nature of the acceleration technology, Brain Burst was at most a fighting game. The fighting that had taken place up to that point in the South Ikebukuro crater had been extremely gruesome, but still, it didn't fall outside of the sphere of gaming, albeit just barely.

It was true that if the Yellow King's ambush had succeeded and he had managed to hunt Niko or Kuroyukihime, the two of them would have had Brain Burst forcefully uninstalled, and they would never again have experienced the pleasure of visiting the Accelerated World. But that would have been the end of the game, and their everyday lives in the real world would have continued on after that.

If the voice just now indeed belonged to the Burst Linker called Chrome Disaster, then inside that blackened silver armor, the boy by the name of Cherry Rook, the player supposedly enjoying this game, no longer existed.

Kuroyukihime said that Enhanced Armament encroached on the mind of its user. Haruyuki half believed and half doubted that, but the fact that the humanity of the person wrapped in the armor had already been largely lost was clearly communicated by that short utterance. And that phenomenon was likely not limited to the Accelerated World. Whoever was inside that armor couldn't possibly be living peacefully in the real world.

"Niko...he's already—"

"Don't say it." The Red King astutely guessed the meaning conveyed by Haruyuki's quavering tone. "We...we might still be in

time. If we can destroy the armor here and now, then maybe—"
She didn't finish her whisper.

"Ruuooo...Oooooooh!!" Chrome Disaster howled ferociously
again, as if to destroy the hope Niko expressed. Changing direction abruptly, he faced the Yellow King.

He brought the large sword in his right hand up to his shoulder
and stretched out his left in front of him, five fingers in the shape
of enormous claws.

And then something surprising happened. Despite the fact that
the Armor voiced no attack name, one of the red avatars gathered
very close to the Yellow King was sucked into Chrome Disaster's
left hand at an alarming speed. The Armor fingers bit into the
torso of the unfortunate duel avatar with a metallic *clang*.

"Eeaah!"

Even as a high-pitched scream escaped its throat, the red type
tried to turn the rifle in its right hand toward the Armor's head.
Haruyuki realized abruptly that it was the long-distance type
who had been protecting the jamming avatar.

The muzzle of the rifle glittered, and a bluish-white beam was
very nearly discharged at point-blank range. But just as this was
about to happen, the right arm gripping the gun was ripped off
at the base. The beam grazed Chrome Disaster's helmet and
streamed off in vain to the rear. Haruyuki hadn't even been able
to see the slash that took off the arm.

And then, "Rooooo!!" In tandem with this cry, Chrome Disaster opened wide the fangs lining his hood. With a chomp, the red
avatar's right shoulder was swallowed up, lost to the darkness of
the maw.

"Aauuuuughn!!" The wail of distress that burst forth was so
brutal it made Haruyuki want to cover his ears. The pain of damage in the Unlimited Neutral Field was twice that of the lower
field. Most likely, this red type was now experiencing the same
level of pain his body would in the real world: that of being
devoured by a wild animal.

The dozens of enormous teeth easily pierced the avatar's armor.

A semicircle was ripped off from shoulder to chest, and the severed left arm dropped to the ground.

"Aaaaaaaaaah!!" The head of the avatar flailed at the intense anguish of having its stomach gouged out and losing both arms.

Finished chewing and opening wide again, Chrome Disaster's "mouth" then swallowed the flailing head whole.

Was the scattered spray accompanying the wet squishing a spark effect, or fragments of armor—or the avatar's flesh?

The screaming abruptly ceased. A few seconds later, the remains of the avatar, having lost its entire head and been drained of all strength, finally melted into a pillar of light and disintegrated.

My vision is crazy wobbly, Haruyuki thought. It took him a brief while to realize the reason for that was his knees were shaking so hard that they were knocking together.

That was not a duel.

It wasn't violence, either, nor slaughter.

It was predation. Simply an instinctive behavior, to take in the flesh and blood of the captured avatar along with their burst points.

At the same time as the up-and-down movement of the black fangs stopped, Haruyuki saw a deep red light running along the seams of the blackened silver armor. A phenomenon akin to stolen points, but also some kind of energy as well. Most likely, it was Drain, the health gauge absorption ability Kuroyukihime had mentioned the day before.

"Rooooo!" Chrome Disaster raised his head and howled from deep in his throat.

"You mad dog...It appears I have no choice. It is regrettable, but the program is canceled. Everyone, get to the leave point in Ikebukuro Station and retreat!!" the Yellow King shouted. As the order was given, the dozen or so remaining Yellow Legion members faded to semitransparency, apparently using some kind of special move.

The avatars, now hazy shadows, evacuated the crater with

remarkable haste and retreated to the northwest. Although it was already clear that his plan had been ruined, the voice of the receding Yellow King drifted back to the field in a final sneer.

"Heh-heh-heh! Red and Black, I'll invite you back to our wonderful, delightful carnival one day! That is, if you still have the will to fight after being eaten by this dog! Heh-heh-heh... Ha-ha-ha-ha-ha!"

Had they assessed the situation calmly, they could've adopted a strategy of interfering with this retreat: get Chrome Disaster to attack them and then take the head of the Yellow King. But Haruyuki couldn't move a single finger, much less say anything. It was all he could do to simply stand atop Scarlet Rain's armor plate, cowering like a small animal under the glare of a predator.

Fight that? Fight that, render it helpless, and hit it with the Judgment Blow at point-blank range? And I'm supposed to help with that?

No way.

I can't do it. I mean, it's taking everything I have to just stay here and not run away screaming.

As his knees and teeth chattered, Haruyuki watched as Chrome Disaster hunched over motionlessly. It was the pose of a carnivore unable to resist chasing down and slaughtering its prey; in this case, the members of the Yellow Legion running away, scattering in all directions.

Haruyuki prayed they could just let him go with the Yellow Legion. However.

Behind Chrome Disaster, as he began a fierce dash—

"Death by Piercing!!" Kuroyukihime's voice rang out boldly.

The sword of her right arm nocked in her left thrust straight ahead, accompanied by an enormous noise like a jet engine. The violet glittering encasing the blade expanded and extended in a straight line nearly five meters long, coloring the world around her dazzlingly.

The incredible attack power released compressed the virtual air, and the view of the other side was distorted like a heat shimmer. The high-pitched sound of screeching destruction roared—but what was immediately cut off was just the horn extending from the right side of Chrome Disaster's helmet.

Despite being targeted from behind in the best possible opening Kuroyuki would get—as it was the verge of taking pursuit—the blackish silver armor slid to the left, as if turning to mist, and evaded the attack.

The horn, whirling high up into the sky, dropped down, and pierced the surface of the blue-black ground with a *thud*.

"So. You dodged that," Kuroyukihime uttered, almost admiringly, bringing the right arm she had thrust forward back to her body.

The tip of the large sword in his right hand clanged. It carved out the arc of a half-circle in the ground as Chrome Disaster turned around and returned what was clearly a roar of anger from between his enormous fangs. "Yurooooo!"

Raising his sword and setting it on his right shoulder, the diabolic knight glared directly at the jet-black beauty. From the depths of the jaw, slightly open beneath the hood, the deep red light of his eyes flickered repeatedly.

"K-Kuroyu…" A hoarse voice stole out from Haruyuki's parched throat.

Are you going to fight it? I mean, even if the Red King did ask you—With that? Face-to-face…

It was true that Chrome Disaster was still at level seven. Even if she was defeated, she wouldn't end up losing Brain Burst, unlike when a King was her opponent.

But she would be eaten.

In this Field, where a sensation of pain could be greater than that in the real world, her avatar would be devoured still living. Such agony as that was beyond comparison to that of taking a slug from the gun in Haruyuki's training room.

And it wasn't just a matter of the sense of actual pain. The screams of the long-range avatar that had been caught and slaughtered by that thing a few minutes earlier were marked by despair. Despair at its whole self helplessly assimilated into a predator's overwhelming power.

No way. I don't want that thing to eat me. If that happens, I'll just run again—

The strength abruptly drained from his legs, and Haruyuki fell to his knees on top of Scarlet Rain's armor. He hurriedly tried to stand again, but his body didn't move. It was frozen, stiff down to his fingers, refusing to listen to his commands.

What's going on? What's wrong with me? I was talking so big and saying all that stuff when Kuroyukihime was down, and now... I'm so pathetic, I can't even move.

The more panicked he got, the more petrified his body became. It was almost as if his nervous system had been detached from the limbs of his avatar.

Haruyuki could only keep taking shallow breaths below the mirrored surface of his helmet when he heard her.

"A Burst Linker without the desire to fight cannot move his duel avatar." Kuroyukihime's clear voice reached him from where she and the black-silver armor still faced off on the edge of the crater. "It's exactly as the little girl there said before. I don't want to acknowledge it, but I regret that betrayal of two years ago. I feel that it was an unforgivable crime. And because of that, I was deeply afraid in the bottom of my heart of my own desire for battle—the very belligerence that seeks victory."

With her sword arms still at the ready, her guard still up, Black Lotus's blue-purple eyes glanced at Haruyuki.

"However, Haruyuki. You are the opposite. You fear defeat. You are under the impression that your own worth drops with each loss. This is the cause of your poor form recently in the Territory Battles."

Her words gouged, mercilessly, deep into his heart.

Still on his knees, Haruyuki forced his eyes open wide and gritted his teeth.

It's not an impression! It's the truth! he shouted in his mind. *If*

I lose, I don't get anything. The value of my—of Silver Crow's—existence is in continuing to win with his unique flight ability. Just gain levels, increase the territory of Nega Nebulus, and meet your expectations. I mean, if I don't win, if I don't get stronger and stronger, then you'll—one day, you'll give up on me...

"I'll return the words you said to me earlier, Haruyuki!" With a sharp gesture of her right hand-sword, Kuroyukihime uttered a shout that bordered on ferociousness. "Do you really believe... that the bond connecting the two of us is at most on that level?!"

Then she immediately started to cleave at Chrome Disaster. Almost as if she was trying to tell him something.

Disaster's broadsword welcomed Kuroyukihime's left sword-arm as it struck down from directly above, absorbing its tremendous impact. Shining, spherical energy welled up and burst on the surface of the black-and-silver armor, turned into countless points of light, and then scattered.

Both fighters, violently knocked back, held their ground, digging into the surface of the earth, and attacked again at exactly the same time. Disaster gripped his broadsword in both hands and swung it horizontally. Kuroyukihime met this with a right roundhouse kick.

The bold moves, crashing into one another and tracing out deep red and bluish-purple arcs, really did cause an explosion this time, drilling out a small crater on the spot. Both were sent flying in opposite directions, and Chrome Disaster's left hand, open all the way, was turned precisely toward Kuroyukihime, raising as she tumbled along.

That attack!

But, unable to move or speak, Haruyuki only held his breath.

The special attack that dragged the enemy over through a mysterious attractive force and held them. If he hit her with that, she'd be pulled into a close-contact situation, and without being able to fully swing her swords, she would just, in a manner of speaking, be chewed up.

Tnk!

A silver light seemed to flash between the two.

At the same time, Kuroyukihime placed a large lump she had gathered up at her tiptoes when he wasn't looking—a mass of rock made out of the fragments of the ground from the earlier explosion—and kicked it up, into the center of her right leg-sword.

The boulder was propelled into Chrome Disaster's palm. As he tried to shake free fingers that had bitten deeply into the hard surface, Kuroyukihime charged at full speed.

The piercing, metallic screech of impact burst forth, and the upward-thrust sword of her left leg at last found a home, digging into the armor of Chrome Disaster's chest.

Incredible, Haruyuki murmured in his head, forgetting momentarily the despondency strangling him. *How can she fight like that when her opponent is that terrifying? She might be a higher level, but the difference in power's more than made up for by the Enhanced Armament; they're basically even in terms of the force a single blow packs. I mean, if she makes a single mistake, she'll be eaten up by those huge fangs for sure and drown in intense pain and despair. Why can she—It's almost—*

Like she's having fun.

Because she's confident she'll win? Can she move so freely like that because she's sure she's stronger than her enemy?

No, that can't be it. Despite the fact that Yellow Radio, level nine like her, still had ten or so subordinates left, he fled without even hesitating. And there's absolutely no way you could say that decision came from cowardice. Chrome Disaster's not a regular Burst Linker anymore. He's a bigger threat than that enormous Enemy we saw on our way to Ikebukuro.

As if to support Haruyuki's thinking, the crazed knight unleashed a terrifying skill. Reddish-black light coalesced around the wound in the Armor that Kuroyukihime's sword had opened and proceeded to repair it to a smooth polish right before his eyes.

"Yurooo…" The Armor, a low voice like laughter spilling out, counterattacked with a sudden ferocity. The sword in his right hand came down at a speed that made it impossible to see, cutting the sky and the ground in a straight line. Kuroyukihime, on that trajectory, dodged uncharacteristically, but the tip of her armor skirt broke off at the left hip and fell with a faint *clink*.

But Chrome Disaster's attack didn't stop there. The enormous sword, the blade of which was probably a meter and a half long, was brandished again and again at a speed that made it seem weightless. Black Lotus dodged as if dancing or deflected the blows, but in short order, chinks were carved here and there across her beautiful armor.

She was gradually being pushed from the west side of the crater to the north in an onslaught that seemed like it could go on forever. Yet there was no sign that Kuroyukihime's fighting spirit was weakening in the slightest.

The swords of her limbs swelled with violet light, and whenever she found a small gap in Disaster's movements, she threw in a sharp counterattack. The wounds carved into her opponent's armor were quickly restored by that malevolent red light, but she thrust her sword out, cut, and plunged the blade in again and again with an accuracy that was startlingly effortless.

It couldn't have been that she wasn't feeling the terror. They were essentially equals in attack power, speed, and precision, so the fact was that, at some point, an opponent with the ability to automatically heal his own damage would overcome her resistance. If she got hit with even one heavy attack and her ability to evade dropped, in that instant she would be snatched up by her opponent, and some part of her body would be bitten off. Her pride as a King would be taken, and she would crawl on the ground as just a hunk of food for the beast.

And yet—Why…

"Why…why don't you run?!" A croaking screech ripped itself from Haruyuki's throat.

After all, running away wouldn't lower her value as the Black King. The Yellow King had run away, and he was sure she had said that the Seven Kings of Pure Color had worked together to finally put an end to the former Chrome Disaster. It was only natural to pull out here. And more than that—

He didn't want to see it. He absolutely did not want to watch her get destroyed and eaten, screaming.

"Please run, Kuroyukihime!" Haruyuki shouted again.

However, the massive iron sword rained down from on high with such speed and timing that it allowed no evasion.

Kuroyukihime caught the blow with crossed sword arms, but, unable to repel it the way she had up to that point, she dropped a single knee. The fierce impact roared like thunder, and fissures radiated outward in the ground around her.

"Yurooooooo!!"

Chrome Disaster howled loudly, perhaps convinced of his victory. He used all his weight to lean forward on the weapon gripped in both hands. With each hard metallic creak, fine sparks flew out from the contact point of the three swords.

It was the same scene as her battle with the Yellow Legion's warrior avatar, but this time, the one on the defensive was clearly Black Lotus. The light of the bluish-purple aura enveloping her sword arms gradually faded and began to flicker irregularly.

Soon, both swords would be cleaved through, and she would take serious damage. Disaster would pounce on her the moment she fell and maul her at will until her HP gauge ran out.

"Why…didn't she run?" Haruyuki murmured feebly.

It likely wasn't to protect the immobilized Haruyuki. Because it had been Kuroyukihime herself who initiated the offensive, striking at Chrome Disaster when he was about to go after the Yellow Legion. In other words, Kuroyukihime had chosen to fight that armor, and with absolutely no chance of victory to boot.

Haruyuki knew that this had been their original objective when diving into the Unlimited Neutral Field, but the situation was already very different from what they'd assumed. Takumu was dead and wouldn't be able to come back for another half an hour at least, and the essential Scarlet Rain was seriously damaged and incapacitated.

So, why? What exactly was she—

"This…this is my place, Haruyuki." Unexpectedly, her words rang out.

Black Lotus looked up with violet eyes, blazing in the blades pressed within an inch of them, but said in a quiet but profoundly leaden voice, "I have exposed you to something unsightly here. As your teacher…and as your 'guardian,' I wouldn't be able to look you in the eye in the real world if I left things like that."

Chrome Disaster's blade was getting closer to her with each passing moment. Haruyuki swallowed his breath and squeezed a trembling plea from his throat.

"P-place? But…if you lose, it won't…mean anything…"

"You're misunderstanding. Feed your clever retreats to a dog! There's no value in things like that! Once you dive into the battlefield…there is only fighting with all your heart, toe-to-toe with whosoever your opponent might be!!" Kuroyukihime's words, uttered so brazenly on the doorstep of defeat, hit Haruyuki like a hammer.

In his mind, the sense of acceleration that had visited him countless times in battle up to that point returned in a dazzling flash.

That time, just a few minutes earlier, when he'd dodged the protective laser attack in order to take down the jamming avatar. When he'd slipped through the Red King's fierce antiaircraft barrage. And three months earlier, around the time when he'd just become a Burst Linker and caught Ash Roller's motorcycle; or when he saw through Cyan Pile's special attack…

Inside, I wasn't lusting for victory or frightened of defeat. I was just lost in the battle. Without being aware of anyone's eyes on me. Right. It wasn't defeat itself I was afraid of. It was being laughed at by the gallery when I lost. Being compared with Takumu. And I was scared senseless of disappointing her. Not only in the real

*world, but even in the Accelerated World, all I've worried about is
how people will see me—What...*

"I am such an idiot." Murmuring, Haruyuki put all his strength
into his open right hand, frozen helplessly.

They creaked and groaned in protest, but he managed to clench
his fingers tightly.

He raised this fist straight into the air and hit his own cheek as
hard as he could. Accompanying the dull sound of the impact, a
burning pain ran through his molars. This sensation of scorching heat raced along his entire virtual nervous system, diffusing
as a signal to the limbs of his avatar.

He raised his head abruptly. On the northern edge of the crater,
Black Lotus was offering her final resistance to the lethal blade.
The dull-colored edge was grinding the crossed arms and pushing the backs into her forehead. Scattering sparks illuminated
armor pitted with damage.

"Kuroyukihime!" Haruyuki cried. He spread his wings, to
which the power had just returned, and threw himself into flight.
Gliding at full speed just barely over the bottom of the crevasse,
he hit Chrome Disaster's blind spot and flew up from the crater's
edge.

"Unh...Ooooh!" Haruyuki howled. The punch he'd thrown
at the black-silver armor was just barely blocked by an upraised
right gauntlet.

But the instant Disaster took one hand off his sword, Kuroyukihime thrust both arms up with a battle cry.

The sword rebounded with a *thud*, and Chrome Disaster was
pushed back several meters. But he maintained his fighting posture, immediately readying his sword low again, the fangs below
the hood chattering fiercely.

"Rooo! Roooooo!!" The growl was colored with anger.

His whole body shaking with fear, Haruyuki confronted the
beast head-on, keeping Black Lotus behind him. No doubt using
every bit of strength she had left, Kuroyukihime had poked one

arm into the ground like a cane, but soon she used it as a crutch to stand and took her place to Haruyuki's left.

"Well, Haruyuki. Now, then, shall we lose with grace?"

Unconsciously, he smiled bitterly and nodded. "Yes, Kuroyuki-hime." He crouched, widened his stance, and took a half-baked karate-style pose.

Next to him, Kuroyukihime yanked her swords up in a motion seemingly appropriate to the situation.

A second later, several things happened in succession.

Chrome Disaster raised his sword with a violent roar of rage.

Something glimmered on Haruyuki's left as he was focused on trying to anticipate the coming slashing attack.

Kuroyukihime's right arm flashed with exceptional speed, striking Haruyuki hard in the chest with the edge of the blade.

As he was sent helplessly flying in shock, and tumbled along the ground, a wall of crimson light rose up before his eyes.

Only after the terrifyingly large explosion—a detonation that sent him flying a farther ten or so meters—did Haruyuki grasp that this was a beam attack launched to his right from the center of the crater. He instinctively raised both arms to protect himself from the heat and impact wave that surged toward him, but even so, the HP gauge in the upper left of his field of vision was ground away. Upon his attempt to move, an unpleasant metallic scraping came from all over his body.

He was overwhelmed by a wave of anguish so acute it was as if every nerve he had was scorched from the intense heat of the flames, and it took his breath away as he lay there, legs splayed as he had fallen. Unable to even scream, his body convulsing, a raging storm of question marks swirled in his head even as he waited for the pain to recede.

How on earth—The Yellow Legion long-range types should have all retreated. Did they come back and jump into the fight? Even if they did, though, what was that power about? That was no gun.

That was artillery so overwhelming it could have been from the main armament of a tank—no, a battleship!

Propping himself up on his right arm now that the feeling had finally returned to it, Haruyuki wobbled as he raised his torso—

—and saw something falling with a stiff crunch. Deeply cracked, mutilated black armor. It was cruelly scorched, its transparent gloss gone. Of the four swords, the left arm and leg had been split in half, and cracks raced along mirrored goggles in a spiderweb pattern.

"Ku—" Haruyuki groaned hoarsely and dashed forward, forgetting his pain. "Kuroyukihime!!"

When he lifted her up in a daze, black splinters scattered from every part of her body. The completely limp avatar was so light it shocked him, and the bluish-purple sparks crawling around the damaged areas looked almost like blood spilling.

But another heavy metallic sound came from in front of him. Abstractedly lifting his head, he saw the figure of Chrome Disaster kneeling on one knee a short distance off. The destruction there, too, was severe: the black-silver armor was covered in soot and deeply dented in several places. The interior of the hood-shaped helmet had sunk once again into an indefinite darkness, and the broadsword, having perhaps flown off somewhere, was nowhere to be seen.

The damage had even changed the terrain.

New, smaller craters had been dug out of the northern edge of the South Ikebukuro crater, which had served as their battlefield up to that point, and thick smoke rose up from fires twinkling and burning in various places. Apparently, some percentage of the power of the bombardment had escaped to the north, and the buildings had been cut down at the roots, as if a new avenue had been created that cut across Green Street.

Nervously, Haruyuki finally turned his head to the south. He was already half expecting the scene that met his eyes, but he didn't want to believe it. Even after logically determining that it couldn't be anything else, his heart strongly rejected this conclusion, and the conflict materialized as tears distorting his vision.

"Why...why, why...Niko?"

The main weapon, the right arm of the fortress avatar, the Red King Scarlet Rain, who he had thought too severely damaged to move, had been raised and was pointed straight at the center of the new crater. The residual heat moving heavenward from the large-diameter gun was a haze distorting the surroundings.

He could no longer doubt that the attack launched from that gun—most likely, a top-level special attack—had swallowed Kuroyukihime and Chrome Disaster whole, causing enormous damage.

Haruyuki gritted his teeth and stared at Niko's eyes, peeking out from a gap in her armor plating. But those red lenses didn't even notice Haruyuki, or Black Lotus in his arms.

"Why?!"

Even at Haruyuki's scream, the Red King remained silent. Instead, the thrusters on her back and bottom lit up and began to slowly ease the enormous body of the Immobile Fortress forward.

Once she started moving, she was surprisingly fast, and she soon covered the radius of the crater.

"Rooo..." The low whimper came from Chrome Disaster, curled up like a wounded animal. Sensing the approach of the Red King, he got up on all fours and retreated to the north. The red automatic recovery light could be seen covering gashes all over the armor. But it seemed that his wounds now were too deep and could not be so simply healed.

The crimson fortress in pursuit of the wounded and escaping knight appeared over the lip of the crater. Moved to tears at her majestic appearance, Haruyuki could only stare.

"Why..." The trembling query escaped his throat once more, and the forward momentum of the fortress stopped abruptly. The avatar towering in front of him looked up, and with a deep breath Haruyuki cried, "Niko! I mean, Scarlet Rain!! You haven't forgotten, right? If she's defeated by you, Kuroyukihime...Black Lotus will lose all her points!!"

Kuroyukihime was still unconscious in his arms. And just looking at the extent of damage, it was clear she didn't have much left in her HP gauge.

At Haruyuki's reproach, the Red King replied curtly and hollowly. "So what?"

Haruyuki was rendered speechless, and the childish, cold voice continued to pummel him. "For a Burst Linker, all Burst Linkers other than yourself are enemies. You get defeated by an enemy, your points decrease. When they hit zero, you're forced to leave forever. And that's that."

"B-but...we...you and us..."

"Are friends?" With a heavy *thud*, Scarlet Rain's main weapon struck the scorched earth. A voice, sharp like a blade, cut through air tinged with a final afterglow. "Your softness makes me puke! Listen, I'll teach you one last thing. In the Accelerated World, you trust nothing and no one!! Partners, friends, armies...and even the guardian-child bond, they're all nothing more than illusions!!"

The incandescent blaze of a cry ripped through the air, and in unison, all of the Red King's weapon containers, which had taken serious damage, broke off. From the center of the Enhanced Armament melting into the air, a small avatar appeared, descending to the ground.

The crimson armor of the little avatar maintained its ruby-like shine, but her left arm from the elbow down had been savagely ripped off, and now small sparks scattered from it. Although she should have been in pain, Niko stood tall in a movement betraying nothing. The avatar glanced passingly at Haruyuki. On the other side of the lenses of those cute, round eyes, an inferno swirled.

"After I take care of him, I'll finish the two of you off together. If that's not your thing, better run now. The next time we meet... it's as enemies."

Having coldly communicated this fact to him, the Red King

turned her gaze forward again. She pulled out the handgun on her hip with her right hand and started walking, yanking back the slide as she did.

At her destination, Chrome Disaster was crawling northward even now, light the color of blood seeping from the wounds covering his body. That he could move even that much despite having been closer to the blast's epicenter than Kuroyukihime really spoke to his astonishing endurance. However, he could slink no faster than about half of Niko's current gait, meaning escape was no longer possible.

Still holding the injured Kuroyukihime in both arms, Haruyuki's blurred gaze was held by the shadows of two avatars steadily growing closer. Judging the situation rationally, he should have considered the possibility that he should, based on her earlier pronouncement, run toward the withdrawal point in either Ikebukuro Station or Sunshine City right away.

But Haruyuki couldn't move. Or rather, he didn't want to move. If he ran now, something wrong would be established as fact. That's how he felt.

Near the exit to the road—created by the enormous beam mowing down a block's worth of buildings—Niko had finally caught up with Chrome Disaster, and she casually raised her right foot. The knight avatar was kicked to the ground with a rough *clang*, and Niko perched her left foot on his head.

Haruyuki felt it was an indescribably sad scene.

It was true that the demonic armor had to be destroyed. And it might also have been a fact that she'd had no choice but to aim for the moment right before he started grappling with Kuroyukihime to actually hit this thing, given its transcendent reflexes, with her special attack.

But—in that case, what was the other night about?

Niko and Kuroyukihime sleeping, arms wrapped around each other in Haruyuki's living room, as if they were both looking for something in the other. The two girls, making him feel a bigger bond, one that surpassed even their shared destiny that, as Kings, they would have to fight one day. Was that sight, so precious Haruyuki almost wanted to cry, merely one night's illusion? Was it just a meaningless coincidence?

Scarlet Rain pressed her gun to the back of Chrome Disaster's head.

Unable to bear the sight of what came next, Haruyuki ducked his head. But he didn't hear the gun report no matter how long he waited.

Instead, a weak voice spoke next to his ear. "...Hon. Estly... This is why... I despise children..."

Kuroyukihime's voice, wounded, shaking with pain. But there wasn't a hint of anger there. Haruyuki lifted his face with a gasp and stared into the ebony goggles so close to him.

Inside, a very faint violet light shone. Suppressing all the feelings welling up, Haruyuki whispered, "K-Kuroyu..."

It was in that instant he heard a metallic screeching.

Shifting his gaze, Haruyuki saw Chrome Disaster, upper body arched back, right hand thrown out. And Scarlet Rain, fragments of armor scattering from her left arm.

Dancing, high up in the sky, was the crimson gun.

"Wh-why didn't she shoot?!" Haruyuki cried involuntarily.

She should have had plenty of time to deliver Chrome Disaster the Judgment Blow, the immediate execution of a member by the Legion Master. Wasn't it for exactly this purpose that she had gotten Kuroyukihime tangled up in her special attack and even gone so far as to toss them coldly aside and say such terrible things? Why on earth would she hesitate now?

The response to the questions making his head swim came from Kuroyukihime in his arms. "...That. Little girl...is just sulking. It's hard...She's sad, throwing a tantrum..."

"Wh-what?!"

Shocked, eyes covering the distance between the girl in his arms and the one on the other side of the wreckage, he saw Chrome Disaster's right hand flash like lightning, seizing Niko by the neck.

The arm, which appeared to have recovered a fair bit of power, slowly hoisted the small avatar. Niko grabbed the gauntlet with her right hand but offered no other resistance, simply dangling there limply. Almost as if she had given up on everything and resigned herself to this fate.

"That girl in particular...More than anyone else, she wants to believe. In the ultimate bond of a Burst Linker...," Kuroyukihime murmured.

"B-bond...?" Haruyuki asked in response, dumbfounded, his eyes opening wide.

"Y-yes. I can tell. Those two...are guardian and child. The Red King...is Disaster's...no, Cherry Rook's child."

Guardian and child?! Those two?!

Up to that point, the thought hadn't even crossed his mind. But now that she had said it, there was one thing that made sense to him.

Niko had tracked in detail Cherry Rook's location in the real world. Haruyuki had assumed it was some kind of Legion Master privilege, but that wasn't the case. Niko simply knew Cherry Rook in the real. As her only "guardian" who had passed Brain Burst along to her himself.

Further overwhelmed by surprise and rendered again speechless, Haruyuki shifted his gaze back to Kuroyukihime's placid expression. She raised a ragged right hand and patted him on the shoulder. "Come now, what are you doing? I'm...fine. Go and help her...Niko...our friend."

Tears welled up in Haruyuki's eyes, tears he didn't try to hold back. He didn't know why, but some huge, hot thing born in his heart pushed its way up. He nodded vigorously. "Okay!"

Haruyuki gently settled Kuroyukihime's body back on the ground and stood up. With a sharp *clack*, the wings on his back were fully deployed.

He aimed for the top of Niko's shoulder where she was clutched in Disaster's right fist. It would also bring him close to the monster's jaw. He took a deep breath and clenched his right hand.

"Yaaaaah!" He shouted a cry and then kicked hard off the ground. After running toward takeoff for a few seconds, he vibrated the metal fins of his wings as hard as he could. His feet pulled away from the ground, and Haruyuki plunged forward, just skimming the surface of the earth, becoming nothing more than a beam of silver light.

On the other side of the rubble road, the crazed armor drew closer to Niko. He held her before his red eyes, ready to tear into her flesh, his own "child" Linker. Haruyuki clenched his right fist tightly, readying it at his side.

"Stoooooop!" Screaming, Haruyuki slammed a fist enveloped in dazzling light into the center of that stygian maw.

His silver radiance ripped into the lurking darkness with a *crunch*. After a moment's pause, Chrome Disaster flew back, head thrown off to the side, as if flicked away by an explosion of repulsive force. He bounced on the rubble and tumbled along for another ten meters before falling, limbs askew.

Haruyuki folded up his wings and landed, glancing up to see that he had used half of his special-attack gauge with the Punch. Presently, he looked down at the crimson avatar on her knees beside him.

Holding her throat where Disaster had clutched it and coughing violently, Niko lifted her face and glared at Haruyuki, fire in her eyes. "Y-you...Why..."

"I came to help." The heat rising up from the depths of his body made his voice unusually rough. "We're...friends, okay?"

Swallowing her breath for an instant and stiffening up, Niko squeezed out hoarsely, "You jerk...Just a small fry and here you are...acting all big..."

"You, too. You're supposed to be a King. How long are you gonna mess this up?" With the tip of his toes, Haruyuki kicked up the crimson gun, which had fallen near his right foot, and grabbed the barrel midair. He held the grip out to Niko as he continued, "You're the only one who can help him; the only one who can help Cherry Rook, Niko. For him, Brain Burst is nothing more than a curse now. You have to set him free."

Behind the round, cute lens, a glimmer wavered as if in hesitation. But a second later, her right hand stretched out and wrapped firmly around the grip of the pistol.

"Yeah. I know. I *know*, okay?" Muttering as she stood, the Red King brought her left foot down on the ground loudly, as if to crush something. She focused her gaze straight ahead.

Chrome Disaster, having been sent flying, was only now raising his torso. With his right hand, he covered his face where he'd been struck by Haruyuki's Punch and whined restlessly. He apparently didn't have enough strength left to stand. The red glow attempting to repair the damage covering his body had disappeared almost entirely, replaced with particles the color of pitch, dripping out of the wounds like blood.

"Cherry," Niko called to him quietly as she advanced. "Let's end this already. There's no point in going on with a game that's just pain and suffering."

From between the fingers covering his helmet, the flickering blink of Chrome Disaster's red eyes was visible. The left arm that had been thrust into the ground lifted shakily, and the palm of his hand was turned up to the sky, as if to say *I surrender*.

For a moment, Haruyuki wondered if he had come to his senses. However...

Suddenly, without any kind of preliminary movement, the blackish-silver avatar whirled upward diagonally, with a speed that belied its weight.

"What?!" Haruyuki cried as he watched Disaster attach himself to the steel frame protruding from the top of a nearly destroyed five-story building. Whipping around backward, he leaped again, as if sucked up by the sky itself.

As he stared at the figure receding with each passing second, Haruyuki shouted, "Flight ability?!"

"No, it's a long-distance jump!" Niko replied, tense. "He's going to try to log out at the withdrawal point in Sunshine City. If we let him get away now, we won't get another chance."

Cherry Rook, wrapped in that armor, probably already understood that his Legion Master and "child," Niko, had tracked his movements somehow. He was certain to deal with that once he logged out, and if he did, they wouldn't be able to use this Unlimited Neutral Field ambush strategy again.

Haruyuki gritted his teeth, stared directly at the Red King, and said, "Niko. This time you can shoot, right? The Judgment Blow."

"Shut up. I'll fire. For his sake."

Finally, Haruyuki's turn had come: time for Silver Crow to run down and capture Chrome Disaster as per their original plan. All he had to do now was fly. Praying that was the case, Haruyuki told her bluntly, "I'll keep Disaster in check until you catch up."

Speechless for a moment, Niko shook her head in tiny increments. "Y-you can't alone! Not only are you hurt, but he can still move like that. If you get caught, he'll be the one eating *you*!"

Haruyuki glanced over at the jet-black figure lying at the far southern edge of the crater and then quickly brought his gaze back before saying, forcefully, "Then you've got until he eats me!"

Making the rubble clatter, he reoriented his body, spread his wings, and took off in a straight line.

Flying from the devastated cluster of buildings and giving everything he had to increasing his speed, a dully glittering avatar entered his field of view. Already three hundred meters off to the northeast, the fleeing beast continued to move farther away with incredible long-distance jumps from rooftop to rooftop.

Haruyuki glanced down to see the crimson avatar starting to run in the same northeasterly direction. Taking a deep breath, he flew faster, accompanied by a roaring *whoosh*.

He stuck both hands straight ahead and surged forward, slicing through the virtual air. Soon enough, he'd passed Green Street, and he continued accelerating along the intersecting Shuto Expressway No. 5.

Soaring on the horizon, Sunshine City was already directly ahead. Naturally, it was no longer the gray skyscraper from the real world. A bluish, jagged steel material interwove to make up the truss structure, and the look of it piercing the dark clouds, eclipsing everything else, gave it the appearance of an enormous tower that was home to the King of Hell. The shopping mall at its base had also been transformed into a desolate park, and here and there in the cracked, tile-covered space, pitch-black trees spread out deformed arms.

At the end of the large stairway cutting through the park from the road to the tower, he could see the structure's entrance, filled with a hazy, pale blue light. That was probably the leave point. If Chrome Disaster managed to get that far, they'd never get the chance to capture him in the Unlimited Neutral Field again.

Disaster continued leaping in a zigzag across the tops of the buildings on the main street, pitch-black blood particles dropping in his wake. He was so incredibly fast that it was impossible to believe he was just jumping, but as expected, he was slower than Silver Crow in flight.

I caught him!

Haruyuki held his breath and planned the timing for a sudden drop. Above all else, he had to knock the Armor into the ground and stop its advance.

Maintaining sufficient speed and having positioned himself directly above his opponent's blind spot, Haruyuki entered a full-throttle dive the instant the Armor landed atop a new roof and launched itself toward its next target.

Haruyuki stuck out the toes on his right foot, turning himself into a sharp wedge, and streamed downward. Perhaps noticing the whistle of the wind, the Armor's helmet looked up with a start. But he wouldn't be able to dodge midleap. The tips of Haruyuki's toes, glowing with a fierce radiance, piercing the lacerated back of the Armor—

"Wha—?!"

The instant before he connected with the mutilated Armor, something impossible happened.

In midair, Chrome Disaster, without giving any warning whatsoever, abruptly diverted his trajectory to the right. Haruyuki's Kick missed its target, accomplishing no more than a scraping sound. Had he allowed the momentum to carry him, he'd have buried himself in the base of the tower, but he braked with every ounce of strength in his wings and just barely managed to decelerate in time.

Landing on both feet with an enormous *thud*, Haruyuki looked up, still dumbfounded, at Chrome Disaster flying off to the right.

What was that?! No matter how fast or long the jump, as long as it was still a jump, it just wasn't possible to change trajectories in midair. After all, had it been possible, then it was basically the same as being able to fly, like Haruyuki.

He hurried to take off again and pursue Disaster. The avatar was already close enough that he could probably reach the Sunshine City site in another two or three jumps.

The method of it was unclear, but given that his opponent could alter his course in midair, Haruyuki wasn't likely to land a straight dive-kick. In which case, the only thing to do was court the risk of being caught himself and launch an attack while following him closely.

"Aaaah!" With a small battle cry, he accelerated and closed the distance until he was just behind the blackish-silver back. When he did, the Armor once again whirled, this time to the left, and Haruyuki was forced into a hard turn. His avatar groaned at the centrifugal force bearing down on him.

Gritting his teeth, he began beating his fist desperately into the Armor's back when Chrome Disaster again did the impossible.

This time, he sank straight down. Haruyuki's Punch sliced the air, and having overtaken his enemy, he dove, twisting his own body to target where his opponent would land.

Only in that moment, when both his feet made contact with the roof of the building, would Disaster be forced to stop before launching into the next jump. Haruyuki continued holding the figure of Disaster descending desperately in his sights, dimming because of his own reckless maneuvering, and calculated his timing.

The Armor arched its body, yanked its face up, and stretched out its right arm, allowing Haruyuki to bear witness to a sight that stunned him a third time.

The metal avatar, supposedly incredibly massive, suddenly decelerated in midair. Almost as if gravity had reversed direction, it stopped instantly in empty space and then shot directly up again. His aim off yet again, Haruyuki sliced through the atmosphere vainly with his right foot and flipped his body—

Both eyes wide, he finally saw it.

The momentary glimmer of an extremely fine red line between Chrome Disaster ascending at a steep angle and the rather tall building for which he was headed.

It wasn't a beam. The light was a reflected afterglow shining through the gap between buildings.

It was a wire.

In the back of Haruyuki's mind, he recounted flashbacks of the strange gripping technique Chrome Disaster had shown off earlier. That technique—the way he had forcibly yanked the Yellow Legion long-range avatar and the rock that Kuroyukihime had kicked into the armor's opened palm—and Disaster's long-distance jumping and midair maneuverability came from exactly the same thing: an extremely thin wire with an anchor attached. It was launched from the palm of his hand at the target to retract it, or was launched at a fixed object to hoist himself toward *it*.

As Haruyuki watched, Chrome Disaster ascended, wire winding at ridiculously high speeds, and disappeared onto the edge of a building.

Rising once more to give chase, Haruyuki focused his thoughts to calculate his next move. To interfere with that jump, all he had to do was cut the wire stretched out in the air.

But he probably couldn't disconnect it with a hand chop or a Kick. It easily supported that heavy avatar—and while accelerating on a descent, to boot. He had to assume that the wire's anchoring power and load-bearing ability were absolute. There was even the possibility that it could not be cut and, in fact, might do him damage.

Rolling seriously through these thoughts as he gained altitude, Haruyuki caught sight of Chrome Disaster landing on an arched roof. On the other side, separated by only a road now, was Sunshine City. His opponent would reach the portal tower with one more leap. What could he do? How could he stop him?

Disaster stretched out his right hand, aiming for the blue-black wall of his destination. His sharp fingers opened into claws. In the center, the light of the wire firing flashed.

"Right!!" Haruyuki shouted at the revelation that came to him in an instant. The strategy that popped into his mind was basically suicide, but he had no other cards to play.

He poured every bit of energy he had into the silver fins that constituted his wings and plunged straight ahead toward Sunshine. Particles of light enveloped his small avatar, drawing out a tail in space like a comet. He quickly overtook Chrome Disaster, crossed the road, and flew on.

More! More, more! Accelerate!

The faster he moved, the more the color of the world changed; everything was decelerating in relation to himself. Now just a dazzling laser shooting forward, Haruyuki was sure he saw it: the wire launched from Chrome Disaster's right hand toward the exterior wall of the tower, and the microscopic hook at its end.

"Aaaaaaah!!" With a howl, he applied a final burst of acceleration and dove at a shallow angle, mingling his flight trajectory with the wire sight.

He heard the faint snap through his body and felt something bite into the center of his back. An incredible force tried to haul Haruyuki back, but he fought it and pushed himself to the limits of his acceleration to keep charging ahead.

He felt the weight suddenly. Chrome Disaster's body at the other end of the wire was floating on its back in midair. Without even looking back, Haruyuki saw vividly in his mind the Armor connected to him, flying through space at the same speed.

When landing normally, Disaster avoided crashing into whatever he'd hooked by adjusting the force reeling in the wire. But dragged along like this, the Armor had no technique for decelerating on its own.

Before him, the exterior wall of the enormous tower piercing the sky drew closer. Haruyuki glared at it, a combination of countless pieces of thick steel, and swallowed his fear as he timed his strategy. Too early and he would end up giving Chrome Disaster enough time to land safely; too late and he would crash into the tower himself.

Right. Now.

"Gah!" Screaming, Haruyuki shot straight up at the steepest angle he could manage. Every joint in his body squealed, pain lancing through them. The sharp end of one of the steel girders grazed him from chest to stomach. Orange sparks flying, Haruyuki ascended along the wall of Sunshine, easing up on the acceleration at the same time.

And Chrome Disaster's enormous body collided against the wall of the tower with an impact so loud that the whole of Ikebukuro shuddered.

The tower itself rattled, and broken fragments of glass, steel, and stone scattered with the force of an explosion. The aftershocks of the energy unleashed turned into bluish-white sparks, crawling through the air.

The wire stretching out from Haruyuki's back trailed into a massive breach around the tower's tenth floor. There was a rumbling roar, and he stared, awestruck, as a river of water surged from the hole. Straining his eyes, the water appeared to contain strange, aquatic creatures of varying sizes. The afterglow lighting up their scales red, they danced in the sky and fell to the park on the first floor, splashing about.

Haruyuki finally realized that in the real-world Sunshine City, there would have been an aquarium around this spot. Most likely, that had been re-created here in the Accelerated World, and the crashing Disaster had shattered the tanks.

Toward the end of the outflow of giant fish and amphibians, something that looked like a lump of metal popped out of the hole and was caught, limp, on one of the twisted girders.

Chrome Disaster. In such bad shape, he was nearly unrecognizable. Half of his left arm had been torn off, and his right leg had been smashed like scrap iron. His armor plating was furrowed and crushed, wholly lacking its former sheen.

From innumerable lesions, a near-terrifying amount of black liquid spewed, melting into the air and disappearing before it even hit the ground. Given his condition, it was amazing Chrome Disaster didn't disappear from the field that second.

Haruyuki blinked his eyes tightly, told himself that this was not the time to let these feelings out, and went to lower Disaster's body to the ground, using the wire that still connected them. Niko would probably arrive soon.

He ascended slightly, and the taut wire hoisted up the Armor's right arm.

"Rooooooooooo!!" Suddenly, a howl emanated from the beast at an unspeakable volume.

From inside the hood-shaped helmet of Chrome Disaster's abruptly raised face, a countless number of very long fangs appeared and opened wide.

His right hand snared at the air like a claw, and Haruyuki's body was yanked back irresistibly.

After unexpectly dropping several meters, Haruyuki put every bit of force he had into pumping his wings to resist the demonic pull. The straining wire screamed. Before his eyes, the hungry fangs snapped open and closed.

"Nngaaah!" Wailing, Haruyuki desperately fought back. Chrome Disaster's "predation" had a damage recovery effect. If he got eaten now, this thing would be all healed up and go after Niko again, and then Kuroyukihime.

Tearing his gaze away from the terrifying maw, Haruyuki looked straight up.

The sky of the Unlimited Neutral Field, night approaching, was almost entirely covered by inky black clouds, but between the breaks, he could faintly see stars. He reached out his right hand to a remarkably large red star among them. Making a tight fist, Haruyuki cried out.

"Ngaaaaaaah!"

The air roared, and the thrust of his silver wings increased the metallic attraction. Flying perpendicularly as if popping out, Haruyuki started scrambling up the exterior wall of Sunshine tower rapidly, the Armor still dangling below him. The shock wave rippled the wall like a wave, and the glass followed, shattering.

Reaching the summit of the tower mere seconds later, he kicked at one of the strange thorns stretching out horizontally from the edge and used the reaction to change his orientation, turning back toward Chrome Disaster, still borne along by the wire.

"Nngaaah!!" As he yelled, he drove a right Kick into the Armor's throat. The lower half of the helmet went flying with a sharp metallic clatter, and the obsidian fangs crumbled.

Still in the same posture, he began plummeting at full speed. The silver avatar and its blackish-silver counterpart became one, streaking toward the ground like a falling star.

Then...

The darkness inside Disaster's helmet disintegrated with a puff. What appeared inside was a simply designed mask with a light pink hue. The horizontal ellipses that were its eyes blinked hazily, and a small voice—that of a boy—spoke, a lingering innocence in its tone.

"I...want...to be stronger. That's all..."

Continuing to dive even now, Haruyuki opened his eyes wide. He met the other's, almost as if trying to peer in, and the peach-colored avatar pressed further, "You...you can understand that, right? You want...power, too, don't you?"

Hearing those words, Haruyuki felt an intense heat well up deep within him.

Rage. Overwhelming fury.

"You wanted to be strong?" Haruyuki said, still concentrating all the thrust of his wings into the right foot piercing the Armor's neck. His question instantly swelled to a shout, which practically erupted from his throat.

"So you're saying that gives you the right to do whatever you want?! You're saying that makes putting on that armor, attacking huge numbers of avatars, and even trying to eat your own child—eat Niko—totally acceptable?!"

Their dive had already passed the tower's halfway point. If he didn't pull out soon, he'd be in trouble, too. He knew that, and yet he couldn't stop the words rushing out of him.

I want to be stronger. He had, in fact, been repeating those words over and over like a spell for a while now. He felt inferior to pretty much everyone and had become completely obsessed with his ridiculous training. But coming to the field today and fighting his way through more battles than he could count, Haruyuki finally understood that he had forgotten something important.

Strength was definitely not relative.

Superficial standards like winning or losing duels, or being higher or lower than someone, had no value.

It was him. The sole, absolute standard was inside himself.

"It's not just you!" Haruyuki mustered every scrap of vocal strength he had to shout. "I mean, Niko...and Kuroyukihime... and Taku, and the other Burst Linkers...and Chiyu, and the kids at school, the teachers, too, everyone thinks that!! 'I want to be stronger, I want to live strong...I want to be able to stand up and face all the hard things myself,' everyone thinks that!!"

Fragments of the Armor, unable to withstand the speed of their descent, peeled away, immediately turning into light particles and disappearing. Even the darkness leaking from the countless wounds emitted heat the instant it touched the wall of air and burned up.

The avatar contained in the helmet said nothing more.

Without even trying to decelerate or withdraw, Haruyuki plunged forward as one with the Armor.

The two entangled avatars crashed at a terrifying speed into roughly the center of the large staircase that stretched out from the entrance of the park to the tower, causing a final, massive explosion.

8

The fact that Haruyuki still had about 20 percent of his HP gauge left, even after being swallowed up in a pillar of fire that reached up to the sky and then jostled by the shock wave, was because he had taken almost no damage in the impact itself.

Punching out an enormous crater by crashing into the large staircase at Sunshine City, Chrome Disaster's armor—the Enhanced Armament—was finally completely destroyed. The armor broke into thousands of metal fragments and went flying, and from its core, particles of thick darkness jetted straight up, acting as a cushion and repelling Haruyuki's avatar back into the sky. He felt the wire on his back severed, perhaps struck by shrapnel.

Tossed about like a scrap of litter in the enormous explosion, Haruyuki curled his body up intently and endured the damage whittling down his gauge. He somehow managed to break free of the intensely hot sphere and descended haltingly, thin lines of smoke trailing from all over his body. Unable to stand up again once he'd landed, he crumpled to his knees.

When he raised his face, the pillar of flame mixing orange and black was just beginning to diffuse into the atmosphere and disappear. The embers pouring down like rain bounced off gray tiles and withered trees, making their surroundings glow red.

The large staircase had been pitted near the middle in the

shape of a mortar blast, and in the center of this, he could see a small avatar lying half-buried on its side. The cherry-pink armor was completely scorched and absent its left hand and right foot. Extremely faint light in the elliptical eye lens, which seemed humorous somehow, blinked irregularly and disappeared.

Such a powerless and pitiful figure. He found it incredibly hard to believe that this was the avatar that had put on the evil armor and slaughtered so many so ruthlessly.

Crouching, unable to move, Haruyuki only heard the sound of the small footsteps approaching him from behind. His left shoulder was slapped lightly.

"You did it, Silver Crow. Now leave it to me."

Haruyuki stared silently at the back of the Red King as she stepped forward and then descended into the crater.

He thought about standing up and following her, but he quickly reconsidered. He got the feeling that the final conversation between those two was something he shouldn't overhear.

The two duel avatars, the same red family and nearly the same size, one prostrate, the other standing, appeared to exchange words for a brief while. Finally, the red girl-shaped avatar knelt down beside the light peach boy-shaped avatar, held up the ragged body, left arm severed, and hugged it tightly.

The gun in her right hand raised softly.

The barrel pressed against the boy's chest.

Despite its impressive name, both the sound and the light of the Judgment Blow were modest. But the instant the virtual bullet pierced the avatar, something happened that Haruyuki had never before witnessed.

The boy avatar disassembled into countless ribbons, each one a luminous, minute series of code. All the information that made up the duel avatar by the name of Cherry Rook unraveled, divided, and melted into the sky of the Accelerated World.

Roughly ten seconds later, there was nothing left in Niko's arms.

The crimson avatar, slumped down on the spot, threw her head back to look up at the sky, which was painted almost entirely black in the twilight.

Haruyuki wobbled to his feet and started walking toward the explosion's epicenter, dragging his right foot, which had suffered a fairly serious injury. A few seconds later, he arrived behind Niko and stopped to her right, but a mixture of every type of emotion tripped him up and prevented any words from coming out.

Finally, Niko blurted, "Me and Cherry, we don't know our parents."

He couldn't grasp her meaning right away. When his breath articulated the question in his heart, her words returned, quietly.

"And by 'parents,' I don't mean where we got our copies of Brain Burst, okay? I mean, the real world…our real parents. I told you before that my school's a boarding school, right? The truth is, it's a 'school for the total care and education of abandoned children.'"

Haruyuki could only listen respectfully to the words Niko, still plopped down on the ground, dispassionately uttered.

The policy of taking in newborn babies unconditionally had started in hospitals and similar places at the beginning of the century. As a step in the countermeasures against the acceleration of the decreasing birthrate and aging population, this policy had become law around the year 2030, and welfare institutions that doubled as schools were established in every region. And it was true that there was one such school in the Red Legion–controlled Nerima Ward.

"I-it's 'cos of this personality. Even at school, I don't fit in. I was always playing VR games by myself. But three years ago…this guy two grades ahead of me suddenly starts talking to me, right? He says, there's an even better game, asks if I wanna try it." She let out a small laugh before continuing.

"An invite like that, and I still let him direct. But, you know, he was just so sincere, all red in the face, you practically laughed. And that didn't change after I became a Burst Linker, either. He taught me all these things super seriously, and when I got in trouble, he'd be a shield and protect me and stuff. But soon I caught up with his level. And then I passed him. And before I knew it, I'd somehow gotten to level nine. And once I was pushed into the Legion Master thing, I was frantic, too. It's almost like I didn't even care about what he was thinking or the problems he was having. In the real…When we'd meet at school, I didn't even notice he was acting weird."

Niko's right hand scratched at the ground. Facing down, shoulders shaking, the young King squeezed out a thin voice. "He wanted to stay my 'parent' forever. And he wanted me to stay his 'child.' That's why he sought power. He lost to the temptation of the Armor of Catastrophe. I-if I had just said something, just told him. That levels and stuff don't matter, you'll always be my only 'parent.' That that would never change."

Back still rounded, little, softly weeping Niko crouched over…

For a moment, Haruyuki couldn't find anything to say.

The Burst Linker "guardian-child" relationship. Connected in the same way with Kuroyukihime, Haruyuki had thought he understood the weight of that. But for Niko and Cherry Rook, for these two who didn't know their real parents, it was no doubt the only indelible bond they'd made. And Niko had severed that with her own hand. She'd had no other choice.

Haruyuki worked to swallow back the things welling up in him, kneeled down, and placed a gentle hand on Niko's shoulder.

"Niko. It's true, Brain Burst isn't just a game. But…it's not the whole of our reality, either."

Thinking, he started to talk, and the bitter sobs quieted slightly. "I mean, I'm always scared of being powerless. I'm scared of being abandoned by her. But…I know the real her. I know her face, her name, her voice. No matter what happens, that bond's not going anywhere. I mean, it's not digital. It's carved into my heart. Which is why—Which is why you can still be friends with him again in the real world. You should be able to. I mean, you and us, we're in different Legions in the Accelerated World, but in the real world, we managed to become actual friends."

The low sobbing continued for a while longer but finally melted, as if swept up by the slight wind blowing away the twilight. Her back shuddered conspicuously one final time, and Niko wiped her avatar's eyes with her right arm before brushing away Haruyuki's hand, still resting on her shoulder.

"Friends...you say?" Her voice was hoarse and shaking, but it had reclaimed just a little of its impudent tone. The childish King stood abruptly, looked down at Haruyuki with red lenses, and spoke. "Were you born yesterday?! At best, you managed to become one of my subordinates! Don't get carried away!!"

"Wh-what?!" Haruyuki was about to continue in protest when a cool voice from behind interrupted.

"Hey. Just who is whose subordinate?"

Whirling around, Haruyuki saw the ashen avatar, her entire body in tatters but standing solidly—Black Lotus.

And the indigo-blue avatar Cyan Pile supported her left arm.

"K-Kuroyukihime! Taku!!" Crying out, Haruyuki practically flew over to them. "A-are you okay, Kuroyukihime? And Taku, how—" he started to ask before he finally remembered.

Immediately prior to entering the battle with the Yellow Legion, Takumu himself had explained it. Burst Linkers who die in the Unlimited Neutral Field were resurrected in the same place after a one-hour standby penalty. Which meant that much time had already passed before he'd even realized it.

"Taku...honestly, you were totally crazy to do that," he grumbled.

Takumu spread out a hand and replied, "You say that, Haru, but look at the terrible shape you're in. Going after Chrome Disaster by yourself...I mean, that's beyond crazy."

"I take after our master."

And that master separated herself from Cyan Pile and hovered on one leg to stand immediately before Niko. Kuroyukihime waved the tip of the sword of her right hand and uttered in a somehow arrogant voice, "Now then, Scarlet Rain. Don't you have something to say to me?"

Right fist trembling for a while, the Red King finally jutted her face up. "Sorry."

"Come on! Is that it? Honestly, this is exactly why I—"

"Wh-what about you?! We were out there fighting our butts off while you were just taking a nap!!"

"What did you say?"

"What, you don't like it?"

Haruyuki and Takumu inserted themselves placatingly and desperately between the two Kings facing off, red and bluish-purple sparks scattering.

Suddenly, a remarkably strong wind blew down from the enormous tower of Sunshine City, and Haruyuki unconsciously closed his eyes.

"Oh," Niko murmured.

Followed by Kuroyukihime. "Come, Haruyuki. Look. It's the Change."

"Ch-change?" Haruyuki asked in response as he lifted his face to see—

The unbelievable sight of the world rapidly changing around him.

The city, nothing more than blue-black steel and desolate ground unfolding infinitely, was covered in a wave of light like an aura rolling in from the east. Caressed by this curtain, the bleak, naked steel structures of the town were transformed into a series of large trees with thick trunks. Cavities to be used as entrances and stairs winding around the trunks were built into the trees, with suspension bridges reaching out to connect thick branch to branch. The city became an elf country straight out of a fantasy movie.

In the dead of night, the thick growth of leaves were enveloped in a faint blue phosphorescence that illuminated the floor of the forest. As Haruyuki stood there dumbfounded, a rainbow-colored aura drew near, wrapped up the world in front of him with a roar, and faded to the rear.

"Ah! S-Sunshine is…"

In the place where there had been an enormous tower, the castle of the King of Hell a moment before, he saw a tree so enormous it very nearly pierced the heavens, and Haruyuki caught his breath.

The trunk, covered in a golden-green moss, stretched up vertically, gnarled knots popping up here and there, while the top of the tree melted into the clouds in the distant sky above. Here and there along the trunk, terraces—small forests themselves— jutted out, and particles of blue light spilled down to the ground. A majestic presence worthy of the name World Tree.

But why on earth would the field transform like that?

When he shifted his attention to ask the question, Kuroyukihime had the air of a slight smile wafting around her injured avatar as she replied. "Come now, I told you that its affinity was 'chaos' when we first dived into this field."

"Uh-huh, so then…"

"That, in other words, means that the affinity of this world changes at fixed times. But most of the time, it's just brutal. You're lucky. The field almost never shows itself in this kind of beautiful form."

"Uh-huh." Haruyuki filled his lungs with air that had adopted a sweetness in scent and flavor and nodded several times. It had been a tough, painful series of battles, but for the first time, he felt glad to be here.

I still don't have enough power to fight here. But I'll get strong enough so that one day, I can fly freely through this world's skies. And I'll probably keep losing again and again in very uncool ways, but… one day, for sure.

"I'd ask you to pick us up and fly again. But when the Change happens, the Enemies are completely repopped. Loitering's dangerous right now. We'll just be good kids and go home."

"Let's." Kuroyukihime nodded at Niko's suggestion. "Whoops! Before we do, though, I nearly forgot something important." Looking around once, she continued in a more severe tone, "Everyone.

Open your status screen and check your item storage. If the Armor of Catastrophe is there, you must get rid of it. So the same thing does not happen again."

Haruyuki's eyes flew open.

Right, we have to check that at least.

When the previous Chrome Disaster had been subjugated at the hands of the Seven Kings of Pure Color two and a half years earlier, the Kings supposedly did the exact same thing. And they'd all reported that the armor hadn't been transferred.

However, that had been a lie. There was no proof, but the armor had been dropped into the Yellow King's storage. The Yellow King had concealed this fact and had only recently contacted Cherry Rook, who belonged to the Red Legion, and given him the armor. To have him break the nonaggression pact due to the poisonous nature of the armor, and then take compensation for this "crime" with Niko's head.

Just as Kuroyukihime had said, the same tragedy must not happen again. Haruyuki stretched out a hand, touched his HP gauge, and moved from the open status screen to the item storage.

The window was completely empty. He nearly burned a hole into it with his gaze, but there wasn't a single line of text there.

"I don't have it."

Haruyuki gave his answer, lifting his head, and was followed by Niko's "Me neither," Takumu's "Nor me as well," and shakes of their heads. Finally, Kuroyukihime murmured, "Nor I," and the four of them fell silent for a moment.

Cherry Rook, the fifth Chrome Disaster, had definitely had Brain Burst forcefully uninstalled with Niko's Judgment Blow. When its owner lost all his points, the Enhanced Armament was supposedly transferred with a fixed probability to the storage of those who had defeated the owner. In which case, this time, not having been transferred, it had finally been completely destroyed. Probably.

Since it was impossible to see anyone else's status screen, there was always the possibility that someone was concealing the armor like the Yellow King had. However...

"It's gone, this time for sure," Haruyuki declared in a clear voice.

Niko assented right away. "Yeah. We're not that jerk Radio, and...I don't think anyone here's stupid enough to fight him, fight Disaster, and then go and make the thing their own. The Armor of Catastrophe is gone. We totally destroyed it."

"Uh-huh. I could see that explosion from South Ikebukuro. That's probably proof it was annihilated, right?" Takumu also nodded.

Finally, Kuroyukihime declared firmly, "Good. Settling things with the Yellow King will have to wait until next time or later, but in any case—mission complete. Now, perhaps we should go home and raise a glass?"

"Ooh! Okay, let's have champagne! Champagne!"

"Idiot. Children drink juice."

Quarreling once again, the two Kings began walking. Takumu and Haruyuki followed them, grinning wryly.

At the root of the World Tree, a large cave opened up illuminated by the same blue light he'd seen when it was a steel tower was shining inside. They headed toward the swirling, shining withdrawal point, and walking last in the line, Haruyuki's ears—

A voice that somehow wasn't—

"Huh?" He turned around automatically, but of course, there was no one there.

"What's wrong, Haru?"

At the sound of Takumu's question, he hurried to turn again and shook his head. "No, nothing! Aah, I'm like ten times more tired than after a regular duel. I'm starving. I can't go on..."

"Hey, come on! You know, in the real world, we ate cake, like, just a few seconds ago."

"Gah! I forgot..." Bantering with his friend, he slipped through the entrance enclosed by the thick tree trunk.

The base of the World Tree turned into an expansive semi-sphere of a dome. In the center, a blue portal, which contained a view of the real-world Ikebukuro, floated like a mirage. Following his friends and moving forward a few steps, Haruyuki turned around just one more time.

Must be imagining things, he murmured in his head before quickly facing forward again.

But the instant he leaped into the slowly rotating portal, the strange voice rang out behind his head once more.

This is what he heard:

Want to eat.

9

Haruyuki glared intently at the steel holes created by the eight spiraling grooves of the rifling.

Saturday. Four PM.

He was in the middle of the public Territory Battle to protect Suginami Area No. 3, controlled by the Black Legion, Nega Nebulus.

A three-person team with a balance of blue, red, and purple had come to challenge them. It was a lineup that had often been coming to attack for a while now. Which was to say, they were also the opponents to whom Haruyuki had clumsily lost repeatedly.

The one he was particularly bad with was a sniper-type avatar in a dark red cloak, equipped with a large antiaircraft rifle. It would conceal itself on the rooftop of a building quite far from the front line and launch incredibly powerful bullets with terrifying precision.

Since of the three members of Nega Nebulus, Kuroyukihime and Takumu were actively close-range types, Haruyuki necessarily had to take on the enemy sniper, being a high-maneuverability type. That said, because he didn't have any long-range attack power, he needed to fly in close once he'd determined the sniper's position.

But in the Territory Battles up to that point, Haruyuki had

been ignobly shot down time after time, unable to dodge the enemy sniping in the course of closing the distance. To compensate, he was forced to join up with Kuroyukihime's powerful battle abilities, and every weekend, he fell victim to fierce bouts of self-hatred.

And now again from the roof of a building a kilometer ahead, the black gun muzzle was precisely trained on Haruyuki flying hard.

Since approaching in a straight line was the equivalent of saying *Please shoot me*, Haruyuki carried out maneuvers as randomly as possible to escape the enemy scope, sometimes even entering the shadow of some cover on the ground. But no matter what the technique, at the end of it, the large-diameter rifle always snapped back onto Haruyuki without the slightest delay.

When are you going to shoot? Now? Now?

Here and there passing before his eyes at high speeds were the figures of people in the gallery. Especially right after he started playing, Haruyuki had been pretty popular as the possessor of the sole flight ability, but now that walk-throughs had been studied, the gallery was mostly exposed to scenes of him crashing awkwardly. And they were disappointed—that would have been better, actually. Lately, he thought they had gotten past that and likely reached the sneering stage, and everything got hot inside his head.

And on top of that, in the battlefield to the rear, Takumu and Kuroyukihime, taking on the enemy close-range types, were probably casting their eyes his way during the pauses in battle. Wondering if today would be the day he took care of the sniper or if they would have to follow up yet again.

Just when are you going to fire? Hurry up and shoot already. And set me free from this ridiculous pressure. In desperation, Haruyuki unthinkingly started to drop into a headlong advance.

His eyes popped open.

This is just a repeat of last week. Didn't I learn anything?

Obviously, no one gets stronger overnight. And just because I practiced a bit doesn't mean I can suddenly dodge bullets now. But I can totally change the way I think anytime.

It's not like I'm fighting to look cool for the gallery. And it's not for Takumu's approval or Kuroyukihime's praise.

It's for me. I'm fighting because I want to like myself, the menial, weak, thickheaded me I hate so much, just a little more than I did yesterday.

In which case—

"You're not running!!" Haruyuki scolded himself in a low voice and focused more on seeing with his eyes.

Don't look at the gun barrel. That antiaircraft rifle's not the enemy. The avatar holding it, finger on the trigger. The Burst Linker moving the avatar. The will to attack itself, sent out by that brain—feel it!

Haruyuki mustered every drop of willpower, took his eyes off the gun, and stared straight at the right eye of the enemy sniper peering through the scope.

And for some reason, he got the sense the enemy was shaken.

Immediately, a flash of orange light flickered from that direction, and a glittering bullet was released from the rifle's maw.

Before he even saw it close in, drawing out its spiral vortex, Haruyuki shifted the angle of his right wing slightly and twisted his body. The bullet lightly grazed his right side with a whine and flew off harmlessly behind him.

One-point-five seconds later, before his enemy had finished pulling the rifle's bolt handle, Haruyuki was driving a Punch into its jaw.

"Well! Nice work avoiding that!"

The instant he returned to the real world, his back was slapped, and Haruyuki leaped out of his chair. Turning around, he saw the smiling face of Kuroyukihime, who had burst out a step ahead of him.

It was their usual table at the back of the lounge, adjacent to the student cafeteria at Umesato Junior High. Late on a Saturday afternoon, there were no other students to be seen. Takumu had apparently dived into the game from the roof, so he wasn't there, either.

"Oh yeah. Probably just lucky."

Tucking his chin in as he spoke, he got the usual "What am I going to do with you?" face.

"That wasn't luck. It was superb timing. You must have had some trigger to anticipate it?" Kuroyukihime sat up on the table, crossed her arms, and stared him down.

After faltering a moment, he replied. "A trigger...I guess it was just, the moment I looked at the scope instead of the muzzle of the rifle, I got the sense that the sight shook. And then it was like my reflexes took over and I dodged," he mumbled, and Kuroyukihime snapped a single eyebrow up.

"Oh? Hmm...Yes, I see...It was that, then, was it?"

"What do you mean, you see?"

"Oh, well, that sniper. I had thought he was just too good at maintaining a line of sight. Most likely having an ability you could call 'eye tracking,' perhaps."

"Eye tracking...?" Haruyuki asked in response, blinking furiously.

"Mmm. That is to say, track the eyes of an enemy looking at the gun muzzle and automatically sight."

"What?! Th-then, that means that up to now, I've been getting shot down precisely because I've been staring so intently at that gun muzzle?"

"It does."

"Th-that's..."

Seeing Haruyuki slumping back into his chair, mouth hanging wide with shock, Kuroyukihime laughed gently.

"Don't be so discouraged. Regardless of any tricks, being able to dodge a bullet moving that fast is clearly the result of your efforts. This last month or so, your reaction speed has visibly improved. Have you been doing some kind of practice in secret?"

"Oh. Y-you can tell?"

As he shrank into himself even further, the slender, black-stocking-wrapped legs were nimbly crossed in front of him, and Kuroyukihime moved her beautiful face, where neatness and cleverness coexisted, into a faint smile.

"Naturally. I'm your 'guardian.' What kind of practice have you been doing?"

"Uh, umm, well." Haruyuki resigned himself and explained the specifications of the training room he had constructed.

Instantly:

The crown of his head was struck, and Haruyuki let out a cry. "Gaah?!"

"Y-y-you idiot!! Avoid a bullet with no one pulling the trigger at that close range?! And with pain at maximum?!" Kuroyukihime shouted, her expression fiery, and her right fist trembled momentarily.

She studied Haruyuki, who was sprouting tears and frozen solid, let out a long breath, and abruptly grabbed his head with both hands and pulled it close.

"Wh-wha—?! K-Kuroyukhime, wh—" When he started to hyperventilate at the softness communicated from the other side of her uniform, she changed suddenly, and he heard a calm voice above his head.

"I told you, didn't I? That no matter what happens, I have no intention of harming my relationship with you. Trust me. That is an order."

"O-okay." When Haruyuki went limp and simply nodded, she released his head and grinned.

"I'll say this because it's now, but the reason I accepted the Red King's request this time was because I thought perhaps it could show you that winning or losing isn't everything. Don't push yourself too hard. Get stronger for me bit by bit. I prefer it like that. Now. Shall we be on our way?"

Haruyuki stared at the figure dressed in black as she stood up, retrieving her bag from the table, and nodded deeply once more.

"Me, too. No matter what happens...I won't hurt you again."

He didn't say it out loud but made sure to mutter it under his breath.

"Hmm? Did you say something?"

"N-no, nothing!"

And then he pulled himself up from his chair and hurried to follow after his guardian, his king, his classmate—the person he loved.

Opening the door to his condo, a tiny trace of sweetness lingered in the air that enveloped Haruyuki.

Although the dim hallway, returned to silence, was a sight he should have been used to, it made him sad somehow. The two Kings had only stayed here two nights, but it didn't look like he'd be forgetting the experience any time soon.

"I'm home," he murmured, taking off his shoes before opening the door to his deserted living room.

His mother was supposed to be back from her overseas business trip that morning, but she'd apparently just dumped her suitcase and headed to the office. She had unbelievable energy.

Taking off his uniform jacket and hanging it on the back of a chair along with his tie, Haruyuki noticed an icon blinking in the corner of his visual field. As usual, his mother had left a message on the home server.

He played the message back with a voice command while he pulled a bottle of oolong tea out of the refrigerator. An indistinct noise reached his auditory system, followed by his mother's voice.

"Haruyuki, I'll be late today, or I might not make it home at all. Send the clothes in my suitcase out to the cleaner's for me, would you? Oh, and sorry, but we're babysitting again. This time, it's my coworker's kid, and it's just for one night, so watch out for her, okay? Please? She should already be there by the time you get home. Okay, thanks."

What did she say? Haruyuki froze, glass of oolong tea still tilted. *No way. It can't. I mean, come on.*

He took a gulp from the glass and then put it down. He held his breath and looked around quietly.

The living room, the kitchen, completely deserted. The lights were even off, and the air was still. Haruyuki had frantically cleaned up last night, so there wasn't a trace of the terrible spectacle of the retro gaming tournament of two days prior.

Holding his breath and letting his eyes race around, he heard—

It was faint, but it was definitely a voice laughing somewhere.

"No. Way." He moaned as he flew out of the living room at lightning speed, dashed down the hall, and pushed open the door to his own room at the end of it.

And then Haruyuki took a deep breath and let out a scream. "Waaaah?!"

On his bed.

Flopped back, legs crossed, buried in a mountain of paper manga from the last century smuggled out of his hiding spot, and flipping through one of them—a girl in a pure red outfit.

"N-n-n-n—"

The girl glanced at the trembling Haruyuki, lifting her head. It made the hair tied up on either side swing, and she smiled.

"Welcome home, big brother!"

"Wh-what are you—?!" Haruyuki shouted and crumpled on the spot, pointing at the girl—Immobile Fortress, Bloody Storm, the Red King Scarlet Rain, Yuniko Kozuki—mouth flapping before he finally manage to get words out. "Niko. Why are you here?"

"Don't make me explain the whole thing again. The whole fake-mail thing." Abruptly returning to her other tone, Niko raised her torso. She flapped a volume of manga—definitely not educational, the kind with people dying and explosions—and grinned. "And this is some good taste you got here."

"O-oh, thanks—*No!!*" Panting frantically, Haruyuki slumped over and shook his head from side to side. "This is seriously too much! The exact same social engineering in one day, I mean…"

"Come on. I figured I should at least say thanks, so here I am."

He hurriedly bobbed his head at Niko, who was pursing her lips sharply. "W-well, that is very thoughtful. Thanks."

He would definitely be roasted whole in her overwhelming firepower the next time she was in a bad mood that erupted into a duel. "You're welcome," Haruyuki quickly managed, his lips spasming into a smile. "So that's all you needed, then? You can make your way out through that door—"

"Oh, is that your attitude? Hmm. And here I was thinking I'd give you a follow-up report, and this is how you are?"

"I-I'm listening! I'm listening!" Haruyuki dropped to his knees to sit formally; after glancing down at him from up on the bed and bringing the slender legs stretching out from her cut-off jeans up to sit cross-legged, Niko gave him a sharp look. But luckily for him, she continued to speak without making trouble.

"It's about Chrome Disaster."

Haruyuki swallowed hard and switched tracks. He would have to report back to Kuroyukihime on everything she said henceforth.

"Last night, I notified the Five Kings, including the Radio jerk, that I had executed Disaster. And so anyway, that's the end of that. Although personally, I'd like to make some kind of fuss about Yellow swiping the Armor. Unfortunately, I've got no proof, so…"

"Right." Haruyuki nodded slowly. Timidly, he continued, "So then, um, what about Cherry Rook?"

Niko fell silent briefly and looked up at the winter evening sky peeking through the south window. Narrowing her deep green eyes, blinking her long lashes once, she answered quietly. "He said he's moving next month."

"What?"

"Some distant relative stepped up after all this time saying they wanna take him in. All the expenses at our school are covered by taxes, so students can't say no to offers like that. He said he's moving to Fukuoka."

"He is? That's far."

"Yeah, I guess. So he was in a hurry. Once he moves, his only connection with me would have been Brain Burst. And on top of that, there are almost no Burst Linkers outside Tokyo. If you can't fight, you can't level up. And then his impatience got eaten up by the Armor..." Making a gesture like she was swallowing something back, Niko smiled faintly.

"But maybe because Brain Burst is gone, today he was...he looked like the old him, from when he first started talking to me. Even though he hadn't been coming to class lately or talking to anyone, today he actually chatted with me. And, you know, I was thinking. Even if he's not a Burst Linker anymore, even if he's moving to Fukuoka, the VR world isn't just the Accelerated World, right?"

She turned her gaze on him, and Haruyuki nodded deeply.

"Y-yeah. Of course."

"So, like, I hadn't thought about it before now, but...I figured I might try some other VR game. One I could play for a long time with him. If you know any good ones, let me know."

"Right, okay." He nodded, again repeatedly, and then replied: "Well, you can take whichever ones you want that I have here. Although I am kinda biased when it comes to genre."

"Ha-ha-ha!" Niko smiled and abruptly turned away, digging around in a small backpack off to her side. She pulled out a brown paper bag and tossed it up, and Haruyuki hurried to catch it in both hands.

"Wh-what's this?"

"Yeah...It's, uh, a thank-you. You scarfed it down the other day, all 'so gooood,' right?"

Craning his neck and opening the paper bag, the smell of sweet butter wafted up. He could see the faces of several golden discs from under the white paper towel wrapping.

Dazed, he pulled out one of the cookies, still a little warm, and timidly asked Niko, "What? A-are you sure—?"

"What? If you don't want 'em, give 'em back!" She glared at him, and he hurriedly shook his head.

"I want them, I want them! Th-thanks. I was just a little sur-prised." Turning his face down, he bit into the cookie in his hand.

It was sweet and fragrant and a little salty.

The taste of reality, he thought. *This is the flavor symbolizing something in reality. And that something's the fact that me and Niko can be friends in the real world, for real.*

"Hrng." A strange noise slipped out of his throat.

Curling up his body as best he could, desperately hiding his face, he took another bite of the treat. He heard a high-pitched cry from on top of the bed.

"Y-y-you're crying! I-idiot! Go to hell!!"

He lowered his face into the bed, and listening to Niko's voice continuing to berate him, Haruyuki kept chomping down the cookies, a little saltier now.

END

AFTERWORD

It's been a while, or maybe this is the first time. Reki Kawahara here. Thank you for reading *Accel World 2: The Red Storm Princess*.

I was told about two billion times that the afterword in the last volume was "too formal!" or "pretentious!" or "who are you?" so this time, I'd like to do it with a tiny bit more delicacy.

About twice a week, I get on my good-for-nothing bike and ride out to a farm not far from my house, about thirty-five kilometers north along the river. Last year, two kittens were born on this farm. And of course, even these kids, who were such cuties as first, grew up at an incredible speed (lol). Before I knew it, they had gotten so huge, and for the most part, that's fine, but what bothers me is that when I eat some sweet bread on a bench at the farm instead of an extra meal, they come flying at me really forcefully now, demanding some bread with loud meows.

I feel like it's not a particularly good idea to give cats bread, and more important, I'm very much not interested in having my precious calories taken from me, so, crafty me, I decided to bring some of those little dried sardines with me along with the sweet bread and give them those. What a good person! Go ahead and compliment me!

However. The sardines I offered up so confidently (domestically made, no less) were only sniffed at by the cats and ignored.

Then they started clamoring—*Who would eat such a fish? Give us a break, give us the bread.* You can understand my amazement, I'm sure. Until that time, I had believed all the writings stating that these creatures called cats universally loved sardines. But that was not the case. Cats who have been raised not eating fish will end up not liking fish.

The result of all this being that I now spend my days being squeezed by this gang for approximately 10 percent of my precious sweet bread.

The moral of this apparently pointless story is that things you think may make others happy may not necessarily make others happy. Yes...Even so, I do hope you all enjoyed this book, which I worked hard in my own way to write.

Illustrator, HIMA, and my editor, Miki, you have again helped me out so much.

Thank you to my friends on the IRC channel, who cheer me up when I tend to lose heart so easily, and everyone who sent me encouraging messages on the website.

And you reading this far, you have my deepest gratitude.

Reki Kawahara
March 30, 2009

ACCEL WORLD, Volume 2
REKI KAWAHARA

Translation: Jocelyne Allen

ACCEL WORLD
© REKI KAWAHARA 2009
All rights reserved.
Edited by ASCII MEDIA WORKS
First published in Japan in 2009 by KADOKAWA CORPORATION, Tokyo.
English translation rights arranged with KADOKAWA CORPORATION, Tokyo,
through Tuttle-Mori Agency, Inc., Tokyo.

English translation © 2014 by Hachette Book Group, Inc.

Yen On
Hachette Book Group
1290 Avenue of the Americas, New York, NY 10104

www.HachetteBookGroup.com
www.YenPress.com

Yen On is an imprint of Hachette Book Group, Inc.
The Yen On name and logo are trademarks of Hachette Book Group, Inc.

First Yen Press Edition: November 2014

Library of Congress Cataloging-in-Publication Data

Kawahara, Reki.
    [Kurenai no Bofuki. English]
    The red storm princess / Reki Kawahara ; illustrations, HIMA ; [translation, Jocelyne Allen].—First Yen Press edition.
        pages cm—(Accel World ; Volume 2)
    ISBN 978-0-316-29636-6 (paperback)—ISBN 978-0-316-29655-7 (ebook)   [1. Science fiction. 2. Virtual reality—Fiction. 3. Fantasy.] I. HIMA (Comic book artist) illustrator.   II. Allen, Jocelyne, 1974– translator. III. Title.
    PZ7.K1755Kaw 2014
    [Fic]—dc23
                                                    2014025099

10 9 8 7 6 5 4 3 2

RRD-C

Printed in the United States of America